SILVER GUILT

SILVER GUILT

Judith Cutler

This first world edition published 2010
in Great Britain and in the USA by
SEVERN HOUSE PUBLISHERS LTD of
9–15 High Street, Sutton, Surrey, England, SM1 1DF.
Trade paperback edition published
in Great Britain and the USA 2010 by
SEVERN HOUSE PUBLISHERS LTD

British Library Cataloguing in Publication Data

Cutler, Judith.
    Silver Guilt. – (A Lina Townend mystery)
    1. Antique dealers–Fiction. 2. Aristocracy (Social
    class)–Fiction. 3. Theft–Fiction. 4. Detective and
    mystery stories.
    I. Title II. Series
    823.9'14-dc22

ISBN-13: 978-0-7278-6852-7   (cased)
ISBN-13: 978-1-84751-238-3   (trade paper)

All Severn House titles are printed on acid-free paper.

Severn House Publishers support The Forest Stewardship Council [FSC],
the leading international forest certification organisation. All our titles that
are printed on Greenpeace-approved FSC-certified paper carry the FSC logo.

Mixed Sources
Product group from well-managed
forests and other controlled sources
www.fsc.org Cert no. SA-COC-1565
© 1996 Forest Stewardship Council

Typeset by Palimpsest Book Production Ltd.,
Grangemouth, Stirlingshire, Scotland.
Printed and bound in Great Britain by
MPG Books Ltd., Bodmin, Cornwall.

ONE

'**A** television set!' Griff quavered, in a voice far older than his usual one. 'My dearest Lina, why in the world would we need a television set?'

I kept my face blank. How many households in twenty-first century Britain didn't have a TV, for goodness' sake? You really weren't part of the world if you didn't have one. But I knew Griff wasn't just afraid it would spoil our domestic evenings, listening to the radio so he could explain about music, or reading books or plays together – all part of his scheme for educating me. He'd embarked on this the day when, aged seventeen, I left the care of his old friend Iris, the only foster mother who'd managed to find anything to love in me, and become a sort of live-in apprentice, sharing his cottage in the Kentish village of Bredeham. Griff thought he was supposed to be looking after me, but Iris assured me that it was my job to look after him. At first our set-up had horrified the villagers, who muttered things about paedophiles (him) and yobs (me). But then they remembered he was as gay as they come, and saw that I was quite tame, really, and now they accepted the arrangement without comment.

What Griff really feared was not the arrival of the TV but something else.

I opened my mouth and shut it again. To be honest, I thought we both needed a bit of the sort of education only television can bring, but I didn't want to provoke him by saying so. Not when I'd already upset him by accepting the set as a present from my father.

In the ordinary way of things, few people would find anything to worry about when a daughter accepted her dad's gift. But though Lord Elham was what Griff described as my natural father, there wasn't much that was natural about our relationship. Although he'd known I existed, he'd never bothered paying maintenance, and lost touch altogether. When I'd burst into his life years later, he saw me more as a way of selling a pile of antique china than as a human being worth cherishing. I'd never found him lovable, and often struggled even to like him.

Although he knew all this, Griff was still afraid of losing me to him.

Griff wasn't legally my adoptive father, or even my adoptive grandfather, much as we'd both have liked that. But he and I loved each other. Deeply. He was far more caring than most parents, and hurting him was the last thing I wanted. If ever Lord Elham gave me anything – which wasn't very often – it always made Griff afraid I'd leave our cottage and move into Bossingham Hall.

It was time that I said something. 'You know what Lord Elham's like. He can't imagine life without television any more than he could imagine life without champagne or Pot Noodles. The only time I've ever really seen him upset was when his old set died.' In fact Lord Elham had been so frantic I'd taken him out to Curry's to buy a huge flat screen model. Because of all the precious, stealable things he had in his apartment, there was no way I'd let them deliver it, but it was so big I'd had to use our larger van to transport it. I didn't think he'd be able to tune it himself, but he'd managed, and had even set up a free view box, chuntering all the time about not being allowed to have a satellite dish because of living in a grade one listed building.

Griff still said nothing, so I giggled. 'You know what'd make him as mad as fire? If we could get Sky on the set and watch the cricket.'

'You mean the test matches and one day internationals?' At last he started to perk up.

'If eleven men play with bats and balls, they play on Sky,' I said. 'We'd have to have the dish tucked right out of the way, of course, because of living in a conservation area. Any idea where we could put it?'

'The old bugger's let you come over, then?' Lord Elham bleated next time I rang his doorbell.

For some reason my father had never got round to telling me to call him something less formal, which meant I never called him anything at all to his face and referred to him as Lord Elham even to Griff. He lived in Bossingham Hall, a stunning Palladian mansion in a village six or seven miles south of Canterbury. Or at least, the part of Bossingham Hall that the trustees now owning and running the place allowed him – one of the wings, which was actually big enough to house three or four families. In theory he wasn't supposed to have access to the rest of the house, but in practice he could wander in when he wanted, via a door with a touch access lock, provided he took nothing out. Security cameras were panning round all the time, not just on the days when the public were allowed to pay their tenners for a good nose round. Anything the experts thought was worth stealing was alarmed.

'I'm awfully short of everyday champagne,' he announced. 'So you'd better find something good today.'

He meant I was to hunt through his hoard. Before the trustees had settled everything legally, he'd managed to spirit out of the main house a mass of china and furniture that filled a dozen or so vast rooms and would have kept the *Antiques Roadshow* team busy for five years, maybe ten. At first he'd only let me look in what was once a filthy kitchen and equally disgusting living room. As he came to trust me, he let me explore others, though he still kept me out of a few. Goodness knows what he had in them, or what he thought I'd do with my finds.

Wherever I went, I found tottering stacks of china, pictures stacked against walls, and piles of first editions, though nothing as valuable as the incredibly rare copy of *Natura Rerum* that had brought us together in the first place. Only a couple of copies were known to exist in the world, and I'd found one of them in his possession. I'd managed to persuade him it would be safer in a museum. Now it lived in the British Library, which had purchased it for what I thought was an eye-watering sum but which the experts handling the deal assured me was a snip. The money was now in trust for me and his other thirty or so illegitimate children, but we couldn't get our paws on to it until we were thirty. Neither could he, of course. A long story . . .

Lord Elham held the door open and waved me inside. Because of Griff's training I meticulously wiped my feet on a mat I'd found in the former butler's pantry.

'So damned middle class, Lina! Still, with no servants to mop up . . .'

I looked him in the eye. He still hadn't got it into his

booze-soaked, vitamin-deprived brain that I owed my very existence to what he still thought of as the Lower Orders.

He changed tack. 'So what's in that basket of yours?' he demanded, sounding just like a two-year-old expecting a treat.

'Carrots, broccoli, onions, garlic, ginger, soy sauce, free range chicken. We're having a stir-fry for lunch.'

His face fell. If only I'd brought a batch of Pot Noodles in a new exciting flavour. But he didn't say anything, just shrugging and leading the way into the kitchen it had taken me weeks and weeks to get clean. After I'd emptied the junk, I'd scrubbed it from top to bottom. It was so shabby, there was nothing for it but to turn to and paint it. So I should have been pleased to see it still pristine. I wasn't.

'You're supposed to be cooking properly, you know,' I said, plonking the basket on the table and peering into the bin. 'Just as I thought! Ready meals and empty Noodle pots!'

'But I can't cook.'

'Neither could I till Griff taught me.'

He winced.

'Have you put the bottles ready for the bottle bank?'

He pointed to three flat-pack supermarket bottle carrier boxes I'd installed in a corner.

How could anyone get through eighteen whole bottles in less than a fortnight?

'The idea isn't that you have to fill all the boxes, you know,' I said. 'It's that you put all your empties for me to take away.' Though I suppose it was the same thing for him.

'I don't know why they call it a bank,' he grumbled. 'A bank's something you get money out of, not put money into.'

Which said more about our stations in life than he realized.

'I've put some plates in the sink for you to look at,' he said to divert me, grabbing a tea towel and polishing champagne flutes he'd left to dry on the draining board. At least I'd trained him to do that much. 'They're soaking in cold water, like you said.'

I nodded, reaching under the sink for some of the lightweight rubber gloves I kept there. Since his only attempts to wash up had resulted in damage to a Limoges sweet dish that even I couldn't repair, I'd persuaded him that the only way to wash china he wanted to sell was wearing these gloves – which were obviously too small for him.

Ten minutes of hot soapy water revealed nothing more than plates far too tatty for our stall. I'd have to get a mate who did bottom of the range collectors' fairs to try to shift them, but we'd be lucky to get twenty pounds for the lot.

'No?' He'd been peering hopefully at the pile like a pasty-faced, balding spaniel. But he didn't want walkies, not outside at least. He wanted a stroll through one of his Aladdin's caves of ill-assorted goodies. But why the urgency? Griff said that to describe his usual mode as laid-back was to indulge in hyperbole, a word he'd printed for me in my vocabulary book. So why this sudden urge for action?

'Not much champagne there, I'm afraid,' I said. 'A bottle at most.'

As I dried and stowed the gloves, I pondered. The champagne flutes had been in pairs. The empty food packaging had been in pairs. Had he had a visitor?

If so, who?

One possibility was Titus Oates, of course. Titus was a dealer at the very dodgy end of the antiques market, but he'd done me a couple of good turns in the past, one of which had certainly kept Lord Elham out of jail. On the other hand Titus preferred not to make house calls, preferring to do business in pubs still without CCTV. He operated using prepaid mobile phones and no one I knew claimed to know his home address.

Another possibility was Robin Levitt, the local vicar. Robin might, twenty years ago, have modelled as a golden-haired cherub. He was still very attractive in a sweetly innocent way, but packed a good punch when required. I suspected Griff would have carried a torch for Robin, had he not had a long term partner. As it was, Griff insisted that Robin carried a torch for me, and would no doubt declare that any pastoral calls on Bossingham Hall were only made in the hope of renewing our acquaintance. I thought better of Robin than that. If anyone needed a spot of redemption it was Lord Elham. But I couldn't imagine Robin quaffing champagne and tucking into Healthy Option ready meals while he was wrestling for the old guy's soul.

There was no point in asking outright. Anything like that and Lord Elham clammed up immediately. So I humoured him. 'OK, let's find something better to sell.'

'Can you do your trick?'

'It's not a trick; it's a gift.'

Since I'd gone to live with Griff he'd taught me as much as he could. The trouble was, being in care I'd been sent to a lot of schools, and I'd never bothered going to any of them very much. So even though I was desperate to pick up Griff's learning, my head often found it very hard. Funnily enough my hands didn't. If he found a chipped or cracked plate that needed restoring, he asked me.

But there was one thing Griff didn't need to teach me – couldn't have, even if he'd wanted to. How to be an antiques diviner – like a water diviner only without a twig. Somehow, don't ask me how, I knew if there was a valuable ring in a tangle of tatty old costume jewellery, or a Bow figure in a basket of assorted china.

This was why Lord Elham was so welcoming today. A shortage of champagne meant I had to pick something out to sell for him. Apart from the green tea I sometimes managed to force down him, champagne was the only thing he drank – I mean, even for breakfast, though I had persuaded him to mix it with orange juice. So he needed to sell some of the goodies crammed into his rooms. My job was to pick out small but valuable items. Then I would clean them, which was always vital, and restore them if necessary. Did I want to use my divining gift today? Probably not. All the same, it wanted to be used. For no reason I found myself drifting towards the stairs, an area I'd not much bothered with before. I didn't go up, but turned to the door on the right.

Usually Lord Elham opened doors eagerly; this time he asked reluctantly, 'Are you sure?'

'You haven't started forging again, have you? Because if you have, I really do not want to know. Any dealings you have with Titus are strictly your own. When you go to prison, I don't want to be an accessory to the fact. OK?' I turned on my heel, generally giving the impression that I was about to leave. Actually, I was so strongly drawn to whatever was in that room that you'd have had to drag me away, but I was learning to deceive – no, Griff had taught me a better word than that. I was learning how to *dissemble*.

Don't ask me what I expected to find when at last he unlocked and opened the door. But what I certainly did not expect to find was a cigarette stubbed out in a Victorian Worcester saucer.

Not just a fag end. A spliff end. Amongst all his sins there was one Lord Elham didn't number, and that was smoking, even the legal sort of cigarette – a good job when you consider all the smoke alarms, connected direct to the fire station in Canterbury. I pretended to ignore it, my mind working over-time. Titus had given up smoking long ago, so he wouldn't get nicotine stains on the delicate work he was doing; Robin Levitt wouldn't burn money he could give away to other people.

'Company?' I asked lightly.

He pretended not to hear – Griff called it selective deafness – but started to rummage round the piles of stuff on the floor. I wasn't drawn to any of it, but didn't want to let him down. So I headed to the table that occupied one end. Not drawn? I was positively yanked to one end. What was it? Apart from another fag end in a Spode casserole? A six-sided dish of some sort. I breathed on the edge and polished it with my sleeve, which would infuriate Griff if he spotted the mess it left. Silver. With flower sprays in the border – they were pushed up from underneath: Griff would know the term. There was some sort of inscription I couldn't read.

What I should have done was tell Lord Elham I wouldn't tell him what I'd found unless he told me who his visitor was. But Griff would have been appalled by what he'd call blackmail.

'You really should tell your visitor not to use some-thing like this as an ashtray,' I said severely, patting the poor casserole.

He managed to look greedy and hangdog at one and the same time. 'I will,' he said. 'And now we should have some lunch or I'll miss *Neighbours*.'

TWO

I waited until Griff, who'd been looking after the shop all day, was back in the cottage before I showed him the dish, now gleaming after my efforts with a specialist silver polish. At last he switched off the spotlight and put it down on the Regency occasional table beside his favourite chair. He looked hopefully at the clock, but found it was still not time for his seven o'clock first drink. 'You did get a receipt for this, didn't you, dear heart?'

My heart beat faster as it always did when he asked me if my paperwork was in order. It meant the item was valuable, and he wanted to protect us. 'I always do. His copy's clipped inside the folder I gave him. And I got him to initial it and my copy too.'

He nodded approvingly, but shot a look under his eyebrows. 'You really don't trust him one bit, do you? For all he's your father.'

'Probably because he's my father. So what did I find today, Griff?'

'You tell me.'

'I can see it's silver, with some gilt round here. And I don't know any of the marks underneath, so I presume it's not British. OK so far?'

'Very good. It's called parcel-gilt. As to the marks, I don't know them either. It's very pretty, isn't it? I'm bound to say I think he'd do better to sell it at auction.'

'But then he'd have to pay auctioneer's commission and the tax man might notice. So he'd rather get a thousand less but keep it all – my commission apart, of course. And at ten per cent, Griff, how much am I likely to get?'

He laughed. 'That's a very roundabout way of asking how much it'll sell for. And I really don't know. After all, it's not our usual range, dear one. Though you might be able to inveigle one of your admirers into selling it for you, especially if we can find out all about it. Speaking of finding all about things—'

When Griff changed gear with a clunk like that I knew he was going to say something I didn't want to hear.

'That man Habgood's been on to you again, has he?' I snapped. I didn't know whether to be furious or fascinated. Arthur Habgood was a fellow antique dealer, who ran a twee outfit called Devon Cottage Antiques. He was desperate to prove that I was his granddaughter; in other words, that it was his daughter whom Lord Elham had seduced. When I told Habgood that I didn't need a grandfather, he rather sadly pointed out that he'd rather like a granddaughter. But I wanted an honest grandfather. Once I'd sold him a heavily restored

plate, at an appropriately low price – only to see him triple
the price and try to pass it as perfect. So I wasn't at all sure
that he'd be any better as a grandfather than Lord Elham was
as a father. However, since, if he was my grandfather, he'd
be able to tell me all about my mother, I hadn't quite shut
the door on his regular pleas.

'He's repeated his offer to pay for a DNA test,' Griff
continued, bravely, obviously afraid that Habgood would lure
me down to Devon but determined to be fair. 'It wouldn't
hurt: it's only a matter of—'

'I know what a gob swab is,' I said. 'But it's not that sort
of hurt I'm worried about.' Let him chew on that. 'Now, who
do you suggest I wheedle into selling this here dish?'

He took a deep breath, the sort he always took when he
was about to suggest something I wouldn't like. I braced
myself.

'You know that Aidan's sister is something of an expert on
silverware?'

'His sister? Does that make her a Lady or an Honourable
or something?' I didn't sound very enthusiastic. Aidan and I
had never really liked each other, and why should we? He
was Griff's long-time lover, and saw me as a horrible brat
taking Griff's energy and draining his emotions. As for me,
deep down I was angry that anyone should have known and
loved Griff longer than I had. Illogical, I know, but all the
same . . . Plus Aidan was filthy rich and spoke with several
plums in his mouth.

'No need to look so mutinous. Being born with a silver
spoon in her mouth doesn't mean she hasn't worked as hard
as I have for a living. Anyway, she's coming down to stay
with Aidan this weekend. He's invited us both to dinner
tomorrow evening.' After a long silence, he said, 'Please say
yes, my love.'

I'd rather put pins in my eyes and pull out my toenails. But
I'd come to realize that for Griff's happiness, a bit of self-
sacrifice was sometimes in order. Besides which, I could pick
someone's brains for free. So, a bit late, I smiled, as if I'd
been thinking about clothes and nothing else. 'Do you think
that Christian Dior number would be over the top?' I'd found
a wonderful New Look outfit in my size that for some reason
the dealer had grievously underpriced, perhaps because it was

not just small, it was designed for someone short. In other words, Dior might have pinned it on to me himself, all those years ago.

'I don't think silk is ever over the top. Just chic. But you must be careful not to overdo the accessories. You'll come?' he prompted, with a beam I found impossible to resist.

'So long as Aidan isn't cooking.'

'Let's hope it's Nella. She learned at finishing school.'

Not the finishing school I went to, I'll bet.

'You may find her manner a little offhand. If you want to put it in that vocabulary book of yours, I think the best word's brusque. Don't let it put you off, my love. Or her accent, which is a good deal more Upper than either Aidan's or your father's. If you find yourself going into prickle mode, retire to Aidan's cloakroom till your hackles have dropped. Promise?'

To do Aidan justice, he'd actually booked a cab to collect and return us, so that Griff could relax what he called his self-denying audience – or something like that; I must look in my vocabulary book – and I could risk more than a sniff at a glass. If he was prepared to go to so much effort to make Griff happy, then I must try even harder to like him. It wasn't so hard with a pre-dinner glass of champagne – which was as good as Lord Elham's daily tipple, but not up to his celebration vintage stuff. He might be a rotten father, but when it came to bubbly Lord Elham took his responsibilities seriously.

Then Aidan's sister emerged from his top of the range but rarely used kitchen, flourishing a couple of plates of dinky nibbles. She could have been anything between fifty-five and seventy, iron-grey hair cut so severely it declared to the world that Lady Nella Cordingly was too busy for any colour and blow-wave nonsense. But it must have cost a bomb to make it fall like that. Her dress was also beautifully cut, but a rather unkind lime green. It screamed aloud for sheer stockings and elegant heels, but got black tights as thick and pilled as a toddler's and aggressively flat black shoes.

'Nella, you know Griff, of course.' Aidan paused while they air-kissed, the plates tilting ominously. I couldn't stop myself from grabbing the nearest, lest the perfect little canapés – at last I remembered the proper term – landed on the perfect silk rug. 'And this is his – ah – protégée, Lina.'

'Indeed.' The 'ee' sound went up and down like a hospital temperature chart, but never managed to reach the point marked 'enthusiastic'. 'How do you do?'

At least Griff had told me never to reply, 'Fine, thanks,' so my 'How do you do?' was all right. And I'd taken the plate with my left hand, so I was able to shake hands properly. Then I did the obvious thing. I held the plate so that Aidan and Griff could help themselves. What I wanted to do was take one myself, but wasn't quite sure if Nella would approve. She was still following me with her eyes, as if I were some animal in a ring and I might or might not get a rosette. Perhaps the Christian Dior really was OTT.

A silence gathered and fell. Was I doing something wrong? If only they'd start talking again.

At last she sat down, putting her plate of goodies on the table beside her and helping herself before swigging champagne. Perhaps I should put the other plate beside hers. Offer it to her first? By now I was practically weeing myself, I was so nervous.

I shot Griff a look, but he had that horrible ins . . . incrust . . . unreadable expression on his face that always made me want to scream. But I knew that screaming would certainly earn no brownie points, so, putting my plate between Griff and Aidan, I moved back to my chair and picked up my champagne flute. Just to show there was no ill-feeling, as Iris used to say, I raised it to my lips, but didn't actually sip any of it. Sober, that was the watchword.

At last Griff smiled approvingly – I'd got it right, without his needing to prompt me! – and he said, 'Lina's been asked to sell a silver dish.'

'Provenance?' Nella barked.

'Good but confidential,' I said.

She ignored me. 'Not your usual area, Griff.'

'That's why we brought it along for you to look at, Nella,' he said, with something of a bow.

'So why should anyone ask you to sell something you don't know about?' She addressed Griff.

Brusque, Griff had said. I'd have had her down as bloody rude, all the more peculiar when Aidan was always so wordily polite.

'Lina's got a kind heart. And she's a divvy,' he added, with a huge grin at me. 'If she finds something, I know it's good. She's only operating on commission, but naturally wants to make the seller as much as possible.'

Nella turned to me. 'So what made you pick it out?'

'The owner asked me to. So I did.' I flashed a smile at Griff.

'Just like that? Well, I suppose you could see it was silver gilt.'

'She couldn't see anything when she brought it home,' Griff corrected her. 'It took her a good hour to get it back to this state. Her restoration work on anything beats mine hands down.'

Holding it by two of the corners, she twirled it round so that it looked like a gold orb.

'Well, you picked well. Have you really no idea what it is?'

'I've been hunting round the Internet a bit. But maybe I've been looking in the wrong places. I know it's European, of course. But that's all.'

'Seventeenth-century Hungarian. If I take it to a LAPADA fair I should get you between five and six thousand. Nearer six. Minus my commission, of course.'

'That would be a lot more than we'd get at the fairs we go to,' I said. 'And of course, it's not the sort of thing we usually handle, so we might not attract a buyer looking for something like that.'

'I'll take that as a yes, then, shall I? Good. Now, more nibbles, anyone? Aidan, my glass is empty – what's happened to the bloody shampoo?'

Although I was technically a guest, of course, I made myself as useful as I could, my efforts with the canapés having attracted a couple of approving nods. I always left Griff and Aidan on their own together as much as I could. And although she was so . . . brusque . . . she seemed glad to have my help, even if it was just to clear the starter plates from the dining table and transfer the vegetables from the steamer to the appropriate dishes.

'So you've become Griff's apprentice? Well, he needs one. So long as you don't start telling mops and buckets to clean the floor.'

What was she on about? And then it dawned on me. Mickey Mouse!

'You mean like *The Sorcerer's Apprentice*?' I hummed a bit of the music, and her eyes widened. 'He teaches me all sorts of things,' I said. I couldn't quite call her Nella, but refused to call her ma'am.

'And what do you do in return? Apart from sniffing out goodies?'

'I keep an eye on him,' I replied seriously. 'He doesn't drink half as much as he did. And I make him take some pills the doctor's given him for his – oh, dear, I never can pronounce this right . . . Chol . . . chlor . . . The tablets are called statins, anyway.'

Her smile made her look a bit like a frog. 'I didn't quite mean that. I meant professionally.'

'Oh, you mean like the restoration work? And driving our van – his eyes aren't what they used to be, and even with glasses he hates driving after dusk. And I set up at fairs. Is that the sort of thing you mean? Oh, and I clean the house. He pretends to – he's got this fluffy duster on a stick – but my last foster mum told me always to use a damp cloth. And he always skimps the kitchen, so I do that and the bathroom too. I love seeing everything coming up shiny.'

She frowned as she squeezed some baked potatoes to see if they were cooked. 'I hope you don't over-restore.'

Where did that come from? Because I'd said I liked cleaning? What a weirdo. But I mustn't let my hackles rise. 'He's got these friends near Wolverhampton who restore stuff for museums. They taught me – a mini-apprenticeship. And it's our policy to tell anyone wanting to buy if I've repaired anything.'

'*Our*?' she repeated, as if she hadn't heard the word right.

'Yes. Griff said it was better for taxes and stuff if we were proper business partners. He got a solicitor to do everything.' He'd also insisted on giving me something called Power of Attorney, in case he was ever really ill and needed, he said, someone reliable to switch off the machine. But she didn't need to know that, not if the idea of a business partnership shocked her. Aidan knew all about it, since he shared the Power of Attorney, but if he hadn't told her, I didn't think I ought.

'Hmm. Now, can you reach that pie out of the oven? I've

got more arthritis than I like in the old wrists and I'd hate to
drop it. Made it at home and brought it down with me. Wouldn't
dare spill anything in here, would I? Does Aidan ever use it?
He always was one for show. The best pony though he hated
riding, the best tennis racquet though he was rubbish at serving
– that sort of thing.'

'At least in Griff he made a good choice,' I said firmly, reaching
the pie out as I spoke and carrying it through to the dining room,
where Griff had seized all the place mats and was putting them
in a heap to protect the wonderful Regency table.

The pie was full of tough meat and mushy vegetables.

It was only as I cleared the plates and loaded the dishwasher – Aidan's stuff was expensive, but also very practical
– that I returned to the subject of Nella's wrists.

'How do you manage if you're handling valuables all the
time? Especially something that can be heavy, like silver?'

'Let's just say it's a good job I don't deal in china. Does
he prefer cheese or pud first?'

I was startled. Didn't brothers and sisters know things like
that?

'Your brother likes cheese first, but he always gives way
to Griff, who likes dessert first. And I like cheese second too.'
There were some cheeses I wasn't at all sure about, but I'd
never had a dessert I didn't like.

'Dessert it shall be, then. Bloody hell, this dish was heavy
enough when it was empty – and now it's full of sherry trifle . . .'

I took it from her, as if I was just inspecting it. 'It's
Stourbridge lead crystal, isn't it? From the days when
Stourbridge actually made things. Thomas Webb?'

She put her hands on her hips. 'Is that divvying or
knowledge?'

Which would she respect more? 'Knowledge,' I said truthfully. 'I recognize the pattern.'

'And where did you take your degree?'

Hadn't she noticed what I said about my apprenticeship? I
didn't think she was the sort of person who'd like to hear that
I hadn't got so much as a GCSE. 'Griff thinks learning on
the job's best. And what he can't tell me I can pick up from
books and the Internet. There's a lot of time to kill at fairs
and in the shop.'

'And you put it to good use?'

'Fairs are best. I can read about something and then go and see it for real. And some of the dealers are very kind.' Some weren't, of course. Some would peel you alive if they thought they could sell the skin. And some were real crooks, who wouldn't let you get near anything, because everything they handled was fake or stolen.

'So why didn't you find out about that dish for yourself?'

'Because it only came into my hands yesterday, and I spent the whole of today trying to repair a Chelsea figure for a client. Someone had broken off the poor lady's hand and lost it, so they asked me to help.' I spoke modestly but she should know how much skill it took to model a limb from scratch.

But if I hoped for a nod of acknowledgement, I was disappointed. 'Who?' she barked.

'A private collector. Not someone who'll try and sell it as perfect.'

'Do they drink proper coffee or decaf?'

It seemed the interrogation was over.

THREE

As I had predicted, the television and its magic Sky dish had brought the world of international cricket into our sitting room. Lord Elham was so jealous that any day now he'd invite himself over to watch.

One day, with no fair, no sales and Griff minding the shop, I headed for Bossingham with a batch of home-made casseroles to put in the freezer I'd made him buy. He might not be cooking himself, but at least I could guarantee that my stuff came without any supposedly nasty additives. Griff wasn't especially happy, but he conceded that I needed to practise cooking as much as I needed to practise reading and writing.

This time I found no trace of any visitor, which was surprising. Lord Elham didn't do cleaning or tidying, and yet the fag ends had disappeared. Even the kitchen bin was empty, the first time I'd known it not to be stinking.

'Your visitor's been back?' I said, trying to appear more interested in a pile of jewellery than in his answer.

I must have been too convincing; he came and stood beside me and started reminiscing about who had worn the pendant or necklace I was holding. Since I was interested in what was, after all, my family, even if they were the other side of the blanket, it was a very good ploy. I got so absorbed in the relationship of the woman in this locket to the man who'd owned that fob that I got completely sidetracked.

There were a couple of rings which might fetch something, but I always hated flogging anything so personal. And the stones weren't up to much either, considering their provenance. Since my divining-sense seemed to be on strike, I left everything where it was, taking just a pair of hideously fiddly Derby potpourri vases that might, when clean, fetch about £800 and left him to watch *Neighbours* in peace.

I was just cleaning one of the vase lids when the phone went. I left Griff to answer it. It was usually one of his old friends, and they could talk for hours about their days on the stage. Once or twice when I'd picked up the phone I'd not recognized the name at the other end, much to my embarrassment and probably the ageing star's as well.

At last I'd finished the lid and its mate, too, so I decided to nip down and make a cup of the green tea I'd read somewhere would do Griff good. He wasn't at all keen at first, but drank it to please me. In fact, I rather think he'd started to like it, because sometimes he drank it even when I wasn't there to nag him.

'Don't you want to know who was on the phone?' he said.

'One of your old muckers?'

'Not exactly. It was Nella.'

'Aidan's Nella?' I asked stupidly, as if I knew any other Nellas.

'Indeed. It seems she's in a hole. Her assistant has broken her ankle, and won't be back at work for six weeks. Which, given Nella's bad wrists, is a disaster, when there's a big show in the offing.'

'She just needs a couple of heavies.'

Griff laughed. 'I think we can trust her to ensure that her property and her vehicle are well-guarded. But she needs someone to help on her stand at the next NEC event, and she wondered if you might like to go, just for the experience.'

'The NEC? Antiques for Everyone? We always do that. Together.' And if it was a choice between working with Griff and working for her, I knew which I'd prefer. Every time.

'No, loved one. The Fine Art and Antiques Fair. A LAPADA fair. A few select dealers, with a guaranteed time line. Punters wanting to buy instead of bringing their junk along and expecting us to give a free valuation.'

'When?'

'This week.'

'I'd stay in our caravan?' I was obviously wavering.

'Oh, no. Nella has a property up there.'

I froze. 'The same sort of place as Aidan?'

'Not quite. I'll take that as a yes, shall I?'

'No! No, don't. I'd rather stay in our caravan, Griff. Honestly. I can drive up and park actually in the NEC.' Our caravan was a home on wheels. It was where Griff and I had spent some lovely evenings with dealer friends. We'd even gone on holiday in it a couple of times. It was safe. Staying in a posh house would be anything but safe.

He took my hand. 'I know. But it would look very strange if you did, especially as Nella's home is near Leamington, no distance from the NEC.'

'But eating with her . . . Sharing her bathroom . . . And what if she has a guard dog?'

'You've already eaten with her and lived to tell the tale. She's probably got more bathrooms than you can shake a stick at. No dogs or cats to worry about. And her husband is a very pleasant man, who will, I have no doubt, treat you with every courtesy.' He gathered me to him and hugged me. 'My darling child, you are young and beautiful and people like you. Nella tells me you're a credit to me. I said you were a credit to yourself.'

'Let me think about it,' I said, meaning there was no way I'd agree.

'You haven't got long, my love. She wants you to catch a train tonight. She'll reimburse you for your train fare, which will be considerable without prior booking discount. She'll meet you at Birmingham International, so you won't have to worry about changing trains after Euston.'

'Tonight! But what do I take?'

'Your best suit and three or four tops. Those lovely patent pumps. That's all you'll need for the day. For the evening, that embroidered skirt, a pair of trousers and a selection of fancier tops. Clean undies. Diamonds. Make-up. Your eyeglass. Your sponge bag. Your mobile phone. Use that wheelie case I gave you for Christmas.'

'What about towels and—?'

'I'm sure you'll find the largest, fluffiest towels in the world. And a bathrobe. My darling, I promise you that you are going to have a wonderful time. And even if you hate it, the fair only lasts four days.'

I'd never travelled by train on my own before, and only occasionally with Griff, so it was a good job I hadn't had time to worry about that, too. As it was, I got into the London train from our village with about a minute to spare, spent the whole tube journey being afraid of going round for ever and ever, like some underground Flying Dutchman, and then being sure that I would buy the wrong ticket and fetch up in Newton Abbot. OK, wrong station for Newton Abbot. Some travellers took off coats and scarves and even their shoes for the journey. I was so afraid of being whizzed past the NEC and into darkest Brum that I kept my coat on and my case beside me. My bag never left my lap. I did risk reading. Griff had found me a book on silver, which I studied as if I had to take an exam on it. I didn't want to let Nella down. More to the point, I didn't want to let Griff down.

She met me in her car, which seemed reassuringly small. Her husband was away, working in The Hague, she said, which ought to have meant something but didn't.

'So if you don't mind, we'll eat in the kitchen. Warm there. Here we are,' she concluded, pulling into a circular driveway in front of a lovely double-fronted house – the Old Rectory. 'Drink now or do you want to freshen up first?'

'If freshening involves a loo, I'd like to freshen,' I said.

'In that case I'll show you your room.' She opened the front door and dived through to silence the burglar alarm. 'Straight up the stairs.'

I would have spent ten minutes stroking the banister rail if I hadn't had to follow her. Her clothes weren't so much casual as scruffy, her moccasins worn right down the back.

She installed me in a big square room, with a huge double bed in the middle and a single one at the side. 'Bathroom's next door. Come down when you're ready.'

The bathroom might be measured in acres but the towels were thin and grey. No bathrobe. For a moment I thought even my father would be shocked, but I told myself I was exaggerating.

Nella hadn't left a trail of breadcrumbs or a piece of string to guide me, so I just had to guess and pray she wouldn't mind if I got it wrong. I wasn't going to hang about worrying. I might freeze to death if I did. I turned on the huge cast iron radiator before I set out, but apart from a few hostile clunkings, it didn't seem about to deliver anything else.

Once you've slept on the streets, you learn how to keep warm. So I rolled myself in the old-fashioned eiderdown from the big bed and cocooned myself on the smaller. But I wanted to cry. Why had Griff sent me up here to this arctic house to stay with a woman who must have had antifreeze running through her veins? Why had I agreed to help a woman who'd produced undercooked rabbit pie, which I'd always hated on account of their little white tails, and a strange lumpy mash of all sorts of root vegetables that were supposed to be good for you? Why had I got to get up before six so I could go and set up a stall full of items I knew nothing about and cared less? I'd have put my head down and cried, except I'd learned a long time ago that there's nothing worse than tears for leaving your cheeks cold, and maybe chapped.

'You don't half owe me, Griff, you old bugger,' I muttered. And then I remembered one more thing. I'd managed to squeeze Tim the Teddy into a corner of my case, and he was probably as cold and pissed off as I was. So I pulled him into bed with me and for all our grumblings we fell asleep remarkably quickly.

FOUR

'Now, Lina, what you have to do is this,' Nella said. 'Forget you've spent hours arranging things and adjusting lights. Imagine you're a punter. What do you see? For God's sake, don't just stand there: do it properly. Go out into the foyer and turn round and come back into the hall. Look at the other dealers' displays. Then look at mine. And tell me what you think.'

Mine, not ours, I noticed. Well, it was her stall. Argentia Antiques. The name board was in tasteful silver on a black ground, with Lady Petronella Cordingly in smaller but distinct letters underneath. So I mustn't get stroppy. As for the display, I'd done the donkey work, of course, but that was what I'd come for. I'd unpacked thousands of pounds' worth of metal and given it a last polish and placed it exactly where Nella had told me. Only I'd never got it exactly right. She'd tweaked every last salver. So I was glad to get away from her for a bit, before I lost my temper.

Very well, what would a punter see? The entrance hall was a big carpeted space, with a bank of tables on the left; behind them sat well-dressed ladies (they'd definitely call themselves ladies, not women) with extravagant hairdos. They were pretending that they were doing real work when all they were doing was checking pre-bought tickets and handing out expensively produced guides to the stands. The ticket office proper was the other side.

Some burly Brummie men checked tickets; later they would be checking people as they came out. Every punter had to show the documentation from people like me to prove that he or she had bought whatever it was, not just nicked it. One of the men spotted me and winked.

'Bloody brass monkey weather! Is it any warmer in there?'

'Got to be, hasn't it?' said one of his mates. 'People are supposed to leave their coats over there. You get back in, my wench, before you freeze.'

I nodded, ready to take his advice. There were loos and a

restaurant upstairs, apparently, but I wasn't interested in those. It'd be a sandwich on the hoof for me, if the fairs Griff and I did were anything to go by. On the other hand, the coffee at a little stall off to the left smelt good. Probably better than that in the flask Nella had prepared for us. But I didn't think I'd earn brownie points if I returned with a paper cup.

So as Nella ordered me to do, I checked out the competition – and rather enjoyed it, too. One furniture stand had nothing except stunning Regency furniture, all genuine by the looks of it – not to mention the prices. Then there were areas devoted to pictures. I wouldn't know a fake Hockney from a real one, but the price tickets suggested the Hockneys – and the Lowrys – were spot on too. I fell in love with a sketch by Laura Knight, but my affection would have to be unreturned. No, not unreturned. What was the word? I'd put it in my vocab book. Unrequited, that was it. Then there were loads of big unaffordable gilt-framed jobs, all undemanding and unexciting – the sort of thing you'd buy if you had a lot of cash, a lot of wall and no confidence. There was some beautifully lit jewellery, some military stuff, a grand piano on a little platform, a bigger refreshment area – and yes, here was Argentia Antiques, looking extremely pleased with itself. To do Nella justice, she'd been right to make me move things from where I'd put them. She herself looked smart but not chic. On the other hand, I should have used those loos I'd spotted to clean my nails and apply what Griff always called slap. With a quick smile I burrowed under the skirts of the display stand and fished out my bag from the cupboard there, which also held our coats and my book on silver, just in case I had a chance to mug up. I'd marked my place with a business card.

The loos were as different from the glitter of the hall as they could be – I'd seen more luxurious public ones. Anyway, here I was, clean and tarted up, and ready to face the world.

By the time I got back, there was a man sitting down to play the piano, and a photographer was snapping the great and the good. He even photographed me, so I was glad I'd taken some trouble with the lippie. I remembered to hand him one of Nella's cards.

And then it was action stations. Yes, even the well-heeled punters – £10 a time to get in, as opposed to the fiver or less at the fairs Griff and I usually sold at – managed a bit of a rush. At this stage there was a lot of milling round and peering, before people moved on to the next area. I wasn't surprised. At the sort of prices Nella and her colleagues were asking, you wouldn't be making too many impulse buys. Nella greeted a lot of people with air-kisses. I stood around doing my best to look both decorative (not easy), and knowledgeable (quite hard).

In similar circumstances Griff would have sent me off to sniff out bargains on competitors' stalls. The idea was to find something they really knew nothing about and as a result had underpriced. Any bargains here would have been relative – and way beyond my budget. Nella unlocked the cabinet and showed off a couple of fine pieces. She put them back and locked up again. Another punter. A sale! But nothing that involved me, no matter how hard I wanted to help. The purchaser stood and talked for ages. She and Nella exchanged family news, and at one point photos were shown.

So I stood and smiled until my face started to ache. The pianist switched to slow stuff, as if his fingers were tired. One-two-three, one-two-three: I tried to recall what Griff had told me about rhythms when he'd pushed me round the kitchen in an effort to teach me to dance. Waltz-time. That was it. Thinking about Griff made my feet move in time with the music. Not a lot, not enough to draw attention to myself. Just enough to stop me screaming with boredom. If I'd had better hair I might have been happy to swap with one of the ticket ladies.

Griff would be cross with me. Life was too short ever to be bored, he said. Just look at people if you've ever a spare minute. Learn from them. So I blinked my eyes extra hard and started looking. The two men were there again.

I hadn't registered them consciously before. But now it dawned on me that I had seen two men looking hard at one of Nella's cabinets several times. Of course, people do this all the time. They fall for an item but think it's too pricey. Or they think something might do as a gift, only they're just not sure. But there was nothing wistful or thoughtful about these two. Had Nella clocked them? Had the other exhibitors? On home territory I could have sneaked over to one of our friends and asked them for the low-down. Not here.

Did any exhibitors look as if they'd welcome a friendly natter? Not enough to interrupt a possible sale, that was for sure. Wherever I looked, plastic was being shoved into terminals and codes being inserted.

The men had disappeared. Why hadn't I thought of tailing them?

They were so ordinary-looking, trying so hard not to draw attention to themselves, they must have been up to something. Were they planning to steal something? And if so, what? I drifted over to the display case they'd been most interested in. Well, with nothing in it costing less than £4000, they'd have had a good selection. Perhaps it was time to revise my opinion of Nella, which had fallen quite a lot in the last twenty-four hours. She'd put Lord Elham's Hungarian silver dish dead centre, with a couple of spots highlighting it nicely. It looked really good, worth every penny of the £7250 price she'd written in code on the reverse of the card beside it. She'd be able to drop it slightly if anyone asked for her best price on it – if people did such things at exalted events like this.

I felt eyes on our area again. Male again. This time a very expensive-looking man, probably in his later forties. He wasn't looking at the display or at me, but at Nella. I could have sworn he caught her eye and touched his watch. She responded with a swift smile which he returned.

The pianist played on. He'd moved to a piece by Schubert that Griff played when his arthritis wasn't troubling him – an Impromptu, it was called. I hummed it, under my breath, I'd thought, only Nella stared at me.

I stopped. 'Is there anything I can do?' I asked. 'It doesn't seem right for me to be standing around doing nothing, and it'd look unprofessional to sit reading, even if it is a book on silver.'

'It would indeed. Dear me, I thought you'd have more stamina than this.'

'I can work till the cows come home, Nella,' I said sharply. 'You ask your brother. Aidan knows I'm happy working sixteen-, eighteen-hour days when Griff and I are under pressure and I don't want Griff to wear himself out.'

'So what exactly do you do at a sale?'

What did she think I did? Walk round on my hands? And why had she asked me along if she needed an answer? 'Sell.

Griff reckons I can sell sand to Arabs. Or I might mooch and
buy from other people. Or just keep my eyes open. Which
I've been doing today. Have you noticed a couple of men dead
interested in something in that display case?' I pointed. 'Can't
keep their eyes off it – they've been back three or four times
now. Look, they're both about forty, one quite good-looking
and the other quite steely-eyed.'

She rubbed her hands in very upper-class glee. 'I was going
to ask you to serve while I have some lunch, but if you think
there's a likely sale—'

'I told you, I can sell things. I know the code you use. And
if anyone haggles, I can always call you on your mobile.'

She nodded, bending to retrieve her bag from the cupboard.
'Let me see you put the number in your phone,' she said. She
sounded so like my least-favourite headmistress I could have
head-butted her. Come to think of it, I'd been wanting to hit
her all morning.

Instead I did as I was told. Off she went, followed at a
discreet distance by the handsome man who'd signalled to her
earlier. She had a nice husband, did she, Griff? Well, it looked
as if she had a nice toy boy too.

'It's Scottish,' I told the gentle-faced woman in her sixties
who'd drifted over and pointed at what looked like a toast
rack for five thousand. 'And it's a bannock rack. Shall I reach
it out for you?' Griff had dinned it into me that the greatest
step to getting a punter to buy an item, even if he'd said it
was beyond his price range, was letting him handle it. Would
it work now? Without waiting for an answer, I unlocked the
case, making sure I locked it again. I pressed the bannock
rack into her hand. 'Robertson of Edinburgh. You can see his
mark. And here's the date – 1773.'

She turned it over and over.

'I always think one of the greatest pleasures of an item like
this is knowing how many other people have used it. Like
that spectacle case over there, with the chain to attach to a
chatelaine.' I adopted a really awful Scots accent: 'And do ye
like your bannocks well or lightly done, ma'am?'

I was rewarded by a laugh, but the shake of the head was
regretful. It really was beyond her budget, even when I quoted
the discounted price. But maybe the spectacle case wasn't. I

reached it without her asking, and fished out the spectacles inside.

'Sometimes you can even see through them,' I said, extending the sides and perching the frame on my nose. 'See?'

She tried. And I knew I had a sale. This time I didn't quote the discounted price.

Nella had taken a very long lunch, but her coffers were fuller and her shelves emptier by three more items when she returned. She looked surprised rather than approving, but sent me off for lunch too. My stomach's rumblings would have drowned any protests if I'd tried to make them.

'I'm sure there are lots of cheap food outlets if you take the indoor walkway to the station,' Nella declared. 'The restaurant upstairs is a minimum spend of £12, I'm afraid.'

Patronizing cow.

I nodded, as if I didn't know about the expensive catering that always accompanied posh antique fairs, and mooched off. I'd spent so much effort weaning Lord Elham off unhealthy food I wasn't about so succumb to rubbish now. But a brisk walk in the open air would be nice, particularly if it led me to a salad bar or at least a decent sarnie. As I turned up my collar and pulled on my gloves – if you're dealing with precious goods you don't risk numb fingers – I realized I wasn't the only one on the move. The two guys who'd taken such a shine to our display were going walkabout too. Just for fun I tried to follow them. After all, one young woman head down and hunched against the wind must look much like another.

I was doing pretty well, I thought, until I realized they were leading me to the car park. So that was that. At least they wouldn't be bothering us any more. I could do an about-turn and head back to base. But I didn't see them drive off. All they did was sit in the car and make a phone call. Just on the off-chance – of what I wasn't at all sure – I jotted down their car reg. And then, my stomach saying that exercise was all very well, I turned back. I'd just got level with the courtesy bus shelter when a bus drew up. I wasn't going to get on – well, it was only a step to the hall – but I noticed that Bill and Ben were active again. They were walking briskly back to the hall.

I thought I'd beat them to it – easily. But it seemed the bus had to stick to a ten-minute schedule, and there I sat, fuming.

I found an empty table in the refreshment area and sat down. If I was paying through the nose for my sandwich I might as well take advantage of the facilities. The pianist was still toiling away. He'd moved on to *Porgy and Bess*, and some of Griff's favourite tunes. Tapping my foot, I unwrapped the sandwich – and my phone rang.

It was Nella. 'Come here this instant!' She did not sound happy.

FIVE

The two men I'd tailed were back, both, even the good-looking one, looking stern as they spoke to Nella, who was holding something in both hands. Nella was furious, but also, I thought, embarrassed. Perhaps furious was winning.

She put something down so that she could point at me, her voice carrying easily but foolishly. It was she, not the men, who were attracting attention. 'Handling stolen goods, indeed! It's she you need to speak to, not me. That Townend girl.' The quiver of her hand made her diamonds sparkle beautifully.

A few years ago, I'd have bolted, and to hell with it. That was what feral kids did, and even if I'd never been quite that bad, I spent enough time living on the edge of the law to know a few unpleasant dodges. I could have tripped people, tipped stands, done whatever it took. And don't think I didn't want to now. But I wouldn't. Neither would I burst into tears or wet myself with fear, no matter how much effort it took.

If Lord Elham had taught me anything, it was to look calm, and even be a bit high-handed in dealings with the police. Griff, on the other hand, preferred to woo them, if they were young and handsome enough. I don't think that just now he'd have felt drawn to either of these.

'I'm Lina Townend,' I said, with a smile I wouldn't let

wobble, no matter how hard my heart was thumping. 'How can I help?'

Did I see doubt in the eyes of the younger cop? 'We have reason to believe you are handling stolen goods.'

'Everything else I can guarantee, officers,' Nella declared, cutting across him. 'This is a LAPADA fair, you know. We have to know the provenance of everything. You can check my paperwork. All of it.'

What would Griff do? He'd give another winsome smile, only he'd speak man to man. I'd better speak woman to man. 'You've had your noses glued to the big display case all morning, haven't you?' I asked them both, with a pale copy of Griff's smile. Let them register they'd not been as clever as they thought.

They didn't smile back. 'I repeat, we have reason to believe you're handling stolen goods,' said the older one, his eye decidedly cold.

'That's a very serious—' I'd forgotten the word.

'Indeed it is,' Nella snapped. 'And one likely to ruin my business. Now you have Ms Townend in custody, officers, kindly interview her well away from here.' She made little shooing gestures. 'Security must have a room somewhere, for goodness' sake.'

I was so angry that the missing word came back. 'What do you allege I've stolen, Mr – er—?' After all, they hadn't shown me their warrant cards yet.

'Detective Sergeant Morris, from the Metropolitan Police Fine Art Unit. And this is Detective Inspector Farfrae.' They flashed their IDs in unison.

They looked genuine. I mustn't throw up.

'For God's sake, can't you do this in private?' Nella demanded.

'Whatever,' I shrugged. 'I shan't run.' Not on legs as rubbery as this I wouldn't.

One on either side, they escorted me away from Nella. The punters parted for us. I could feel their eyes burning into me. The kindly security men who'd bantered earlier now silently admitted us to a room horribly like a cell, one looking reproachful, the other coldly angry, as if I'd personally betrayed him.

I held on to the back of the chair they pointed to so I wouldn't fall over.

'Sit down. Now, tell us, Ms Townend, what you've been up to,' Farfrae said.

I was frozen to the spot. 'Am I under arrest?' Not the most sensible question, but it just came out.

'We're just asking you to answer our questions,' he said.

I didn't think there'd been a question. I shook my head blankly. This wasn't going well and I wasn't making it go any better. I swallowed hard. 'When you were looking at the display case, what were you looking at?'

'You tell us, Ms Townend,' Morris said. 'Please, sit down.' It didn't sound like an invitation.

My head was swimming, so I did as I was told. And realized, rather late, what they were on about. I didn't want to dob Lord Elham in, but if it was a choice between him and me, I'd sacrifice him, any time. 'You haven't arrested Nella, who owns everything else, so it must be something to do with that silver dish.'

'At last we're getting somewhere,' Morris said. 'Where did you get it from?'

'Lord Elham,' I whispered. I tried again, louder. 'Lord Elham of Bossingham Hall, Kent.'

'Really?' His voice dripped disbelief. 'And why should this lord give it to you?'

'He didn't give it me; he asked me to sell it for him.' I dug in my bag for my organizer, into which I'd clipped a copy of the receipt I'd given him.

Before I could fish it out, Morris continued, 'And why should a lord ask a slip of a thing like you to sell something as valuable as that?'

'It's a very long story.'

'So why don't you begin at the beginning? You'll find us very patient,' he added, clearly lying through his teeth, as he leaned back on his chair and folded his arms. 'Come on, why should Lord Elham hand over that plate?'

If only Griff were here, to help me sort out the bits they needed to know from the bits they didn't. If only I could dowse for facts like I could dowse for bargains. I pressed my fingers to my forehead. 'Because I'm his daughter.'

Bingo! Morris nearly went arse over tip, and Farfrae had to grab him.

'Lord Elham . . . So you're Lady—?' Farfrae recovered first.

'Plain Ms Townend.' It was time to have another dig in my purse. I came up with another of our business cards.

Farfrae scanned it and frowned. 'So you're an antiques dealer too? In your own right?'

I was back on firmer ground at last. 'Didn't Nella tell you? I'm helping out while her usual assistant is in . . . is incapacitated.' Thank goodness for Griff and my vocab book. I didn't think they would have been impressed by expressions like 'pulling a sickie'.

He referred to the card again. 'So who's this Griffith Tripp?'

'He's a highly respected dealer, officers, specializing in Victorian china. I was his apprentice; now I'm his junior partner. I only came to this fair on what you might call work experience.'

'And to flog a piece of stolen silver, using an equally highly respected antique dealer as a front.'

'I've got a copy of the receipt I gave Lord Elham. Hang on just a second.' Where was the bloody thing? Ah! I unclipped it from the organizer and put it on the table. 'Look. I've given a full and accurate description of the piece. I couldn't put in what I know now, because I didn't know it at the time.'

'So let me get this straight, Ms Townend,' Farfrae pressed on. 'You offered to sell in good faith what you believed to be Lord Elham's property.'

'Exactly. But because Griff and I only do the smaller fairs, we thought it would be better to sell it through a real expert, like Lady Petronella.' It was time to pull a little more rank, even if it was someone else's. 'She told me it was Hungarian, and what it was worth.'

'But you didn't put that on the receipt.'

'How could I when I didn't know when I wrote it? You can't alter things like that. Look,' I added in desperation, 'silver's quite a different thing from china. I could tell you pretty well anything you wanted to know about a piece of Worcester porcelain; I could walk you round the outfits here and tell you who's overcharging and who doesn't know he's got a real earner on his hands.'

The men exchanged a glance; Morris mouthed something.

I waited, but had to continue. 'But silver – I'm still learning. If you check Nella's stand, you'll find a book on the subject – I was mugging up on it so as not to look an idiot if anyone asked. My God, what if people start demanding refunds for stuff I sold this morning? It could ruin her business!' Now I came to think of it, I was being pretty generous even to think of her business. What on earth had happened to *noblesse oblige*? Griff would never have treated a colleague as badly as that in public.

'So why did Lord Elham give you that particular piece?' Morris looked genuinely interested.

'Why not? He's given me loads of pieces, all of which I've issued receipts for. I get the best price I can, and then take ten per cent. Again, it's all written down.'

Farfrae said, 'It's a very formal arrangement between a father and his daughter.'

'I'm not the only child; I want to be able to prove everything's fair.'

'And you live with your father?'

'No.'

'Why not?'

I took a deep breath. 'I live with my partner. Griff. My business partner.'

'Mr Tripp. OK. But most people would leap at the idea of living in a stately home.'

'Not if they have to share it with the paying public and my father.' Damn, I'd let a crack show.

'Why would that be?'

'I like my life as it is,' I said, suspecting he'd keep prying. 'I'm learning an honest trade and a lot more besides. If you found out you'd got a lord as a father would you automatically jack everything in and go and live with him? No? Well, then.'

'But you go and see him and he asks you to sell something—'

'I told you, he asks me to sell a lot of things. The Hall now belongs to trustees, and he's allowed to live in one wing. All the decent china and furniture and so on was catalogued and kept in the rooms open to the public. He got to keep a load of stuff no one bothered to look at.'

'Got to keep?'

Was he trying to say he'd nicked it? I deliberately misunderstood him. 'Furniture, books, china – all left in the rooms he was allocated. Much of it's rubbish. Some isn't. When he runs short of cash, I sell something for him. Everything's

above board, Sergeant.' This was as near the truth as it needed
to be.

'So where was this dish or plate or whatever?'

'In one of the rooms in his wing. It was filthy dirty. He
didn't even know it was silver.'

'You did,' Farfrae said accusingly.

I was ready to cry. But I put my chin up and went into the
attack. 'Look, Inspector, you specialize in fine art – right?
But if someone showed you a body, you'd have a rough idea
what it was, wouldn't you?'

Morris covered a snigger. In fact, I think I was winning
him over.

Farfrae didn't so much as crack his face. 'Why this piece?
When it wasn't your area of expertise? Because it was small
and portable and you could whisk it away without his
noticing?'

'I've shown you the receipt, for God's sake.' If only I could
tell them to phone Lord Elham to confirm what I said. But
this was the time for *Countdown* and he was quite capable of
denying everything so he could get on with the show.

'But why not some china, since you claim to know a lot
about it?'

'Claim! I bloody do! Look, you're experts – OK? In one
of the aisles near the coffee stall – the cheap one, not the one
by the piano – there's a guy dealing with nineteenth-century
Wedgwood. Right? He's got a majolica cheese dome – quite
pretty, with a little knob on the lid. He's set it up for nearly
a thousand – fine if it were perfect. But take another look at
the knob, and tell me it hasn't been repaired. Very well, but
still repaired. Go on. Take a look.'

'That would prove you had sharp eyes, but not that you're
an expert.' All the same, Farfrae was now wavering too.

'True. The reason why I didn't take away anything else was
most of the stuff I could see wasn't valuable, and Lord Elham
didn't have time for me to check through everything.'

'Lord Elham! I thought you said he was your father!'

'He is my father. Look, why don't you stop bullying me
and check a few facts. Even if it's not your area, you've probably heard of *Natura Rerum*.' And if they hadn't they weren't
about to admit it. 'It's an extremely rare philosophical trea-
tise. Basically it was my doing that it was saved for the nation

and now lives in the British Library. If you don't know all about it, get on the phone and someone will tell you the whole bloody story.' My voice cracked, quite horribly. 'I'm sorry. I didn't need to swear.' And Griff had forbidden bad language in his house before 7 p.m. At least he wasn't in the room to hear. 'But I'm so thirsty and hungry. I had to have breakfast at six, and then I spent my lunch hour keeping my eye on you – I followed you all the way to the car park – because I thought you were up to no good. And then I had Nella's SOS, and I didn't feel she wanted me to turn up clutching a half-eaten prawn sandwich.'

'Quite,' Morris said. 'I'll go and get you something.'

I scrubbed my cheeks with a nasty damp tissue. 'And while you're at it you can check on that Wedgwood lid!'

So the soft cop went off, leaving me with the hard cop. The silence between us grew uncomfortable. It was broken only when Morris returned, carrying a tray. Coffee for three, cake for three, and a prawn sandwich.

I nodded my thanks. I was really cross to see how much my hand shook as I tried to unpeel the wrapper. Eventually Farfrae reached across and helped.

As I ate, Morris gave me quite a nice smile. 'I checked on that Wedgwood. You were right. Tell me, are you a divvy?'

My mouth was full, so I had a moment to work out the answer that would cause me least grief. 'Sometimes,' I said at last. 'It isn't something I can turn on or off, like a tap. And it doesn't work with humans,' I added with a sad smile, 'or I wouldn't have had you down as thieves.' And I might have had better luck with boyfriends.

'Did you divvy this?' Farfrae asked, tapping the silverware.

Drat. 'I told you, the rest of the stuff in the room was tat. As soon as I cleaned a corner with my sleeve I knew I was on to something.'

'Would you walk round with one of us and see if you get any vibrations?' he continued.

Double drat. 'Not like a convict between two warders, I wouldn't. These dealers are way out of my league, but I wouldn't want news to get back to my mates.'

'Fair enough.'

Now he was stuck into his cake, I saw my chance. 'Why did you come to the fair?' I asked. 'You didn't know this would be on sale, did you?' For the first time I touched the dish, now wrapped in an evidence bag.

'Where would you expect to see stolen antiques? At an antiques fair.' He had quite a nice smile. 'Even one as care- fully vetted as this. So my colleague and I just had a look round – and found that.'

'Silly question: are you sure it's been stolen? Might there not be another one around?'

'There might. But it seems a bit of a coincidence, doesn't it?' Farfrae chipped in.

'Life's full of coincidences. But if you want to take it away I shall need a receipt for it, you know. To show my father.'

He nodded. 'Standard procedure. You know we'll have to talk to his lordship.'

My first thought was that I'd love to be a fly on the wall. How would Farfrae deal with champagne and Pot Noodles? Not to mention *Countdown*? But what wasn't such a funny prospect was the police taking into custody every single item in the hoard. It'd reduce my income, and really harm Lord Elham's – might drive him to do more forging for Titus Oates. What if he kept his forgery gear at the Hall? I felt sick at the thought. The minute I was shut of the fuzz, I'd better phone him. And Oates, come to think of it. Or would that make me an accessory? Or worse, someone perverting the course of justice, like people who get rid of murderers' weapons and bloody clothes?

'He's not the sharpest knife in the drawer,' I said cautiously. 'He'll probably not have the faintest clue what's going on.'

'I take it his condition isn't hereditary,' Farfrae said with a mocking smile.

I ignored it. 'Part of his condition is that he's a fully paid up alcoholic. And his diet's crap.'

'And the other part of "his condition"?' This time his voice dripped with sarcasm. Which I also ignored.

'Probably does owe something to inbreeding. And a rotten upbringing.' I'd better not mention I thought his sense of right and wrong had been amputated and that he was blessed with an enormous amount of low cunning. Maybe I should give him something else to chew on. 'The press will have a field day if you turn up and arrest the old guy. Especially if they get a photo of him being taken away. He looks like an advert for Oxfam. Before, not after.'

'If he's a common thief—'

'Who does the plate belong to? When was it stolen?'

'It was part of a haul from a house in Kensington. Armed robbery. Last September.'

So he wouldn't see my genuine sigh of relief, I shook my head in the theatrical way Griff sometimes uses. 'You're on to a loser there, then, Mr Farfrae. He's not left Bossingham Hall except with me for the last year.'

But what I didn't say was that someone might have been to see him.

SIX

To do them justice, both officers walked back with me to Nella's stand. She was far from pleased to see any of us, and who could blame her? Farfrae told her that he was sure the whole thing had been a mistake on their part, and that as far as they were concerned I was in the clear.

'Certainly no slur attaches to you and your business. Or hers,' he added firmly.

'So the dish wasn't stolen?' she asked sharply.

'If it was, we are not of the opinion that Ms Townend was in any way involved.'

'But you are quite sure I wasn't? In that case you may take yourself over to all my colleagues and tell them so. I do not want my business ruined.' As they trailed off, like a pair caught poaching, she turned to me. 'As for you, miss, you can take your things and go. You've done enough damage for one day.' She reached behind her table and thrust my bag and coat at me.

I stood my ground, my hands clenched behind me so I wouldn't hit her, the insolent old cow. 'I can't. I can't, not just like that.'

'And why not?'

'Because all my stuff's locked in your house.' I tried to keep my voice down, but didn't quite succeed.

She stared at me, as if her till had spoken. 'Go and wait at the railway station. I'll drop your case off when I've finished here.'

The only words that came were the words of the play-ground. They came loudly, too. 'That's not fair!' But I didn't stamp my foot.

'It's all you deserve. We close here at six. I should be back at the station by – say, eight.'

'I've done nothing wrong! I do not deserve to be treated this way.' I wasn't getting anywhere, so I made myself think of another approach. 'For goodness' sake, my Griff's your brother's lover – what's this going to do to their relationship?'

'You should have thought of that before you tried to palm stolen goods off on me.'

'She's just told you she didn't,' said a voice.

I spun round, hoping it was one of the police officers. But it was a young man I didn't know from Adam, except he was more warmly dressed. I flashed him a smile.

'Ask the policemen!' I said.

'They are irrelevant. If you work in this business you will know that trust is paramount. I can no longer trust you, and worse still my clients may no longer trust me. I'll see you at eight.' She turned her back on me, and addressed herself to her mobile phone.

'At least let her pick up her things from your house,' the young man said, with the plausible sort of smile young men give grandmothers to win them round when they've been up to something. 'I'll run her over there. Piers Hamlyn.' He put out a nicely manicured hand.

She ignored him. And it.

'I'd say yes please, but I don't even know the address,' I said, hating myself for sounding defeated, but suspecting, deep down, that whatever I said, I might have considered behaving much as she had done – my suitcase apart, of course. It must be something I'd picked up from my father's genes. 'Or have a key, of course. Excuse me!'

I thought I saw Farfrae in the distance, and dropping everything, hurtled after him. As it turned out, it was Morris I cannoned into.

Forgetting to lower my voice, I let rip. 'Thanks to you, I've lost my job. I've been sacked like that.' I clicked my fingers. 'I'd go home, but all my things are at Nella's house. What am I to do?' I used a lot of other words too.

'Let's go and talk to her.' Quite kindly, he took my arm above the elbow to turn me round.

Furiously, I shook him off. 'It looks as if you're bloody arresting me.'

'Sorry.' He raised both hands as if in surrender and fell into step beside me.

Sadly, my dishy young would-be saviour had disappeared, but someone had put my coat and bag in a neat pile out of the way of people's feet. Somehow I didn't think it was Nella. I picked them up.

'You again.' Though it wasn't clear if it was me or Morris she was speaking to.

'I gather there's a problem with Ms Townend's property, Lady Petronella.'

'I told her, I'd bring her case to the station.'

He pulled himself up, and said, very formally but very reasonably, 'You will appreciate we can't just leave a vulnerable young woman unattended on the station for nearly two hours.'

'She'd manage.'

Now his voice was sharp. 'If we drive her to your house then she won't have to. Let us know when you're ready to leave and we'll follow you.' I wouldn't have argued with his tone, and, after a moment, neither did she. 'We'll meet you here at six fifteen, then. Another coffee, Lina?'

I nodded, hardly caring. And then I cared a great deal. 'I'm fine. And I can take a taxi to Nella's.'

'Why?'

'Why? What if you're not the police? Or if you're bent? You wouldn't be the first,' I said bitterly.

Farfrae appeared from nowhere. 'I've been checking your role in that book scam, Ms Townend. And I can see why you wouldn't trust police officers, especially those in plain clothes. Now, there's a police office on the complex: the officers there could confirm we are who we say we are.'

'They won't be able to prove you're not bent, though.'

'I'm afraid you'll just have to take that on trust.'

'You're creating another scene,' Nella declared. 'Just go, the lot of you, for God's sake.'

'I'd better have my book, then,' I said, suddenly remembering it.

'What book?'

'The one on silverware. I showed you.'

'Wasn't it with your other things?' She sounded genuinely puzzled.

I shook out my coat and opened my bag. 'It's not here now.'

Morris asked, 'Where did you leave it?'

I pointed. 'In that cupboard down there.'

'Are you implying I've kept it?' She flushed brick red.

Morris eased past her and bent to open it. There was nothing inside but Nella's bag and an empty paper coffee mug. 'Is there anywhere else it might be?'

'Why don't you just accuse me outright of stealing the bloody thing? You're halfway to ruining my business – you might as well finish the job!'

What would Griff say? I breathed very carefully, as if I could hear his words.

'She's right,' I managed to say at last. 'All this attention is very bad. Let's forget it. If you find it, Nella, you can give it to me later.' I walked quickly away, taking Morris by the arm as if he were Griff, needing to be led from the temptation of the bar to the solace of the coffee stall.

We duly tailed Nella back to her house, but she would not let us in.

The officers were inclined to be stroppy, but I pointed out we were a good deal warmer in their car, even though what had started as a sudden shower was fast becoming a sleet storm.

'You're very forbearing,' Farfrae said.

'There's going to be a hell of a lot – sorry, it's not seven yet, is it? There's going to be a lot of bridge building to do,' I said. 'Her brother and my dear Griff are partners in the other sense. Hey, what's she doing?' I was suddenly a good deal less forbearing, as the front door opened and my case was shoved out, open and spilling the contents. I dived for them, gathering them willy-nilly and dumping the lot on the back seat.

'Everything there?' Morris asked, as I shook out soaking garments, and tried to fold them.

'Yes. I think so. No! No, my teddy's not here!' Precious Tim, a gift from Griff. I suddenly found myself doing what I'd wanted to do for the past five hours – bursting into tears.

Farfrae's thumps on her door would have wakened the dead, but she didn't open. Six foot two of him had to fold itself down so he could yell through the letter box. We all waited in silence.

Then an upper window opened, and Tim came hurtling out. She might have aimed him at the deepest puddle.

'Not a nice lady,' Morris muttered, swathing him in a duster he dug out from a door pocket. 'Anything else still missing?

I stowed Tim in my case. 'Only my book on silver. But that's something that can be replaced.'

I finally reached Bredeham on the last train. Other passengers were cannier than me, and made sure they grabbed all the taxis. No buses, of course, not at this time of night. I'd have to walk. Pity it was pitch dark. One of the local councillors had an obsession with light pollution, and refused to admit street lights to the village. But I'd got a little torch and it would only take fifteen minutes to reach our cottage. And there I'd find Griff. I trudged on. At last I could see the porch light he'd left on. I almost ran towards it. Not because I'd been afraid – there wasn't another soul about – but I wanted to be loved better.

I froze. There was a car parked outside, and it was Aidan's. I hadn't quite depended on getting my three penn'orth in first, but I was really daunted by the thought of confronting them both. I knew who Aidan would believe, didn't I?

I sheltered under a tree and pondered. It was a bit of a step to our caravan, parked in a friendly farmer's field, but I'd be warm and dry there. More or less, anyway. And I could phone Griff to tell him I was safe. I certainly had to do that. And soon. The only reason I'd not called before was to spare him an evening of worry. I'd been stupid, hadn't I? Nella would certainly have got on to Aidan the minute she was shut of me, and Aidan – well, it was clear what he'd done. I checked my mobile. Yes, there was just enough signal. I dialled.

'Griff? I just thought I'd let you know I'm back.'

'My child, where—?'

'I'm heading out to the caravan.'

'My dear one, you'll come home now, where you belong.'

'No, it's too late now. I'll tell you all about it in the morning.'

I cut the call and turned off the mobile. So the trundle of the case wheels wouldn't give me away, I picked it up and carried it. There was a short cut across the field, and though even I wouldn't normally risk it at this time of night, it was one way of making sure Griff couldn't chase after me.

Any time I went to school I was told I wasn't very bright, and by the time I got to the caravan I was ready to believe it. There was bloody Aidan's car, waiting for me. In fact Aidan reached me first, seizing the case and wrapping me in a blanket. He even pressed a hip flask into my hand – the one I'd given to him last Christmas, as it happened. I didn't really do spirits, and it had always amazed me how actors on TV could swig a whole glass without choking. Then Griff explained it wasn't really whisky, of course. Aidan's was. And even though everything was so awful I couldn't stop laughing.

'Not let you into the house? Dear me, what on earth did Nella think she was doing?' Aidan asked, dabbing his hand on the living room radiator to make sure it was giving enough heat. Dissatisfied, he threw another log on the fire. Griff had left him in charge while he busied himself in the kitchen.

I'd had enough time on the train to work out my own theory about that, something to do with the handsome man she'd had lunch with, but I could hardly put that forward as an explanation. I huddled more deeply into my bathrobe and shook my head. 'Actually, she was right to sack me.' It was the conclusion I'd made myself come to on the way home. Before that I'd have torn her hair out, given a chance. Not just for what she'd done, but because if Aidan had believed her and Griff had believed Aidan . . . I swallowed hard and lifted my chin. 'I know Griff always says there's no such thing as bad publicity, but a couple of plods descending on you in the middle of a show like that – well, it'd be bad enough at the fairs we do, but sac . . . sacri—?'

'Sacrilege?' Aidan prompted.

'Yes – sacrilege at a LAPADA one. It's a shame I lost that book on silver, though.'

'And deeply ironic that you, having been accused of theft, should be the victim of it.'

'I was never accused of theft. Only handling stolen goods. Just as bad for Nella's reputation.' But I suddenly found I didn't care very much. What did worry me was more important.

Tim. 'Do you think he'll recover?' Being stuffed wet into the corner of my case had left him very bent and matted. I took him from the radiator where he was drying and squeezed him a bit.

'I'll buy you a replacement, Lina, by way of apology,' Aidan said, throwing another log on the fire: he was clearly trying to turn the living room into a sauna.

I shook my head and started to cry again. What was it about my bear that turned on my waterworks?

Clearly miffed, Aidan stalked out, joining Griff in the kitchen. I could hear him exclaiming to Griff about my lack of proportion.

Griff's reply wasn't clear, but he said something about my never having had a bear to call my own – that was why Tim was precious.

Aidan clearly wasn't convinced. 'But it's worth nothing!'

'It depends how one assesses value, doesn't it?'

There was a moment's silence. Then Aidan started again. Even though he was upset, he managed to use the sort of words other people never say, only write. 'What truly worries me, Griff, is that she seems to consider such appalling treatment acceptable. Why isn't she railing and shouting, threatening legal action?'

'Because she's been treated badly so long she's come to expect it as her due? At least this – ah – incident didn't involve violence.' Suddenly the door shut.

I gave poor Tim's ear another tweak and went back to my nest of blankets on the sofa. People didn't like to know they'd been overheard, did they?

Then they both came back in, Griff carrying a plate of cake and three mugs of hot chocolate on my favourite papier mâché tray. He always made the creamiest hot chocolate in the world if one of us was upset. Putting the tray down, he turned and stroked my hair. 'Bears are meant to suffer, my sweet one. Let him dry, and a little titivating will bring him back to life. Perhaps a new ribbon . . .'

'Do you think Elham really did come by that dish honestly?' In trying to change the subject, Aidan put the question Griff would never have asked, out loud, at least.

I pulled a face. 'Who can tell? He wouldn't go out and nick it from someone else's house. In fact, he couldn't have stolen it when the police said it went missing. But I bet the trustees would kick themselves if they knew half of what he's got in his wing.' Despite all that malt sloshing round inside me I wouldn't say anything about those spliff butts. Not even to Griff.

SEVEN

The following day, I overslept, which I absolutely never did. It was well into the morning when I woke, which was only because someone was leaning on the front doorbell.

It was an Interflora delivery. For me. Something that had never happened before in my life. The bunch of flowers was enormous – it filled three vases. According to the note with them, the flowers were from Nella, hoping I'd got home safely and with her apologies for her overhasty actions. 'Overhasty' was a real Aidan word, so I reserved judgement on who'd actually sent it. Especially as there were no lilies, which he always said were vulgar.

Aidan himself arrived soon after a rather late lunchtime – why he'd bothered going home in the first place I wasn't sure, since he couldn't have left much before three in the morning. However, the reason was soon clear. He was carrying a brand new Steiff teddy bear, complete with limited edition certificate and identity button in its ear. It was large enough to have cost him an arm and a leg. I thanked him and promised to treasure it. Treasuring wasn't the same as loving, though. Tim, looking much better after a good brushing, was safe there.

Griff, who was sure I'd get a cold after all my adventures in the rain, went down with a stinker himself, and had to call Mrs Hatch, who looked after the shop whenever we were both busy.

And late in the afternoon I strolled down the lane to get a signal to phone Titus Oates. I didn't want to use the landline. This was a call I'd rather Griff didn't know about. He always worried about me and my father, and this would only make him fret more.

Titus never bothered being polite. 'Lord Elham? Who says

I'm letting the old bugger do any work for me?' he grunted in response to my very timid question.

'No one,' I said quickly. 'But it's possible, if he did just happen to be doing anything for anyone, the fuzz might find out. You know what they're like if they start searching people's places. And if they find things they ask questions.'

'So why would the filth be poking their ugly noses into Bossingham Hall?'

I quoted back at him his favourite sentence: 'That's for me to know and you not to bother trying to find out.'

'That old queer been blabbing when he was pissed?'

'Griff's drinking habits and sexual orientation are none of your business.' I'd rehearsed that response many times to make sure I got it right. Now I patted myself on the back.

'Oooh, la-di-da!' When I didn't bother responding, he asked, 'You're sure the filth'll be paying him a visit?'

'I can't be sure they won't,' I said in my normal voice. 'And you know what he's like if people start asking questions.'

'Depends which end of the champagne bottle he's at. But point taken. Thanks, doll.' He cut the call.

I rocked on my feet. Had Titus Oates really thanked little me? But there was no one around to see my dramatics, so I gave up and nipped into the village Londis, to stock up on blackcurrant juice, Griff's favourite tipple when he was ill. Shaz's face dropped in disappointment as I put the basket by the till and asked for some aspirins, too.

'Oh, you've just missed him. What a shame.'

'Him?'

'This gorgeous bloke. Legs up to here and a bum to die for. Asking for your cottage. He said he'd got something to return to you.'

Last time people had asked Shaz about me she'd been a good deal too generous with her information. She obviously remembered too. 'I know, I know – but he had your business card, see, and someone else would have told him if I hadn't. And he said he'd got something of yours. And you needed it. So off you go! You might just catch him!' She took my fiver and counted out change.

Not a lot of sleep, no make-up, my gardening anorak and shoes I kept for muddy lanes – did I want anyone to see me like this? Especially a gorgeous bloke?

But it had started to sleet again, and I had to go some-where, so it might as well be home.

I didn't recognize the silver Peugeot parked behind Aidan's car outside the cottage. But whoever had parked it there would have had his photo taken by our security cameras – one visible, which was meant to warn people off, and one hidden, to take the photo of anyone trying to smash the other.

Letting myself in, I heard Griff being very polite to someone; in my experience that meant not just a young man but a good-looking one. So how would Aidan react to that? I nipped upstairs to run a brush through my hair and to change my shoes and ran back down, to find, drinking tea from Griff's Edwardian Worcester tea service, my would-be saviour of the day before, a bunch of flowers even more massive than Aidan's at his feet. Piers Something. Putting his cup and saucer on the table beside him, he got up politely as I came in and took my hand as if he was afraid of breaking it.

Still standing, he passed me the bouquet – a lot of lilies in this one – and then, almost shamefaced, he reached behind him. He produced the book on silver. 'It was just lying there between your stand and your neighbour's so I picked it up. I could have asked Lady Petronella to return it, but she was in such a foul mood I thought she'd throw it at me – or even at you. And since you'd left your business card in it, I thought I'd deliver it in person.'

I could see a frown puckering Griff's forehead, and no wonder – we made a point of not having our address on our cards, just our mobile numbers and our website address.

Perhaps Piers saw the frown. He flushed slightly, and said, with a slight bow, 'I had to do quite a bit of research before I managed to run you to earth.' He smiled at me and Griff equally. He had the most beautiful teeth. 'It helped that I'd seen you before. At other fairs.' Perhaps I was hoping that such a handsome prince was going to tell me he'd fallen in love with me the moment he'd first seen me. But he didn't. He added, 'Sometimes I dabble myself.'

I tried to make my face show polite interest. The last few years had taught me that dabbling was not the way to get ahead in the antiques profession. Or even survive. But every-thing about him suggested a silver spoon – perhaps not as grand as those on Nella's shelves or even in her mouth, but

big enough to send him to the public school which had given
him his accent. From the size of his shoulders he'd probably
played rugby there.

No doubt Griff could see the chip that he swore dented my
shoulder doubling in size, so he jumped in. 'I thought your
face was familiar. Now, where did I see you? Was it Shepton
Mallet? Or Stafford?'

Piers blushed again. 'Folkestone? Sutton Valence School?
I'm only starting, you see.'

'Are you local, Piers?' Aidan asked, surprising me. Why
should he want to know that?

'Absolutely. Well, Sevenoaks. And I wondered, Lina,' Piers
continued, dragging the conversation back the way he wanted
it to go, 'since you were so very badly treated yesterday –
who does that cow think she is? – if—'

'The cow's my sister,' Aidan said heavily. 'But she can
behave in a pretty bovine manner,' he added with a charming
smile. Perhaps he fancied Piers too. 'I'm sorry. I interrupted.'

'Not at all. I hope I didn't offend you, sir.'

Sir? What century was he living in?

'Not as much as my sister offended poor Lina.' Aidan
sounded almost fond of me.

Piers gathered himself together for another attempt. 'Quite.
Which was why I wondered, Lina – I hope this isn't too short
notice – I wondered if you would be kind enough to come to
dinner with me this evening. It shouldn't be too hard to get
a decent table midweek.'

Griff and Aidan produced a matching Tweedledum and
Tweedledee smile. Benign, that was the word I wanted. They
were all so formal and correct. Perhaps it came with drinking
tea and eating little cakes. But what was Piers doing, someone
his age, asking me out in front of them?

If only he'd had the tact to email or something. As it was,
I couldn't use looking after Griff as an excuse, because Aidan
would say he'd do that. And I couldn't say I was ill myself.
And why did he suggest dinner? Thanks to Griff I knew my
way round menus and cutlery – even at 'decent tables'. But
it was hard to eat and drink and think, let alone talk too.

He was off again. 'I thought of somewhere like the
Nonesuch. I know the name's a bit pretentious, but the food
and service are supposed to be excellent.'

Griff said as smoothly as his snuffles would allow, 'It's all of thirty miles away. How were you proposing to ensure she returns safely? A young man taking a young lady to supper doesn't in my experience wish to stay on the wagon.' When he spoke like this I always wondered which book he'd been reading. Dickens? Jane Austen? Then I thought I detected a tiny wink – was he just winding up Piers to see what happened?

Piers thought quickly on his feet, I'll give him that. 'Quite. So I thought I could leave the car here, and take a cab there and back. I wouldn't drink very much, and could drive myself back home.'

'I fear my poor home has only two bedrooms, Piers, or you would be a welcome guest.'

Old liar!

Piers continued, eager as a puppy dog, 'Or if I did have too much, then I could always get the cab to take me back to the Nonesuch and stay over. Or just stay there and put Lina in a cab home.' Clearly, he was very keen on this date, even if a bit hazy on the details. Equally clearly, he didn't depend on profits from sales like Folkestone and Sutton Valence to pay for his social life. He beamed. 'In fact, if Lina preferred, I could book us both rooms there, and return her to you in the morning.'

My sudden sneeze was genuine. 'What Lina would prefer,' I said, with a little bit of sarcasm to show I didn't like being discussed as if I wasn't there, 'is a quiet drink at the Nag's Head. Maybe a bar snack there. But there's no point in going for *haute cuisine* if I've got what Griff's got. I wouldn't taste a thing. Trouble is,' I added, 'I may give it to you, too, Piers.' I reached for the tissues and sneezed, pretty unromantically, again.

To do Piers justice, the prospect of a head cold didn't seem to worry him, and he stayed and talked antiques with Griff – Griff talked, he listened – until Aidan was clearly bored. By then my nose was already glowing red, so he knew what he was in for. At last, it was opening time – the Nag's Head didn't go in for all day service – and we set out, on foot, through the thickening sleet. He offered me his arm and made sure he sheltered me under his golf brolly, so I gave him a few more brownie points.

Away from Griff and Aidan, not to mention Nella, he became

quite funny and nice, talking just like an ordinary person, and I found I was enjoying myself. We had a pint and one of Dave the landlord's wonderful chicken pies apiece, with a plate of genuine home-made chips. What Griff called comfort food, though I didn't allow him to eat it more than once a month.

We agreed it would be a nice idea to email each other, and see each other the next time we were at the same fair. And he planted ever such a chaste kiss on my cheek. I was sorry that my snuffles prevented a nice snog. I thought he might kiss quite nicely.

This cold didn't just drip. It made you sneeze without warning. I'd have been a danger in the shop and didn't dare try restoring any of the china that needed my attention. And I didn't risk visiting Lord Elham, because his diet was so bad he might have caught flu from a fly, and I didn't want his death on my conscience.

In any case, it was better to give him and Titus the chance to spirit away any forgery equipment that might be hanging round. As for the owner of the spliffs, well, he might pay another visit and leave enough evidence for me to tackle Lord Elham about him.

Piers and I texted each other quite a lot, and rather sooner than I expected I was getting a row of 'xxx's. I'd better send a few back. With his background, his education and his income all a bit close to Aidan's, I still wasn't sure he was my sort, but there was no one else on the horizon at the moment, and you never knew what might develop. And what girl in her senses would turn down the chance to be with such a gorgeous bloke?

Soon Folkestone was on us – not a large fair, just a couple of rooms in a big hotel. OK, it was the Grand Hotel, but we and the punters were sent round to a side door. There were a lot of collectibles, not just on Piers' stand either, which made Griff sneer, but some upmarket jewellers too and plenty of middle of the road dealers like us. We went because Griff had some regular customers, including one couple who could be relied on to buy any Mason's Ironstone jugs we found for them, and a woman who collected spectacle cases like the silver one I'd sold for Nella. But not at Nella's price.

Piers was at the far end of the suite of rooms from us, surrounded by what Griff described, quite fairly, as a regrettable collection of Ty Beanie bears in various bright colours. We exchanged a quick kiss as soon as he arrived, and a squeeze of the hand. It was understood that we'd try to have lunch at the same time, and maybe even a nice walk along the cliff top – on a clear day you can see France, though I didn't think there was any hope of that the way the clouds were dashing in. I did have a few doubts, though, about his wearing red cords and a clashing tan body warmer.

'Oh, dear,' Griff sighed. 'Not with those cornflower blue eyes and honey-coloured hair. You'll have to take him in hand, my angel – sartorially speaking, of course.'

Another familiar face was that of Arthur Habgood of Rose Cottage Antiques. I didn't kiss him, or even smile very much, because I knew that as soon as I looked remotely friendly he'd be on at me to do a gob swab for him to prove his theory that his daughter was my mother. Of course, she'd died years ago, which was how I'd been passed round foster parents like the proverbial parcel. At one time I'd have jumped at the chance of having a respectable blood relation. However, there's only so much identity a woman can change at any given time. I'd become someone's daughter, even though my father was far from respectable, and it seemed as if I might become someone's girlfriend. Becoming a genuine granddaughter, as opposed to Griff's honorary one, might be a step too far, as I told Piers over a coffee snatched between setting up and the arrival of the first punters.

'Honorary? I thought you really were his granddaughter.' He sounded quite disappointed.

'Nope. One of the things I don't really tell people unless it's useful is that my father's a lord. I'm his illegitimate daughter.' Griff had persuaded me not to use the word 'bastard'.

One or two guys had even flinched at the term 'illegitimate', and I'd been quietly dropped, but Piers didn't so much as blink. Neither did he ask which lord. 'Some families are a right shower, aren't they? I've got a couple of oddballs in mine. Black sheep. So why don't you want to be Habgood's granddaughter? He seems a nice enough man.'

'He sells damaged goods as perfect,' I said flatly.

Piers' eyes rounded. 'How do you know?'

'Because I recognized a majolica plate I'd repaired myself
and sold him as restored. And damn me if he didn't try to
palm it off as undamaged.'

His jaw set unexpectedly. 'Even so, family's always useful.'

Since this was only the third time we'd met face to face, I
didn't want to start arguing, but I was relieved when the doors
opened and I had to scurry back to base.

For some reason today's fair was incredibly busy; when
Piers was free I was refusing to let a punter haggle down my
price too far, and when I'd extorted another fiver from him,
Piers was up to the eyeballs in turquoise Beanie bears. So we
didn't get to do lunch. The weather was really coming in by
the time we'd finished and packed away, with great gusts of
wind rocking the van and rain slashing into your eyes and
nose. I could see Griff was getting nervous. Since Piers had
to get safely back to Sevenoaks, I allowed myself a little worry
too, and sent him on his way, without much protest. At least
we managed a proper kiss. Which Arthur Habgood had to go
and interrupt.

'Oh, for God's sake—' Piers said.

Habgood just ignored him. 'Lina, I've been trying to catch
you all day. Please – for my sake, for my daughter, your
mother's sake . . . It would mean so much for me to be able
to welcome you into my family. A DNA test wouldn't take a
minute. It wouldn't hurt.'

'It might hurt Griff.'

'It wouldn't change anything between you and Griff.'

'If it wouldn't change anything, why are you so keen?'

'Because – because . . .' He waved his hands around just as
I did when I couldn't explain something I felt deeply about.
Heavens, could you inherit gestures like that?

'OK, I'll think about it,' I told him. But I felt bad, because
I wasn't going to change my mind. Was I?

'Why don't you push off and leave her alone,' Piers said.
'You've had your answer.' He put his arm round my waist
again and kept it there until Habgood had sloped off. 'Now,'
he said, 'where were we?'

And proved me right. He was a very good snogger indeed.

EIGHT

I t wasn't easy to feel sorry for Lord Elham. Ever. But when he phoned me, gibbering with terror, I managed to squeeze a drop of compassion for him. I couldn't make out anything except the word 'police'.

I put my hand over the phone and asked Griff for advice. 'It's my day for the shop,' I said, hoping Griff would say he couldn't spare me. I should have known better.

'You'll have to go over, sweetheart,' Griff said, 'and sort everything out for him. You can't make that cold an excuse any longer, you know.'

I still hadn't told Griff the full story about Lord Elham and the fag ends, or about his connection with Titus Oates. I wasn't about to now. So I just nodded and spoke to my father again. 'I'll get over as quickly as I can.'

'Now, Lina, now! They're putting purple gloves on and looking at everything.'

'Ask to see their search warrant,' I said. 'I'm on my way.'

It was hard to tell who was more pleased to see me, DS Morris or Lord Elham. I grabbed my father by the arm and pushed him towards the kitchen. 'Go and make us all some green tea. I know you don't like it but it's good for you. Off you go.' I turned to Morris. 'Don't say I didn't warn you. Now, do you have a search warrant?'

He flashed something that looked official.   *He should give the occupier a copy!*

'And are all your officers trained in handling delicate china and glass? They'd better be. I know you were kind to me in Brum, but you're still the police and I'm afraid he's still my father. Someone's got to look after his interests, and that someone seems to be me.'

'Lina? Where are you?' Lord Elham wailed.

'I'm on my way!' I wasn't, but still.

'He was offering us champagne,' Morris said. 'All of us. The others have started looking in what seems the cleanest room.'

'Looking but not touching, I hope. You'd have done much better to ask me over first, you know. What are you looking for, and why?'

Looking shifty, he shrugged. 'Acting on information received.'

'About what?' Hell, this was as bad as extracting information from Lord Elham.

He stood up straight and said, 'We have reason to believe that he may have stolen property from the trustees of Bossingham Hall.'

'I told you they let him keep everything that's in here!' Or so he'd said when I'd first met him. I wasn't sure I believed him, but I'd certainly seen nothing new arrive since we'd known each other.

He dropped his official posture and said, 'There's been a recent spate of thefts, Lina – from some of the locked display cases.'

They held a load of rare pieces – English, French and German. 'Which means some really good stuff. But how? They've got an alarm system and CCTV.'

'Quite.'

'A professional, then, maybe stealing to order,' I said.

Morris's eyes opened wide.

'Come on, don't you think we know it happens? That's why reputable dealers won't touch stuff without knowing its provenance.' That was one of the first long words Griff had taught me, and one of the most important.

'Lina!' came a shout from the kitchen. 'Lina! The kettle's not working!'

'Have you tried switching it on? OK, I'm coming!' I turned to Morris, one eyebrow raised. Aidan used the trick, and he'd taught me. Ironic, he said it was. 'You think a man who can't make a cup of tea can deal with sophisticated things like CCTV?'

There was nothing for it but to sit Lord Elham down in front of a schools' science programme – there was no way I'd trust him with *Cash in the Attic* – and walk Morris's team through the rooms they needed to check.

Morris introduced me as Lord Elham's daughter. One woman constable had to stop herself curtsying, and a male colleague definitely touched his forelock. The rest greeted me with a mixture of relief and suspicion.

'I'm his bastard daughter,' I said dryly, forgetting to worry about the word. 'And I don't live here. But I do know the place. I can tell you if anything's been moved or if there's anything in here that I've not seen before. No! Don't touch that jug! It's four hundred years old.'

'And you haven't sold it for him yet?' Morris asked, his own eyebrow raised. Ironically.

I nearly stuck my tongue out at him. 'It's badly cracked and he's fond of it for some reason. Those plates over there are basically post-war tat. None of those glasses matches. I told you it was a mess, didn't I?'

'Even so . . .'

There was a horrible sliding noise. 'I tell you, Morris,' I said, jabbing the air with my finger because I really was alarmed, 'you break one single thing and I tell the press you're hounding a man who's a public benefactor. Trust me, I'll tell you if there's anything you should look at.'

Eventually they got the message, and retired to the kitchen to drink tea. I walked Morris into every room we could open.

I was terrified there'd be gaps where Titus had removed whatever Lord Elham used for the activities I didn't want to know about, but Titus was too wily a bird for that. Everything looked as cluttered and messy as it ought. I thought I could smell pot in one of the rooms, but there were no fag ends lying about. Perhaps Titus had spotted them too, and decided to deal with them. He wouldn't want any impor . . . impertinent questions being asked.

At last Morris came to a halt, spreading his hands helplessly.

'Well?' I asked. 'You want to do a fingertip search, or do you trust me? I can't see anything here I'm not familiar with, and I don't think anything's missing.' I stopped short. This was a room I'd never really given a thorough going over – with so much else in the wing, this wasn't surprising.

The dratted man picked my hesitation up immediately. 'Well? Have you spotted something?'

I shushed him with open palms. And walked gently to a glass-fronted bookshelf, crammed with a jumble of filthy Staffordshire pottery figures. I could have got a couple of

hundred, maybe a little more, for most. But one wasn't
Staffordshire. Nor was it pottery. It was Meissen china.

'I know it sounds silly,' I said, 'but I'd love one of your
scene of crime officers to check that lock and tell me when
it was last used.'

'You *have* found something.'

'Yes, but not what you're looking for.'

Arms folded, we watched Hazel, the Scenes of Crime Officer
– on whom the standard white jumpsuit was embarrassingly
tight – inspect the cabinet.

'Dust of ages,' she said. 'God knows when it was last
touched. I might get some dinosaur's DNA off it, but—' She
pulled a face.

'So no one's put anything in there recently? In the last
twelve months, say?' I said. 'You're absolutely sure?'

'Why?' Morris asked.

'Because I might one day want to get something out of it.'

'Not now?' The SOCO's hand hovered over the lock.

'Nope. I try to limit the amount I sell for him, so I can
ration his booze intake. He's got loads in his cellars, of course,
but he's got some sort of pact with himself not to touch it for
everyday use.'

'Is he all there?' The SOCO touched her forehead.

'Let's just say I'm glad I've got someone else's genes to
balance his.'

Morris looked at me with narrowed eyes. 'Whatever it is
you've found: did you divvy it?'

'I don't think so. I think this time it was just a case of
observation at a level I didn't even notice. Like a batsman
picking the wrong 'un.'

This time his eyes were laughing. 'I didn't have you down
as a cricketer.'

'I didn't know you had me down as anything. Actually,' I
admitted, 'it's not me but Griff who adores cricket. Something
to do with the white flannels, I should think. He's not nearly
so keen on the coloured pyjamas forms of the game.'

'Are you? Because I can usually get tickets for one of the
big games at Lord's . . . if you wanted, that is . . . But back to
this here figure. Talk us through it.'

Not at all sure whether he'd meant to invite me or Griff to
Lord's, and not, for a moment, sure whom I hoped he'd meant,

I thought I'd stick to the antiques side of the conversation. 'You can see most of the figures are a bit crude. And one isn't.'

The SOCO peered. 'That shepherdess?'

'Exactly. And you're not a divvy, are you?' I laughed. 'She's Meissen.'

'And worth—?' Morris prompted.

They whistled in unison when I told them.

'That's why she's staying where she is – until there's a real emergency.'

'You don't feel tempted to take her home and look after her?'

'And have you people suspect I'd nicked her!'

'Point taken. I'd love you to divvy something, all the same,' he grumbled. 'We could go to a fair where you and Griff didn't have a stall and you could try there?'

The SOCO shot me a look I couldn't quite read.

Again I played with what Griff would have referred to as a straight bat. 'Maybe I'll be able to and maybe I won't. It all depends. OK, do you want to do the rest of the rooms?' I asked him and the SOCO equally.

'I should think Hazel's finished for now. But I certainly need to check them out.'

The News had started by the time Morris was satisfied, and Lord Elham was halfway down his first bottle of the day. He waved the bottle at us as we went into his living room.

'Get some more glasses, Lina.'

Morris muttered about not drinking on duty.

'Goodness, this isn't drinking! It's only supermarket piss! Now, tell me, what did you find?' He'd obviously forgotten that he'd been a suspect.

'Nothing to worry us, sir.' Morris found himself holding a glass. 'Thank you for your time, and our apologies for any inconvenience caused.'

'What, did you break something?'

'With Lina watching?' He flashed a glance at me, his eyes crinkled in what I thought was amusement. 'We didn't dare. She knows an enormous amount, doesn't she? You must be very proud of her, sir.'

Lord Elham blinked. 'Oh, I am, I am. And of all the others.'

It would have hurt less if he'd kicked me. So he'd been in touch with my siblings and not told me.

'All the others?' Morris repeated.

All thirty of them. Blood was whooshing in my ears.

'All the other times she's been she's always found something worth selling. How do you suppose I keep myself in bubbly? And she bought me a microwave and this TV. Well, I paid, but she took me out to get it. Very proud all round. Are you staying to get me some lunch, Lina? She cooks very well for all she missed finishing school.'

'Not today,' I said. 'I've got to see a man about a dog.'

His beady little eyes brightened. 'You found something, didn't you? I can read you like a book.'

What a good job he couldn't. 'Something,' I admitted. 'But I left it where it was.'

'Why? You know I want you to sell it! She gets such good prices, officer. She's such a credit to me.'

I didn't dare catch anyone's eye. 'Let's save it for a rainy day,' I said. 'You've got plenty of other stuff to get rid of first.'

I left with the police officers. The team piled into their van, and a uniformed constable sat drumming his fingers on the wheel while Morris hung back.

'The old guy really upset you in there, didn't he?'

'I misheard something, that's all.'

'All the same . . .' He looked at me the same way as our GP when he thought I might have glandular fever. 'Are you sure? Is there some family problem?'

Only about thirty of them. I shrugged.

'Come and have some lunch: there's a pub in the village, isn't there?'

Now why should he spring that on me? And why should I nod cautiously?

The uniformed guy having been sent off with the others in their van, Morris followed me to the Hop Pocket.

'Low alcohol beer,' he sighed, staring at his glass.

'Quite. But you didn't ask me here to discuss hair-shirt drinks, did you? By the way, what should I call you? Griff always says you should never drink with anyone if you don't know their Christian name.'

'Mine's embarrassing, so my friends call me Morris. Well, would you want to be Reginald?'

'Not in this century, no,' I conceded. 'OK, Morris – what do you want? Or would I rather not hear?'

'I'd rather no one else heard. What I said this morning was true. Items have been removed from the public part of the hall, and, as you suggested, by someone who knew his stuff. The only problem I can see is that the easiest place to elude the attentions of the camera is by the access door to your father's quarters.'

One of them, I corrected him silently. I knew of at least two highly unofficial ones. Possibly not even Lord Elham knew them, since if he dropped off while we were watching TV, I used to slip out and explore, for the sheer pleasure of recognizing places I'd been as a tiny child. Until I'd cleaned up his kitchen, I'd often taken plates and other things that were simply too filthy to identify through to the ladies' loos set aside for the visitors who during the summer coughed up a tenner a piece to see a few selected rooms. There was always hot water there. Lord Elham had gone with me through the door he knew about a couple of times to show me rooms he considered he'd lost but which weren't on the public route – his old nursery, for instance. I'd actually been with him when he'd removed stuff from there, but since no one would want his old school books and I valued my own Tim enough not to want to separate anyone from his long-lost bear I'd said nothing.

'So you're not convinced by this morning's visit?'

He seemed to be pulling his hair out by the roots. 'Can you imagine how the case would go? Even the thickest duty solicitor would be able to spot that your father isn't . . . hasn't . . . And the evidence would be hell to gather. And the CPS would go bananas. And if it ever came to a trial, you'd be one of the best defence witnesses he could have. And the press would have a field day.'

'All the same?' I prompted.

'All the same, something's going on. OK, it has nothing to do with your Hungarian plate. On which that vile old biddy's head should be served to you, by way of apology.'

'The flowers she sent were nicer,' I said, not letting on who I thought had sent them. 'A great big bunch,' I added. There

was no point in telling him I didn't think she'd had a hand
in them. Or that I'd had even more from Piers.

'But I don't like people to get away with things, Lina.'

I waited while he gave our order. 'Funnily enough, neither
do I.'

NINE

'You seem to enjoy your outings with Piers,' Griff
observed, rather wistfully, a few weeks later.

I touched his nose. 'You know our pact. If it gets
serious, I tell you. But not otherwise.'

I didn't ever go into details about any of the men I'd seen,
any more than I wanted to know about Griff and Aidan.

As it happens, I was enjoying the time I spent with Piers.
Most of it. We tended to do silly, romantic things that made
me laugh but might have made Griff wince.

One of the trips – easy-peasy – was to London. We met at
Victoria Station, the train dragging in inch by inch and making
me jog up and down with anxiety for over ten minutes in case
he didn't wait. But he did. And had a secret smile about his
face, the sort Griff had when he'd got a treat up his sleeve.

First we did a few touristy things – all my life I'd lived
within a short train journey of London but I'd hardly ever
been there. It was too cold to go on the top of a tourist bus,
so he suggested we walk instead.

'Anywhere special you want to see?'

I tucked my arm in his. 'Burlington Arcade. I love it. Griff's
sold stuff to some of the shops there – you know, things
outside our usual range. And he's got a mate in one of them
who occasionally gets us to sell things that aren't good enough
for him to handle. Only he seems to be nicer about it than
Nella.'

'So I should hope. Anything take your fancy?'

We dawdled along. I stopped short outside one of the posher
windows. So even top dealers handled dodgy goods. But I
didn't want to show off in front of Piers, and since he was
looking pointedly at his watch, I said nothing.

'Are we late for something?' I asked, rather hoping it might be lunch in one of the restaurants Griff took me to.

'We may be if we don't head there a bit smartish.' He grabbed my hand in a far from romantic way and led me hell for leather up Piccadilly.

It wasn't his fault he'd chosen one treat I could really have done without.

A trip on the London Eye.

I'd never admit to being scared of anything, but I just didn't do heights. Never have done. Probably never will. There were some people I could probably have confessed to as soon as I saw what was planned, but somehow I couldn't tell Piers.

I tried to pretend it was the romance of the occasion that locked me in his arms, my face pressed to his shoulder, but I rather gave the game away when I threw up within half a minute of being let out.

The next trip was better. He taught me to skate on a small rink at the O2 Arena, which was great fun, though I think Griff would have been even more disappointed than I was that we didn't see the Tutankhamun exhibition. We also went to some shows, but not what Griff would have called proper theatre. If, however, like me, you'd only ever heard about *Les Mis* and *Mamma Mia* and *The Lion King*, you weren't going to argue.

'How about a trip to France?' Piers asked one evening as we said goodbye at Victoria.

'Wow!' I jumped up and down like a kid.

'I've got a good deal on Eurostar. Start early, I mean really early, from Ashford. Come back late. See a few sights. Would you like that?'

It was on the tip of my tongue to suggest we stayed over, but that side of our relationship was curiously taboo. Not to mention non-existent. He'd explained, in a fairly buttoned-up way, that he'd been badly hurt in his last relationship and just wanted to take this one slowly. I didn't argue. But like a good Girl Guide I got prepared. I did all you might expect someone like me to do to make sure there weren't any other of Lord Elham's descendants to clutter up the place.

The weather was vile – cold and wet – when we left Ashford at some God awful hour. But Piers had splashed out, and we had a champagne breakfast on the train. There was a slight

hiccup as we left Gare du Nord on foot – Piers wanted me
to see as much of Paris as I could, but set us going confi-
dently in the wrong direction. At last, we retraced our steps,
found a taxi, and he haggled, in confident schoolboy French
(quite different from Aidan's smooth but throaty delivery) for
a trip round the city. Clearly we ended up where he didn't
want to be, and we decamped with a few bad words on both
sides. Fortunately Griff had warned me about the amount of
walking we'd have to do and insisted I wore shoes I described
sulkily as schoolgirl sensible – as if schoolgirls didn't wear
platforms and ballet pumps at random these days, whatever
the weather. Griff had also pressed a wad of Euros into my
hand, with instructions to buy something chic, if Piers forgot
I'd never shopped in a boutique before.

In view of the English weather, we'd spent our journey
revising our itinerary. The Louvre, we decided, and then Musée
d'Orsay. We fetched up at the wrong end of a long queue,
outside the Louvre. But we made giggly jokes about queues
and Americans and some particularly severe-looking Russians
and were generally what Griff would have called a disgrace
to our nation.

'Is it my imagination or have we not moved since we
arrived?' I asked at last.

'Not an inch. And it isn't that the queue's just got thicker
– though it has. Bloody Krauts. No, it's OK, they won't understand. I'm just surprised they haven't put beach towels down
everywhere,' he declared, reminding me suddenly of Nella.

'Please, Piers—' I tugged his sleeve. One or two Germans all
too clearly understood. But we were spared an international incident by the arrival of a Frenchwoman, making shooing gestures.
I was too busy assessing her look and wondering how to achieve
it, a bit of a problem given that she was five inches taller than
me and probably weighed no more, to hear what she was saying.
In any case, I'd only been to about three French classes in the
whole of my school life, so I wouldn't have been any the wiser
anyway. *On Grev?* What might that mean?

Piers broke out in a torrent of French, waving his arms just
like Aidan did. So did a lot of people. The rest of us just
looked blank. That soon turned to disbelieving as our compan-
ions translated. It seemed the staff of all the museums in Paris
had decided to go on strike. Today. Starting now.

'Piers, it really doesn't matter,' I said, when he'd used quite a lot of words I never used before Griff's seven o'clock watershed. 'We're here together. The rain's clearing. There are lots of lovely things to do.'

'I've always wanted to go up the Eiffel Tower!'

'Er . . .' I didn't want to remind him of my last attack of vertigo and its messy consequences. 'What about one of those river boat things? It wouldn't be too cold if we sat inside . . .'

As days went, it wasn't great, but he'd done his best, and I decided to giggle him out of his grumpiness with our Eurostar champagne – as champagnes went, not great either – on our way home. We'd just popped back up out of the earth and on to English soil, as I rather pompously observed, when my phone rang.

Without even looking to see who it was, I took the call. 'Morris? Morris!' I squeaked. 'Look, before you start, I've always wanted to say this to someone – I'm on the train!'

I had a sudden cold feeling that Morris estimated to a millilitre how much I'd sunk.

'Sorry,' I said more soberly, 'but I really am, and it always drives me mad when you get on the train and this chorus starts up. *I'm on the train* – you know?' I hoped I sounded like a seasoned traveller.

'I do indeed.'

'So what can I do for you?' I asked, when he didn't seem inclined to say any more.

'Oh, I just wanted a little favour – but if you're in transit somewhere—'

'I'm on the way back. From Paris. Lovely!' No need to tell anyone that the boat trip had made Piers throw up.

'Did you and Griff buy anything?'

'It was me and Piers and no, we didn't.' A bit of bling for me, and a scarf for him. Dead romantic, I don't think. 'Nothing for the business, at least,' I said, and suddenly wished I hadn't. Not sure why, though. I smiled at Piers, who was making winding gestures to get me to cut the call.

The connection died anyway. Morris didn't try again, and I was too busy thinking about passports and things to call him back.

*   *   *

A difficult restoration job came my way, so I didn't worry overmuch when Piers called to cancel a date because his mother was ill. It occurred to me I'd not been introduced to any of his family, and of course I'd made damned sure he didn't meet Lord Elham. So when one day Piers announced that we must be related, I was quite surprised.

I put down my naan bread – we'd managed to get together for a quick and not very good curry in Maidstone while Piers was en route to a Beanie Bear gathering – and stared.

'Related?' Surprised? Actually I was horrified.

'Yeah, I reckon my aunt is your father's second cousin. Too far away for consanguinity to be a problem.'

I nodded, wondering what on earth I was agreeing with. If only I could remember the word, I could ask Griff what it meant.

'You never talk about your family,' I said. 'Not like I talk about Griff, anyway. And you've never taken me along to meet any of them.'

'Hell, Lina, how Victorian is that? Do you want to be presented formally, is that it?'

'Of course not. But you've got Griff's seal of approval, and I just wondered . . .'

Actually, Griff had reassured me when – in a very round-about way – I'd asked what he thought of Piers. He was so low on the Richter scale of passion I wondered if he might actually be gay and using me as what Aidan and Griff referred to as a beard – in other words, making him look like a full-blooded male with standard issue arm candy. Griff said he didn't pick up any vibes, and maybe Piers was doing what he'd said at the start – simply taking things slowly, always, in Griff's book, better than rushing headlong into things you wished you hadn't next day.

Piers got his diary out. Perhaps he'd taken my hint seriously, and I was going to see them. 'Now, when's the next fair we're both at?'

'Detling?' What had fairs got to do with the price of anything? Unless his parents were coming to one to see how he operated.

'Detling? No, I can't do that one – I'm off to Dublin. More family,' he said.

I vaguely hoped he might invite me to go along too. I'd

never been to Ireland, after all, and it might make up for the Paris mess. But then I reminded myself that he knew I couldn't have gone. I was going to be with Griff, getting cold and wet.

'So we must do something really fabulous when I get back,' he declared, stowing his diary and kissing my hands. He seemed to study them. What a good job after all my painting and gluing I'd actually treated myself to a manicure at the village hairdresser's. 'Really, really fabulous. I promise.'

TEN

If we'd been busy, of course, there was no way I could have taken time off to spend time with Piers. But there was no denying it: business was slack. Griff started to take a pile of books along to the shop and spent the empty hours reading. We hoped and prayed things would look up when the weather improved. Meanwhile, I did the restoration work which kept us in profit.

I also had time to think about Lord Elham and the problem he didn't seem to know anything about. I took to dropping in at times he wouldn't normally have expected me. My excuse was that I wanted to make sure he was eating properly, so I'd take plastic freezer boxes full of microwaveable dinners. He quite liked a lamb curry I'd learned to make, and was very keen on my pasta sauce. He ate both with naan bread he kept in his freezer, but I didn't complain. At least while I was there I could make him drink a couple of cups of green tea. It might not do all the Internet said it'd do, but it might do some good. Griff swore it had helped bring his blood pressure down, but I rather thought he was humouring me. Though it has to be said that his GP told me he was actually a lot better since I'd started to bully him. Maybe the same technique would work on my father. It would certainly be better than the prison food he'd get if Morris and his team ever really managed to nail him.

Each visit I made a point of visiting all the rooms in his wing, pretending I was looking for items to sell. Of course I could have sold most of it, but there are fashions in antiques just as in everything else. Lovely mahogany Victorian furniture was at an all time low, and some of our friends who'd specialized in it had actually gone to the wall. On the other hand good jewellery was doing surprisingly well, presumably because of the value of gold. A cynic would say that if you didn't like your ring or brooch, you could always melt it down.

So I'd tell him, truthfully, that there was no call for the cut glass I'd so lovingly cleaned, and that we might as well wait for the market to rise even more before I tried to move the gorgeous dressing set I'd unearthed. So far the Meissen figure had stayed put. Once or twice I thought I smelt pot – that really heavy skunk smell – but Lord Elham always turned the TV volume up if I started asking any questions. Not just about the skunk, or I would have been suspicious. Questions about anything. I even mentioned I was dating a relative only to have him take as much notice as if I'd answered a quiz question properly. Less, probably – he really couldn't believe I could have so little general knowledge. He, on the other hand, was as good as Griff when it came to useless information. They'd have made a really good pub quiz team.

With the coming of spring, Bossingham Hall would be opened up to the public. I knew it was always spring-cleaned first, and wondered if I could get myself recruited as a cleaner, so I could have a good poke round. But several of the ladies working there – running the shop, the tea room and the ticket desk – knew I was not only Lord Elham's daughter, but an antiques restorer as well. Perhaps they giggled over their tea cups that I was having a go at restoring him too. So I didn't dare turn up with my rubber gloves and feather duster. I'd just have to wait until the Hall officially reopened to go and look round.

Unless I used one of my unofficial entrances. I had a couple, both, so far as I knew, unknown to anyone else.

But I hesitated, given Morris's interest and the fact that once outside the main entrance I'd seen several vans with a CCTV firm's logos on them. Security was obviously being beefed up, and until I'd made sure there were no cameras on my access points I wasn't taking any risks.

I excused my cowardice by telling myself I must concentrate on preparations for Detling, one of the biggest fairs in the south east.

Who should I run into the very first morning but Titus

Oates, coat collar up against the wind just like mine. We nodded at each other cautiously, the way people do when they both have information the other person would rather they didn't have. But remembering our last phone conversation, I moved a little closer to him.

'Tell me, Titus—'

He jabbed my chest. 'You never ask questions, doll, remember.'

'You owe me, remember,' I retorted. 'Tell me, do you ever smoke pot?'

'You joking? Do anything to make the filth notice me? Bloody hell, I took you as having your head screwed on.' He turned his back and was about to stomp off.

I took an even bigger risk. 'Well, someone at Bossingham Hall does. It's not me and I can't smell it on Lord Elham's clothes.'

When I first met him, of course, you wouldn't have wanted to get close enough to him to smell anything. Now there were a washing machine and a tumble dryer in the kitchen, and though he grumbled, I saw to it that everything, even his trousers, went through at regular intervals.

Titus stopped dead. 'Bloody hell. Smoking? The whole place could go up like that!' He snapped his fingers.

Given the water sprinklers and the direct line to the fire station in Canterbury I doubted it, but I didn't want to interrupt him by pointing this out.

'Who the hell could that be? He's never said anything to me. Or to you, I take it.'

I shook my head. 'What does he say to anyone?'

'A lot of crap, if he doesn't think he's going to get his fizz. But nothing about visitors smoking pot. Tell you what, doll, I'll get on to it. Keep my ears open. No need to call me – I'll be in touch if I need be.'

From Titus, that was a major offer. Meanwhile, back in one of the barns housing those of us with indoor stalls – there were some poor souls who had pitches outside, in all the elements – I had a job to do. We'd already sold more than we'd hoped, but there was still a lot on the stand, and while Griff worked better with some customers, I did well with people who considered me waif-like and in need of a good meal.

I was just sucking my cheeks and tum in when Arthur Habgood hove into view. He was flourishing something in his right hand. 'Here you are!' he announced, as if he was doing me a favour. 'Now, have you ever done one of these before?'

'A gob-swab? You mean all the times I've been arrested?' I snapped. 'Thanks a bunch.'

His smile disappeared and his eyes blazed. My would-be grandfather didn't see I was making a sarcastic point – he thought I was telling the truth! I was getting less and less keen on being part of his family.

'They say you'd been in trouble up at the NEC,' he hissed.

'Who says?' I fired. 'Come on, tell me who. Because you can tell them that they were absolutely wrong.'

He shook his head. 'I know you were fired from that silver dealer's.' He rifled through a trade paper. 'There – quarter page ad!' He shoved the journal into my hands.

Argentia Antiques wishes it to be known that all alle-gations of criminal activity are completely false. The young person at whom the allegations were specifically directed has left the firm.

In much smaller print it added: *No charges have been brought against this person, who must be presumed to be entirely innocent.*

I felt my face going white, then red, then white again. 'I think I need a solicitor,' I said. And then my head went weird.

I might have needed a solicitor, but what I got was a posse of St John Ambulance people, refusing to let me get up. 'Don't you understand?' I said, waving them away. 'If Griff sees you lot and can't find me he'll be worried sick. Then you'll have a heart attack, not a silly dizzy spell to deal with. For God's sake, Habgood, scoot off and just start talking to him so he doesn't know what's going on. And if you so much as mention that bloody mag to him, I shall sue you too.'

'This is all your doing,' I told Morris, whom I'd phoned in fury. It turned out he was actually drifting round Detling about a hundred yards from where I was standing. Now, muttering about blood sugar, he was treating me to a cup of hot chocolate at the refreshment area, not one of the coffee wagons pulled up outside.

'She's phrased this very carefully,' he said.

'I can see that. I can also see the difference in print size. Font size,' I corrected myself. 'Bloody hell, Morris, what do I do?'

To my fury, he chuckled. 'I didn't think you swore before seven o'clock.'

I jabbed a finger at his chest. 'If you want swearing, Morris, you can have it.' I let rip with some of the things I'd learned on the streets. Not loudly. Maybe they worked better in a quiet conversational tone, because I'll swear he went white.

'I can see why you have to ration yourself,' he said at last. 'Phew, I've not heard anything like that since I was in uniform arresting pr— Since I was in uniform.'

'You mean fine art thieves are polite and mealy-mouthed? I must remember that next time you arrest me. Oh, no – you didn't arrest me, did you? Just ruined my professional reputation.'

He looked from me to the ad and back again. 'Maybe I should have a word with Farfrae. He's here somewhere.'

'Hunting in pairs, are you? Great.'

But he'd turned away to dial, and spoke so that I couldn't overhear him however much I tried.

Being bear-hugged by a policeman wasn't ever on my list of must-dos before I die. But Farfrae embraced me as if I were his long-lost niece. It didn't seem a spontaneous hug, however. More a carefully stage-managed one, with both Griff and Mr Habgood as audience. And Morris taking a photo of the occasion, for good measure.

'What's all this about?' I asked. I might have sounded a bit grumpy.

'I thought the news that you were on very good terms with a police officer might help your injured reputation,' he said.

'But you're a detective – work in plain clothes. It can't do your cover much good if everyone knows you're a cop.'

He put his arm round my shoulders and gave me another squeeze. 'I'm actually leaving the police,' he said. 'I'm going into private security work. Art, not bankrolls. Theft, forgery . . . You never know, I may ask you to work for me from time to time.' This time he kissed my cheek. 'Anyway, that's why I'm doing the hugging and Morris is taking the photos. He's being promoted into my job, but you can't hug him, Lina, because he's staying as a detective.'

'Or you can hug me if no one takes any photos,' Morris put in, with a grin – the sort that made me think he'd be quite nice to hug. But he took a couple of steps back, and disappeared into the crowd, tucking his mobile away as he did so.

'Perhaps you and your grandfather would join us for coffee?'

Both Griff and Mr Habgood stepped forward. Not feeling ready for a big scene, I shook my head, and tucked my hand into Griff's arm. 'We must be off. Look at the punters! Miss the first wave and you can be sunk.'

He looked genuinely disappointed. 'Actually, I'd like to borrow you for a few minutes, if you can be spared.'

I looked at Griff, who nodded cautiously. 'Ten minutes max,' I said. 'And then I'll be back. See if you can push that pretty Derby coffee can!' I didn't say anything to Habgood, who eventually took the hint and mooched off.

'Now what?' I asked, not very graciously.

'I just thought walking round together might help us both.'

'I'm not sure. There's a lot of dealers who think being on hugging terms with the police is being a traitor.' Titus Oates, for instance.

'Not at your end of the market, surely.'

I thought of the man who occasionally spirited items into our cottage at times when I wasn't there. He'd not nicked them, of course, just picked them up very cheap at car boot sales and such. All the same I was sure he wouldn't take to the idea of my hobnobbing with any police officer. But I'd been silent too long. 'You know Griff and I pride ourselves on our provenances,' I said.

He'd picked up the hesitation, of course, but gave no more than a wry smile. 'OK, no more hugging. But the fact is your professional reputation has been horribly impugned, and I can't see you taking legal action – there's no legal aid for that sort of thing for a start. I just thought if we were seen to be on good terms it might help restore your firm's standing.'

'I'd rather you'd talked to Griff first.'

'I did. That's why he came along. No idea who the other bugger was, though.'

'He thinks he might be my grandfather on my mother's side. He's been on at me to do a gob swab for ages. But that ad put him off rather. So it might be a good thing after all,' I said. 'You said "help us both",' I added. 'So what's in it for you?'

'I've never seen a diviner in action. Morris said at Bossingham Hall you found a—'

'Shush. We don't talk about my father and his stuff. OK? So you want me to walk round and pull a big furry rabbit out of a tatty hat. It doesn't work that way, Mr Farfrae. Or does hugging put us on first name terms?'

'Bruce.'

'As in Robert the? The original Spiderman?'

'I thought you said you had no education.'

'Griff's done his best. Anyway, Bruce, I'm happy to walk round and be photographed for *Kent Life* or whatever, but I can't guarantee anything in the way of divining. It's not something you can do to order. So long as you understand that.'

'Why not pick out something in the jewellery line for my wife? It's our wedding anniversary next week and I won't live to see another if I don't give her something special. I thought maybe a ring.'

'Price range?' When he hesitated, I continued, 'Is the sky the limit or do you want something cheap that'll scrub up nicely?'

Then he surprised me. 'When I see it, I shall know.'

'That might take a lot more than ten minutes. I'd better see how Griff's getting on. If he's busy you'll have to wait till after lunch.'

What with regular clients and new customers attracted by the buzz they brought, it must have been nearly half past two when business was quiet enough for me to ring Farfrae. He too was occupied, he said, but he'd be with me as and when he could. He cut the call before I could suggest he made sure of his facts before he leapt in and arrested anyone.

But at least he and Morris had been kind to me, so I tried not to bear a grudge, and even managed a smile when he turned up twenty minutes later.

'Have you seen anything you like yet?' I asked.

He and Griff shook hands as enthusiastically as if they went way, way back. Griff used to be an actor, of course. But Farfrae was pretty good too.

'He's after a ring,' I told Griff.

'There's so many,' he said helplessly. 'Where do I start?'

Griff simpered. 'Don't ask me, sweetie!' Then he said seriously, 'By asking yourself questions. Modern or traditional? Silver or gold? Big dealer with showy lights and big overheads or a smaller stand? Like our friend Josie over there.'

'That little old lady with the bad back?'

'That's the one,' I said. 'She sells a bit of everything. I owe her big time because she used to let me practise repairing things. That's how you get better, working on the real thing. Then she'd sell them – but she'd never, ever pass them off as perfect. I've got to pass the time of day – let's go over.'

Although Josie barely reached my shoulder these days, and her poor hands were swollen and spotted, she gave me a hug even bigger than the police ones. 'I told the others I'd trust you with my life, Lina,' she said in a carrying whisper, 'when they started talking. That woman – I'll have her eyes out if ever I see her again. Though this'll be my last show, the way things are. And my back, of course.'

'Josie, this is my friend Detective Inspector Bruce Farfrae, who also got up Lady Petronella's nose.'

'Petronella indeed. More like "pterodactyl" if you ask me.' Showing her dentures in a snarl, she pulled herself into the shape of some horrid bird.

Farfrae laughed, as if she'd made a clever joke. I joined in politely – I'd have to ask Griff later.

'Mr Farfrae's got a wife who needs an anniversary present. So I told him to start here.'

While he peered at the rows upon rows of rings – I could quite see why he was confused – Josie burrowed behind the stall, coming up with a badly broken figurine, a close relative of the one I'd spotted in Lord Elham's cupboard. 'She's not for sale. One of my regulars asked if she could be repaired, and I said I only knew one person who could do it. Will you have a go?'

'Even for a friend of yours it'd cost, Josie. There's a good week's work there. I'll do it as quickly as I can but—'

'Ah, I heard you'd got yourself a young man. Does Griff like him? Or does Griff fancy him, the old bugger?'

'We tossed for him and Griff lost,' I said. 'You might know him. Piers Hamlyn. He's beginning to deal himself.'

Perhaps she didn't hear me. 'Do you need old Josie to give you some help, Inspector?' She made sure anyone within twenty yards heard her.

He looked totally at sea. 'I don't know . . . All these with three stones, one big and two smaller – they all look like someone dead's engagement ring. And that doesn't seem right, somehow.'

I was impressed. 'Does it have to be a ring?'

He stared, as if I'd suggested flying. 'It has to be personal,' he said, grabbing at firmer ground. 'Nothing anyone else would have given her.'

Josie patted his hand. 'You go for a little stroll, son. Give Lina her head. She'll find you just the thing. Let me know when you've fixed this lass, will you, lovie?'

We trailed round so long I felt guilty, not just for leaving Griff on his own but also for letting Bruce down – twice over. He wanted me to magic a brilliant find from a load of tat, and also to find a perfect present. The trouble was he kept asking me about the stalls and their owners and, apart from fearing I might be grassing someone up without meaning to, my head needed quiet.

Actually, it needed silence, and it needed it now.

I froze. There was something . . . Where was it and what was it? I patted his arm. 'Go and have a look at those prints.'

'But—' And then he decided not to argue and headed off, leaving me in peace.

The stalls here were at the bottom end of the market. There was some stuff I wouldn't have given to Oxfam, even during a famine.

I turned to the nearest. No. The next one. It was selling modern costume jewellery. Gold that makes your skin go green and silver that brings you up in a rash – that sort. I quite like retro and overblown myself, of course, and there might be something to go with my Dior dress. So I rooted around in the mass of dross like a pig after a truffle, which I had always thought meant a nice choccie till Griff explained.

And then I saw it. Unfortunately I didn't want it for Bruce's wife, much as he obviously loved her, but for me. It was a little blue flower pendant. It looked like plastic; some greyish glass chips scattered over it were supposed to be dew. I tucked it back for a moment.

'What's your best on this?' I asked, holding up a brooch I really wouldn't have let into the house. I wrinkled my nose at £15. 'No, thanks. What about this?' – a filthy teddy bear pendant with what looked like a plastic football at the bear's feet. I agreed a tenner, then picked up my flower pendant again. 'Throw this in and I'll give you sixteen.' Eventually I had to part with £18, but I'd done OK. If I knew anything about it the teddy bear was gold and playing with a coral ball. As for the flower, I wanted to kiss it. Plastic? Glass? I didn't think so. Sticking both casually in my trousers pocket, I sauntered back to Bruce. He was beaming and pointing at a print.

'How did you do it? How did you know it'd be there? It's the village where we went on our first date!' he said. 'And they only want £325, so I can take her away for a weekend there, too. Look, they say the colouring's original.'

How could he be so naive? Had all his police expertise gone out of the window?

I said slowly and clearly, 'They only wanted £280 and would have had your hand off if you'd offered £300. But now they've seen you're keen . . .' I shook my head sadly. 'See you back at Griff's stand. And make sure they gift wrap it if you pay full price!'

'You've done very well here, my sweet,' Griff said, when we were back home, looking at my newly cleaned trophies. 'But what if Farfrae hadn't found that print? And wanted to buy his wife a pendant? Could you have parted with either of them?'

'I don't know.' I always tried to be honest with Griff. 'The bear, I suppose. Possibly.'

Griff watched me stroke his nice clean head. 'And what would you have charged for him?'

'What I got it for? Or what it's worth, which must be about £250? Griff, I don't like dealing with friends.'

'And the pansy? Even though I don't know what mineral it's made of, and you're right, it is painted, I know those are very good diamonds. You could sell this for something like a grand, loved one. Eight hundred at least.'

'*We* could sell it,' I corrected him.

He waited.

'I wouldn't have shown it to him,' I muttered, blushing to my ears. 'And I don't know if it's because I want to keep it for myself—'

'Which you're quite entitled to do, remember.'

'Or if I want to sell it at a huge profit. Oh, Griff, have I really got my father's blood in me?'

It was his turn to blush. 'You've got an awful lot of my influence too, angel heart. And – shall I whisper? – I don't think I could have shown it to him either.'

That made it almost better. 'I still feel bad about that print, though. Bruce really thought I'd sent him over to the stand because I knew he'd find something there. And all I wanted was to get rid of him.'

He stroked his chin, as if that would give the answer. 'I really think you might actually have used your gift – you sent him to the print stand but you could just as easily have sent him to the garden memorabilia stand, where he'd surely have drawn a blank.'

I thought of the cracked plant pots and rusty tools and grimaced.

'Exactly. Never knock your gift, Lina. You never know how it will manifest itself. Now, at the risk of sounding like your father, I think you deserve a glass of champagne. You and your gift.'

There was no point in arguing, but I still didn't feel quite right. It hung over me, like a little grey cloud, for a couple of days. Then I had a nice note from Farfrae telling me how delighted his wife was with the anniversary present and asking me to keep my eye open for others of the same village, and little by little the cloud drifted away.

Restoring the Meissen lady for Josie's friend took well over a week. The worst part was making her a new hand, though at least I had the left one to go by. She ended up looking pretty good, and certainly cleaner than when she'd arrived. It always gave me a funny feeling when I returned a figure to its owner, as if I were a doctor returning a patient. She was feeling better, but she'd never be quite her old self, I said. And just to be on the safe side, I gave the owner a complete rundown of what I'd done, keeping a record for myself, too. I used the computer – my own handwriting was still liable to wobbles and slips, especially when I was using a duplicate pad and trying to press hard.

I'd just got back from delivering the figure to Josie when I got another restoration job, one I leapt at. I had a phone message from Mary Walker, a contact at Bossingham Hall – she needed a favour, she said, in a voice that sounded tearful. Would I care to drop in next time I was over in Bossingham? Would I not! Perhaps after all my guardian angel had decided that I hadn't been so very bad at Ardingly.

Mrs Walker was a widow who'd not all that long ago moved to the village; finding time heavy on her hands, she'd become a volunteer guide at the hall – not a terribly hard task, since the wily trustees had screwed the maximum of grants out of the Lottery and other funds, but had managed to keep the public opening hours they had to give in return to a minimum. When I'd first visited the hall, before I'd met my father, she'd wangled me extra time in the place for free, and even stood me tea and cake. Perhaps she'd been kind because she'd been lonely, but kindness is kindness, and needs to be passed on. She was still a guide, and now she'd obviously become one of the spring-cleaning team too.

She was a nice woman, but couldn't stop talking: I suppose it was a nasty combination of having talked for her living as a teacher and having no one to talk to at home. From time to time, when I had to go and see my father anyway, I joined her in the tea room for a scone, but I always cut short the chat by pretending I had another appointment. What Griff called a tactful lie.

I phoned back immediately. Tears meant something broken. And that might mean trouble for her. If she'd broken something herself and was in a hole I'd do any repair for free.

If it was an official breakage, then I'd charge full price, of course.

'They say I must have broken it, but I really, truly didn't,' Mrs Walker said. Her eyes were red and she was on the verge of more tears. 'The trouble is, if I admit it I'm damned and if I don't they'll say I'm lying so I'm damned too.'

That was the trouble with what struck me as a really

amateurish set-up. They didn't seem to have enough insurance and blamed staff personally if things went wrong – which meant the sack.

By now she was weeping properly. 'And I really, really don't know what I'd do without this place to occupy my time. They say I should have got used to being on my own by now, but I can't seem to. Thirty-eight years we were married.'

She needed so much help with so many different things I didn't know where to start. I supposed the obvious place was the damaged plate itself.

We were in what the trustees rather grandly called the administrative hub of the estate, in other words a clutch of underground rooms still painted in cream and green gloss which was filthy and beginning to lift. Whatever had they been used for originally? They weren't the servants' halls or kitchen because those were part of the tour; as for the old steward's office, that was in my father's wing. I'd have to do some research.

Why they'd not been made presentable was beyond me. After all, people spent their working days in them. Computers hummed in one, coats were hung in another and in a third a few chairs even my father might have sniffed at were available for the guides to rest their weary bones, as Mrs Walker bravely joked. She'd laid a large Jiffy bag on an early Victorian burr-walnut card table that had once had something hot placed on it. Surely someone should have had a shot at restoring it? Wasn't there a woodworking version of me somewhere around?

But I was supposed to be concentrating on what the bag held. I eased a bundle of bubble wrap on to my knee.

'It's like passing the parcel,' Mrs Walker said with a pale smile. 'You know, the children's party game.'

It was one I'd never played, not as far as I could remember, anyway. But I smiled and nodded, as if giving the best of my attention to what I could now see was a pretty plate, now in two pieces.

This time my smile was warmer. 'So far, so good, Mrs Walker. It looks straightforward enough.' I put one half down on the table and inspected the other. 'The plate's delft, but I'd say it was English. Possibly Bristol. Late eighteenth century. This pretty raised design, here on the rim, see? It's called *bianco-sopra-bianco.*' I didn't need to say all this but clients sometimes liked me to sound like an expert.

'So it was very valuable, like they say? Two thousand or more?'

It actually might have been, but I didn't want to upset her. 'These chips round the edges – old ones, nothing to do with you – will have taken away some of the value.' I looked again, this time at the break. 'Ah! If you look here, along the edge of the pieces, you can see two different colours.' I held them up so that she could see. 'So I'd say there'd been a crack in it for a long time, and whatever you did just ex . . . exass . . . made it worse. It was an accident waiting to happen. And I can fix it very easily.' I smiled warmly as I packed it up. 'How did it happen, anyway?'

'I told you, I don't know. It was just lying like this when I found it. It was on a table in one of the corridors.'

'Let's go and have a look,' I said, as if I had scene of crime officers' skills. I meant just to help her, truly, but after all I had wanted to check the place over, and I didn't really deserve her watery smile and her gabbled thanks. 'Come on, you know how I love the place.'

She led the way through some of the backstairs areas that always fascinate me more than the grand public rooms. They were freezing – well, that was the servants' lot. But when we reached the state rooms, they were cold too, and felt damp – not what you'd expect in a grade one listed building, where the temperature and humidity were supposed to be strictly controlled.

'This is my corridor,' she said, when we eventually reached a broad first floor corridor running right across the front of the house. 'At least as far as cleaning is concerned.' A long feather duster and a shorter fluffy duster lay on a marble-topped pier table.

'Where was the plate?'

'On the next table. I saw it, dropped everything and ran.'

'Taking the pieces with you?' Morris would have been proud of me. I strolled along the corridor, trying to make myself focus on the task, not on what I was fairly sure was a fake Vigée Le Brun. Did I see any footprints? Was anything else broken?

Total failure, of course. And try as I might I couldn't see

why a plate lying flat on a table should take it into its head to break in two. And then my brain clicked in. 'If you'd dropped it, wouldn't it show up on CCTV?'

'I suppose so.' She looked round vaguely for a camera. 'Oh, over there.'

I tried to attract its attention, but for some reason it didn't track me.

'Shall we talk to the security people and ask to have a look?'

Mrs Walker looked scared, then pulled her shoulders back and put on a brave smile. 'Yes, why not? I've nothing to lose!'

It seemed security was answerable to the administrator, a woman I'd heard of but never met. I wasn't about to meet her today: she had a day's leave. Away from the place when everyone else was working their socks off? I didn't think much of that.

Now what? Mrs Walker was still looking at me as if I had a solution tucked into my trousers pocket. Perhaps I had. A business card.

'Is there a computer I can use? Because I could type a letter saying that in my opinion the break was caused not by careless handling but because of pre-existing damage.' The terms sounded good. I'd seen Griff use them on a couple of insurance evaluations.

It seemed even the computers were sacrosanct. At last, despite being visibly scared, Mrs Walker switched one on and hovered, as if she were acting as look out, while I typed. You've never seen so many typos, but at last I sorted everything out. For good measure, I added an estimate of how much it would cost to repair it, and stapled a business card on to the finished letter.

'You're a star!' she declared, giving me a hug. 'Now, have you got time for a coffee to warm you up?'

I looked at my watch. 'I'd love one. But I really ought to go and see my father.'

ELEVEN

Although it was *Countdown* time, and I knew I wouldn't be particularly welcome, I did nip round to my father's wing to check up on him. It was nice and warm there, too, since he didn't believe in stinting on heat. Especially as the trustees got to pay the bills.

He was too engrossed in the TV show to do more than raise his champagne flute in my direction, so I set off for the kitchen. I was pleased to see sheets in the tumble dryer – I'd have been more pleased to see them blowing on a clothes line, but my sights weren't set very high. He'd even washed up a couple of days ago, but in the sink, still awaiting attention, were several glasses. In pairs again. He'd even emptied the swing bin, which for some reason I thought was suspicious, not good housekeeping.

I took my nose for a sniff for pot round the storage rooms. Nothing in most. Then I caught a gust of skunk in the room with all the Staffordshire figures. And stopped dead. I didn't have to be a white-clad SOCO to see that the door to their cupboard had been unlocked and the Meissen stranger in their midst removed. Somehow I didn't think it was because someone didn't think they belonged together.

Apart from that, only a couple of not very good jardinières had gone – ugly things that I wouldn't have given shop room to. And there was a spliff end stubbed out in a pretty little Royal Worcester ashtray. OK, it was meant to be an ashtray, but it was a William Powell ashtray, dated 1930, and though it wasn't worth a king's ransom, the little chaffinch Powell had painted deserved better than that.

I steadied a pile of books and dusted the top one. I had to sit somewhere to think, and that should do. I didn't think the spliff-smoker was an expert. Unless, of course, he'd hidden the Meissen figure in one of the jardinières just to get it out of the place. He? It might be a she, of course, but I tended to think of cannabis smoking, skunk especially, as a male thing.

So who was it? When the police had been investigating the

place, my father had mentioned something about being proud
of all of them. I'd interpreted that as being proud of all his
wrong-side-of-the blanket brood. Then I persuaded myself I'd
misheard. But perhaps I hadn't. Perhaps one of my half-
brothers or sisters had turned up.

I could have done with a good swig of my father's champagne to help me think. Or feel. One of my social workers
had said I wasn't very good at sorting out my emotions, so I
mixed them up. At least I knew I was mixed up this time.
Why should I be furious? And jealous? When Lord Elham
had sold *Natura Rerum* for all that money, I'd made sure that
all of us were treated fairly: the million pounds plus was in
trust so there was a nest egg for each of us, even though I
was the only one who'd ever cared enough to search him out.

That sounded as if I'd cared enough for him to search him
out. I hadn't. I'd cared for me – I needed to fit a piece into
my pretty thin history. Now perhaps one of the others had felt
the same. I should feel generous and welcoming. A brother
or sister was something I'd never had. We might become mates.

Or had someone simply been flushed out of the woodwork
by the prospect of getting his hands on some of the *Natura
Rerum* bonus? None of us could have anything till the age of
thirty – my puritan suggestion, as it happens. Perhaps one of
us had had the right birthday and decided to make it a special
one, courtesy of the trust fund. And why not? That was what
the money was there for. But I still felt miffed: if it hadn't
been for me Lord Elham might have been in jail and there'd
have been no money. Or I might have kept all the proceeds
from the sale, as Lord Elham had wanted me to do.

So why hadn't I been introduced to this new . . . Sibyl?
(Griff had told me there was an overall term for brothers and
sisters, and I'd even written it down. But I couldn't place it
now.) All the same, why hadn't I met him or her?

I couldn't really credit Lord Elham with tact and diplomacy.
So I couldn't tell myself he hadn't wanted me to be upset.

I tried to put myself into the newcomer's head, not all that
easy given I didn't know anything about him except that he
smoked pot. Had he found out I was selling his father's stuff
and suspected I was lining my pockets? Well, I was, of course,
but only by helping the old guy to make money he wouldn't
otherwise have had. And to stay alive. Let's not forget that.

I was surprised he hadn't died twice over, his kitchen being so filthy when I'd turned up. Not to mention personal hygiene.

I checked my watch. *Countdown* should just be ending. Maybe I could get my father to listen to my direct questions and answer them. But I had as much chance, I reckoned, as I did of getting the number puzzle right. So maybe a sideways approach was best.

Drifting into his room as casually as I could, I accepted a glass of fizz and sat back and told him about my week restoring the figure – just to get the idea of Meissen floating in his brain, you might say. Sometimes my past adventures had upset him, so I didn't dare tell him about Nella's behaviour, and I kept pretty quiet about Piers, too. Sometimes he got jealous if I told him about good times Griff and I had together. Goodness knows what he'd make of the situation if I ever did find I was Arthur Habgood's granddaughter. I had an idea he'd be more upset than Griff.

Lord Elham had never given away much about his own life, and of course I'd closed one subject before he'd opened it by telling him I didn't want to know about his work for Titus. He really didn't see anyone else. Until now, of course.

'How do you get hold of your pot, by the way?' I asked, casually, but with a hint in my tone I wouldn't mind getting some for myself.

If I hadn't been between him and the door I swear he'd have made a run for it.

'Look,' I continued, 'it really is dangerous smoking anywhere inside. If you want a spliff, you should stand in the porch. And make sure you dispose of the nub ends where the police can't find them – you don't want to be done for possession.'

'That's what that Oates cove said,' he croaked. 'He said I shouldn't ever do anything that might attract anyone's attention.'

'Exactly. But you smoke in that room upstairs and leave fag ends everywhere. Not sensible.'

'I told him to use a saucer or something. There are enough of them around,' he added, as if that put him in the clear.

'Some of them are a bit expensive to use as ashtrays. Is that why you got him to use those jardinières?'

'Big pot things? Pot? Get it?' he chortled. 'He said they'd look good in his conservatory and I said he could have them. Didn't look much good to me – not the sort of thing you sell for me.' His smile was a bit on the sickly side.

'Did you say he could have that Meissen figurine?'

He looked from side to side as if afraid the curtains might be eavesdropping. 'He thought he could get a few bob for it – don't like always to be putting on you, Lina.'

He used my name so rarely I nearly dropped my flute.

'You do a lot for me. Don't think I don't know that. Very fond of you, my girl, and very proud too. But it seems this Darren bloke's got some of your talents too. Here.' He stood and dug in his back pocket, producing a fold of notes. 'Ninety quid he got for that. And he wouldn't take any commission.'

'Sit down and listen. One of you has lost a lot of money on that deal. I told you I'd found something that would make a nice little bonus if ever you were really short. That there figure, that Meissen he tells you he got £90 for, was worth £2000 at the very least. OK, I'd have got £200 for selling it, but you'd have got £1800. So either he didn't get enough, so you both lost out. Or he got what it was worth and didn't tell you. In effect,' I concluded unkindly, 'you were robbed.'

Lord Elham never was a very good colour, but now he looked quite ill. 'Robbed? My own son robs me? Darren?'

I poured him some more champagne and held his hand to guide it to his mouth, which was a nasty shade of grey. One day I was going to have to get him to a doctor, wasn't I? 'It might have been Darren that was robbed,' I said. 'But how come you didn't tell me you'd found one of my brothers? I'd love to meet him.'

He put the glass on the table beside him, and actually squeezed my hand. 'I know you would. I told him you would. I told him you were a real expert who'd helped when the police came. But – you know what? – he didn't seem at all keen. In fact, he made a point of asking what times you came round, and it seems to me he made another point of coming round when you weren't here.'

In that case, I reflected dryly, I'd better make a point of being there a bit more often. Or my father could have been lying, to get more company and to irritate Griff. I wouldn't have put it past him.

I nodded, non-committally. 'Tell me about Darren.' I could have bombarded the old guy with questions, and God knows I had plenty to ask, but I'd best wait for him to tell me in his

own good time. At least his colour was better now. I topped
up his glass and sat down, looking patient.

'His mother should have known better. Fancy calling
someone with the surname Harris Darren. Darrenarris. Dear
me. I wouldn't have allowed it, believe me.'

Would he have married her to prevent it? So that Darren
would have taken his own name?

'Anyway, it seems his mother read about that damned book,
and thought Darren ought to get his hands on some of my
lucre. So he turned up one day. Just as I was watching *The
Weakest Link,* too. Told him I didn't have any, not personally,
but if he cared to wait till he was thirty, the trust fund you'd
made me set up would fork out a few thousand. He seemed
a bit miffed. Anyway, he had a bit of a look round, and said
he'd come back. And he did. Bought me some Pot Noodles,
although I'd told him you said I shouldn't eat them. So he
threw the pots straight in the dustbin – disposing of the
evidence, you might say. He smoked a joint or two, and I
gave him those planter things and he sold the Meissen figure.
I shan't half give him a piece of my mind next time he comes.'

It must have been Darren's second visit, since I'd noticed
the pot before. And he must have made a third to bring the
cash. 'When's that likely to be?'

I'd tried to sound casual, but Lord Elham dropped into
shifty mode again. 'Oh, he'll be round sometime, I dare say.'

'Have you got him to sell something else?'

'I'm a stupid old duffer, aren't I?'

'I don't know. Darren may be as honest as the day is long,
but just not very good at selling things. Does he give you
receipts, like I do? Well, then . . . What was his mother like?'

He shook his head. 'Do you know, I can't remember her
at all? Not one scrap.'

'Is she in your book?' He kept a tatty school exercise book
with a list of all his sexual partners, including columns for
any issue, any abortions and any diseases.

'Oh, yes,' he said, so casually I suspected he hadn't looked.
Maybe I should.

'Ninety quid doesn't go very far,' he continued. 'I don't
suppose . . . ?'

'OK. I'll find something. What we really need to do is sell
that silver dish.'

'No takers yet?'

''Fraid not. But I'll keep trying. Now, cricket's quite big at the moment. Have you got any memorabilia you've not told me about? And yes, I will give you receipts, don't worry.'

'So you're afraid this Darren Harris person – dear me, your father's quite right, it is an unfortunate combination – is simply a fortune hunter with no claim at all on the family?' Griff asked, passing me the salad bowl as we sat at supper.

I helped myself. 'What family? The thing is, Griff, the old bugger's brain only works half the time. Remember he showed me how to get into the main part of the house and disable the corridor alarms? What if he's shown Darren? OK, he's got to remember the code he's supposed to tap in, but on a good day even that might not defeat him. Plus I've found a couple of other ways in no one knows about, and if I can, Darren can too. Oh, dear. Perhaps I've just got a suspicious mind.'

'Certain items have disappeared from the hall, and a possibly stolen silver plate turns up in your father's possession. I think you're right to be suspicious. But you must also be circumspect.'

'You mean I should watch my back, right?'

'I do indeed.'

'But I also need to watch Lord Elham's since he doesn't seem able to do it for himself.'

Griff tried not to let his face fall, but I could see he was upset. The front doorbell rang. I went to see who was there.

'Piers! I wasn't expecting you!' I flung myself into his arms, and treated him to a huge kiss, which I fancied he returned, with feeling. Perhaps things would start speeding up at last.

'I know,' he said at last. 'So I thought I'd give you a surprise. Both of you,' he added, as he walked through to find Griff. 'Tara!' He flourished a bottle and put it into Griff's hands. 'I don't know anything about Irish whiskey but they said this was the best. And I got a little present for Lina, too,' he said, looking at me with a smile that melted my knees. 'It's been such a long time and I've missed you so much and I hope you've missed me.'

I suppose I had. In any case, it wouldn't do to tell him I'd been busy doing other things.

'So I found something I hope will remind you of me if ever we're apart for so long again. Which I hope we won't be.'

Griff took himself off, tactfully saying he'd find some whiskey glasses.

Piers fished in his pocket, coming up with a small velvet box with an unmistakable shape. Oh, dear – was I ready for anything like that? I might fancy him, but I didn't think I loved him. Or perhaps it was just that I hadn't learned how to recognize that particular emotion. Perhaps if I got to know him in ordinary everyday situations, not just fun, fairy-tale times, that would help me sort out what I was feeling, not to mention why he seemed to be so smitten with me, but not smitten enough to do more than snog.

'Let's call it – just for the time being – a friendship ring. Just for the time being,' he repeated, eyes holding mine.

I blushed. Deeply. I think he took it for maidenly bashfulness. It was actually an attack of pure lust. For him, to be fair, not the ring that winked at me from the box.

He reached for my right hand, and slipped the ring on the third finger.

'Piers, it's beautiful! It's stunning!'

It was. It was a glowing ruby, the red they used to call pigeon's blood, nearly two carats in weight. It was surrounded by diamonds, some one and a half carats' worth.

'I saw it in Dublin – and like they say – there's only one thing I can't resist and that's temptation. I knew I had to have it and I knew you had to wear it.'

Griff returned, saying all the right things. The whiskey went down well, but not very much of it found its way down Piers' throat: it seemed that it was only a flying visit, and he had to get back on the road almost immediately. Griff didn't press him to change his mind: one day he might have to confront the knowledge that I was bonking my socks off in the bedroom the other side of his bathroom, but I guessed he didn't want it to be just yet.

I should have lain awake thinking about the future, and even the possibility that one day I might have to leave Griff on his own, but Griff pressed so much whiskey on me that I fell asleep the moment Tim found his way into bed and slept the sleep of the just.

TWELVE

When a guy presents you with a friendship ring, it might seem a tad ungrateful to subject it to scrutiny. Especially when the guy seems to think the ring might transform itself into an engagement ring in due course. At least I hadn't done it when he was there – I'd waited twenty-four long hours, actually, before I reached out with my jeweller's eyepiece, while Griff was preparing supper the next evening.

Griff wouldn't ever soil his lips with expressions like *looking a gift horse in the mouth*. But he did ask, as he tasted the green curry sauce, 'More lime, I think. Surely that breaches all rules of etiquette, my darling Lina?'

'I know.' Putting the eyeglass away unused, I slipped the ring back on to my finger, which I wiggled so that it picked up the light. 'I think I was a bit bowled over,' I conceded slowly. 'A jewel like this from a guy I didn't realize was quite so keen on me. For me, Lina Townend!' I didn't mention what I thought it might retail at, because that would truly have offended Griff. Something like £5000, I reckoned.

'There's no earthly reason why Evelina Townend should not own such things. Indeed, possess them as of right!'

How much pre-supper wine had Griff sunk?

'Griff, what was I doing? Seriously? Accepting something so valuable?'

'Piers is, despite his predilection for cords and body warmers, a most dashing piece of manhood,' Griff observed. Then he started to send himself up: 'Those shoulders! That neat bum!'

'Those cornflower blue eyes, perfect complexion and honey-coloured hair,' I continued, as if it really was no more than a game.

Suddenly Griff was sober. 'My sweet one, what else do you know about him? His family, for instance? Is it not time you were taken home to meet them? And don't tell me he's estranged from them, because he doesn't have the air of the cast-off younger son.'

'I know.'

'Does he never mention them?'

I shook my head, preferring not to mention the way he'd snubbed me when I suggested it. I couldn't even remember the long word he'd mentioned when he'd said we might be related. 'All I know is what you know – that he comes from Sevenoaks,' I said, not quite truthfully.

Griff sipped his Pinot Grigio delicately, looking at me from under his eyebrows. 'I hesitate to suggest what you may consider an entirely unromantic course of action. But have you thought of looking up the Hamlyns on Google?' When I hesitated he said, 'Let's do it together, after supper.'

We found a removals firm and a farmer, but not a lot else. Was Piers attached to either of these families? I'd simply have to ask him. And as the wearer of the gorgeous pulsating ruby I was surely entitled.

Piers didn't seem to see it that way, however, when I asked him the next day, at a fair in a hotel near Ashford. 'My family? Why, for God's sake, do you keep banging on about them, Lina?'

'Because I'm interested.' I resolved never to tell him about my Googling. 'After all, you've met my family.'

'Only Griff.'

Only Griff! 'He's all the family I have. I don't count Lord Elham. He's just a responsibility.'

'Even so. I mean, members of the aristocracy aren't ten to a penny, not the old families at least. And if we're related I ought to meet the head of the family – he must be sitting on loads of really great stuff.'

I went very quiet, and let him rant on. Clearly, although he didn't say it in so many words, he'd have liked to get his hands on some of Lord Elham's loot. This was a side of him I'd not seen before.

So I got blamed for not taking him along to Bossingham Hall, when I didn't know if his father was even alive. Fortunately a wave of punters swept in, or I might have snapped at him, though possibly not enough to return the ring with a dramatic gesture. As it was, I turned on my heel and returned to the safety of Griff's stand.

I thought the fair would have been far too small and un-distinguished to attract the likes of Morris, but to my surprise

he strolled in just before I hoped to break for a coffee with
Piers, to wrap my hands round a warm mug and to rebuild
bridges. I didn't like being on bad terms with people, but Griff
said it wouldn't do him any harm to realize that he had upset
me and that he was in the wrong. So perhaps Morris was heaven-
sent. We exchanged no more than a nod – he must be on duty.
But eventually he wandered over and, to my surprise, paid hard
cash for a Ruskin spill vase, not the incredibly precious high-
fired *sang de boeuf*, but a very pretty pale iridescent blue.

I knocked off 10 per cent for cash.

'Without being asked! Lina, are you well?'

'Standard practice, Morris,' I assured him, as I wrapped the
vase in a great deal of bubble wrap. I'd have hated the lovely
fragile thing to get chipped or worse.

He held the Sellotape as I snipped it. 'This is just the thing
for my mother's birthday.' With hardly a pause, he added,
'Any news I should know about? OK, Lina, something's upset
you – what's up?'

I shrugged. I wasn't about to blurt out all about my tiff
with Piers or my fears about Darren Harris – especially in
front of a load of folk with nice active purses.

'Something is,' he insisted. 'Do you want to join me for a
drink when you've packed up?'

'Not round here – just in case, you know . . . If anyone
recognizes you . . .'

'So would I be arresting you or turning you into a grass?'

Griff completed a sale on a nice piece of Gaudy Welsh and
joined us. 'It might be better to continue your conversation
chez nous, Mr Morris. Eightish? I'm sure there's enough casserole for three.'

'Thanks.'

I shoved the vase into one of the sale organizer's official
polythene carrier bags, which should surely become rare
antiques themselves any day now. 'Enjoy your purchase,' I
said in a very public voice, and waved him off.

'Morris seems a decent man,' Griff said, as we left the car
park.

'He's still a policeman. I wish you hadn't invited him. I
want to find out about Darren myself, to—'

'To protect your father? Some might see him as a vulnerable

old man prey to an unscrupulous young fraud. If he is, he needs all the protection the law can give him – not just a daughter, no matter how willing. Think about that, sweet one. And don't worry – I shan't say anything about him to Morris, not without your permission.'

I reached – it was a long stretch – for his hand and squeezed it. If only I could have trusted my father – if only I could have trusted anyone! – as much as I trusted Griff.

Even though the central heating was going full blast, I set a match to the fire and shooed Griff upstairs to have a hot bath. The hand I'd squeezed had been icy, even colder than mine. Meanwhile, I laid the table for three and opened the bottle of red wine that Griff told me would go well with the casserole.

Morris arrived almost immediately. 'Thank God for car heaters,' he declared. 'Why didn't the hotel turn the heating up? Something to do with the hot coffees they were selling, no doubt. Lina, a real fire! What bliss!'

'I didn't want Griff going down with pneumonia,' I said, trying to tease something out of the fuzziest part of my brain. 'He's in the bath with a nip of whiskey.' Some of the stuff Piers had given him, as it happened. 'I don't know if it's a good idea, but he says his granny swore by it, and she lived to be ninety-eight. Would you like a drop yourself? Or Griff's other remedy, hot chocolate?'

He wandered into the kitchen after me. 'Just to get the business end of the conversation over with first, Lina – some more stuff's disappeared from Bossingham Hall. Ivory. Oh, that's better,' he said, holding the mug of chocolate like a hot water bottle.

I held my forehead.

'Are you all right?'

'It's just something I have to . . . No, it's no good. It'll come at its own pace or not at all.' I shook my head. 'Ivory? Not that collection in the display cases in the library? You're joking! They must be worth—'

'Going on for a million, according to my sources. I suppose you haven't seen your father playing chess with a highly desirable set, Lina?'

'My father, play chess?' But it was just the sort of thing Titus Oates might do. No, Titus was a forger, not a thief. What Griff called a subtle distinction, but no less real for all that. 'You mean, in a frogged velvet dressing gown in front of the fire?'

'In his jeans in the kitchen for all I care. Or –' he paused as the drain gurgled with Griff's emptying bathwater – 'in the bath. I take it he'll be down any minute?'

I couldn't stop a snort of laughter. 'He was an Actor, Morris.' I mimicked an old-fashioned thespian. 'An entrance will be made – when you least expect it.'

He joined in. 'At least he'll come down to a nice cosy room.'

Cosy like my father's. Whereas the Hall itself was icy cold. And the CCTV had merely stared back at me.

I sat at the kitchen table. 'Morris. Bossingham Hall was icy cold. It shouldn't have been. Someone was accused of breaking a plate the other day. She didn't: it was so badly cracked it could have come apart any time. Especially if it was sub . . . sugg . . . subjected to changes in temperature. No, don't look at me like that. It's a long story and I'll try to fillet out the important bits.' I took a deep breath and concentrated. 'I think someone's switched off the heating and the humidity protection. Which is pretty bad news. But – and this is where I've been trying to get to – I don't think their CCTV is working either. Has anyone checked their burglar alarms?'

He produced a notebook. 'Why should anyone turn off the heating?'

'Like the hotel did, to save money? Even though they weren't trying to flog poor coffee. Pretty short term savings, but you never know. The whole place is weird,' I said, explaining about the staff quarters and the breakages policy. 'But I can't see how stopping cameras having a nice swivel round is going to save any fuel.'

'Neither do I,' said Morris, writing hard. 'Not when they assured me when I went that it had been serviced recently.'

'I saw a load of security firm vans there one day, so they're probably telling the truth.'

'Do you think one of the cleaners switched things off by mistake?'

'They are not cleaners as in Mrs Mop,' Griff declared, making us both jump, as I'm quite sure he intended. 'And it takes a great big mistake to switch off what I should imagine are three quite separate systems. That wine should be nicely chambré by now, angel heart.'

He and Morris shook hands heartily, and then he turned his
attention to the supper.

'I'd like another look round your father's rooms, Lina.
Unofficial. Could you fix that?'

I shook my head. 'How soon would unofficial become very
official indeed? He is my father, Morris. A pretty crap one,
but my father.'

'What about his other children? Is he in touch with them? He
is, isn't he? You've got too honest a face to dissimulate, Lina.'

'I might well have – if only I knew the meaning of the
word.'

Griff, stirring the casserole, turned and raised an eyebrow.
'Lie,' he mouthed.

'Just give me a name, Lina,' Morris urged. 'Then I can do
all the dirty work and no one will know you've had anything
to do with it.'

'You want me to dob in my own brother?'

'If you know he's nicked a million quid's worth of ivory,
yes, frankly, I do.'

I pushed away from the table. 'I don't know anything of
the sort, Morris. But we do know that someone employed by
the trustees left the hall itself vulnerable.' That was a word
Griff had taught me quite early on; for some reason it had
stuck better than some of the others. I even remembered to
pronounce the 'l' in the middle. 'Couldn't you start there? See
if a trail leads anywhere?'

His face was suddenly as hard as when I'd first seen it at
the NEC. 'Obstructing the police is a criminal offence, Lina.'

My chin went up. '*Obstruct*? I'm not even withholding
information. I don't have any bloody information. All I know
is that one of my father's many sons has turned up in his part
of Bossingham Hall.'

Griff said quietly, 'He *says* he's Lord Elham's son, my dear
one, but have you checked his provenance? Now, Morris, can
I press you to a glass of sherry? Or are you a G and T man?'

I'd have said that Morris was as thrown as I was by Griff's
question. I couldn't yell obscenities at a guest, any more than
the guest could arrest me: that must have been Griff's thinking.

Nothing more was said about my half-brother till the meal
was over, with Morris and Griff chatting away as if they'd

known each other since the year dot. I'd managed to contribute a bit, but not much – I'd been worrying what I should reveal, of course. What if Darren Harris was a fake? What if he was intent on robbing Lord Elham, and maybe even the Hall's trustees? I didn't owe him anything, and rather thought he owed my father a couple of grand.

Griff fussed off to make coffee, leaving the two of us alone. Funnily enough, though Morris didn't present me with a ring, he did remark on it.

'A present from my boyfriend,' I said shyly.

'Do I know him? Is he another dealer?'

'He sells collectibles,' I said. 'Piers Hamlyn.'

Something registered. I'll swear it did. But Morris just shook his head. 'You'll have to introduce me.'

Griff, returning with a cafetière, sighed hugely. 'I was afraid you wanted to question him, too, Morris. You must allow my dearest one a nice boyfriend, even if you may not applaud her taste in brothers.'

I said sulkily, 'I don't even know what my taste in brothers might be. I've never met the guy.' And then I recalled a few of Lord Elham's words – that Darren had made a point of turning up when I wasn't going to be there. If my father was suspicious, dozy old soak that he was, perhaps I didn't need to worry about family loyalty. 'Maybe you'd be able to tell me, Morris, if it's worth scraping his acquaintance.'

Griff smiled and nodded. I'd got the phrase right.

Morris merely nodded.

'Darren Harris. But Morris, if he's not already on your books, leave him till last in your enquiries – please.'

'Consider him left. But if he is on my books, what then?'

THIRTEEN

Though I hadn't heard from him since our disagreement three or four days ago at the Ashford fair, I was still wearing Piers' ring, and collecting admiring looks for it. From time to time I thought about phoning him, texting him at least, but from one of my parents I'd inherited a nasty stubborn streak. As for the ring, he'd probably ask me to give it back, so I might as well enjoy it while I could.

Except there was something about it I wasn't enjoying. Was it my divvy's instinct at work?

I asked myself the questions I'd ask a punter who wanted my opinion. Firstly, what was its provenance? For some things, like pictures and that wretched Hungarian silver tray, which Morris had promised to return next time he saw me, provenance was vital. For a ring like this, it was tricky and hardly worth bothering with, so long as you could see the hallmark on the band. In this case one declared it was made in Birmingham, way back in 1879. So it was the right age to have a silver mount for the stones, as opposed to the stronger platinum claws used later. Why it had travelled to Dublin to be sold, goodness knew. But I thought of all those rings on Josie's stand, and had to admit that rings fetched up all over the place.

So that was all right, then.

Or not.

Was there another problem? Sometimes, as I'd told Morris, it wasn't instinct so much as eyes that operated – like the time I'd clocked the Meissen figure amongst the Staffordshire ones. I'd better trust them now.

Griff was having lunch with Aidan. Good. Knowing it would offend him, I didn't want him to know what I was doing. I switched on my bright work-lights and scrunched my jeweller's magnifying lens into my eye socket. My hands were curiously steady, given what I was doing. I started with the main stone, that lovely pigeon's blood ruby. If anything it was even better under the harsh light than in romantic candlelight. Nothing wrong there. So I started on the diamonds surrounding it. The first two were fine. I told myself I was being foolish. But that didn't stop me looking at the next. And then the next.

When I looked at the next, I could have been sick. It might have been a diamond, but it was so poor it was hardly worth fitting. The next was fine. I worked my way systematically round.

The majority of the stones were good quality. Not nearly as good as the ruby, but good enough. But three were poor. Really, really poor.

When had they been put in? When the piece had been made,

when the general gleam might have stopped lovers' eyes noticing? Or more recently? The ring was so filthy it was hard to tell. Not just dirty, but really filthy – as if someone had done the gardening in it. Twice. A quick slosh round in cleaning fluid made everything come up nicely, but told me nothing.

And now I knew something was dodgy, was I any happier? Surely Piers would notice I'd spruced it up a bit, and would ask why. What would I say? Just that I'd spring-cleaned it? Or that I'd spring-cleaned it because I'd thought one of the stones was loose? That way I gave him a chance to say something. And if he didn't, where was I then? Apart from having a nice clean ruby ring with three dodgy stones on the outside?

This time I didn't put it back on. I tucked it into its little heart shaped velvet-covered box – again, just right for the period – and put it into our business safe. There was a little furrow on my finger, as if the flesh was missing it already. And, oddly, my hand wasn't as steady as I liked when I started work on my pile of restoration work.

I was just wondering what I should graze on for lunch – it was a habit Griff, loving china and linen, utterly loathed, so I only did it when he was out. Cheese or that nice ripe avocado?

The phone rang. Morris.

'Do you fancy a drink?' He named a pub midway between Bossingham and Bredeham – by coincidence called the Halfway House. 'See you there in half an hour?' He cut the call.

What had he been up to? Or what was he planning? He sounded so innocent I was suspicious.

It struck me as I drove over in the larger of our two vans, Griff having taken the other, that I knew nothing at all about Morris. About the same as I knew about Piers, in other words. I was slipping, wasn't I? I used to want to know chapter and verse about anyone before I exchanged much more than the time of day. Here I was wearing one stranger's ring (yes, I'd put it back on, largely because I knew Morris would remark on it if it was missing) and meeting another probably to discuss my father's future. I knew I was exaggerating about both but even so a bit of digging about was well overdue.

'How well are you known at Bossingham Hall?' he greeted me, the moment I'd parked.

'Hey, let me get out of the van,' I protested. 'And a drink might help lubricate my brain.'

For all that, I settled for a J2O, on the grounds that if he annoyed me and I went home I'd be working on precious china, and even if he didn't I was driving anyway. Call me a goody-two-shoes, but our business depended heavily on my having a clean licence. It seemed his did too. He joined me in a fruit juice, and ordered pasta from the specials board for us both.

'Most of the women working at the Hall know me by sight,' I said, 'since I'm Lord Elham's daughter, and they think I'm due a bit of respect on that account. Huh! It's a good job not many of them know him by sight, isn't it?'

'Do you get on with them?'

'Pretty well. Where's this leading, Morris?'

'I was wondering about your doing a spot of undercover work. But it sounds as if that won't work.'

I shook my head. 'Absolutely not.'

'Have you ever thought of becoming their resident restorer?'

'Why should I? I'm too busy with our own business.' I frowned. 'Why do you want me in there?'

'I'd just value a second opinion.'

'Of?'

'A number of things.'

'You've got more experts at the Met than you can shake a stick at, surely.'

'We're quite a small squad, as it happens. Anyway, I shall have to think of something else.'

'Like the strange economies the administrators have been making in the matter of heat and security? I told you, I saw an army of vans out there one day. Surely they were upgrading the system, not switching it off.'

'Apparently,' Morris said deadpan, 'the system's not worked properly since. It kept getting hysterical at the sight of all the cleaners touching things. That was why it was disabled the day you were there. But it's always operational when the house is empty.'

'And the heat? And humidity control?'

'Being spring-cleaned at the same time as the house.'

'Hmm. All very pl . . . paws . . . plausible,' I finished, hoping he didn't notice the relief in my voice when the correct word popped up. 'The trouble is, they're assuming that the thefts take place after hours. What if they don't?'

He waited until the waiter bringing our pasta had gone.
And then a bit longer, while we tucked in. It was very good.
'What times does Darren Harris visit your father?'

'At times I'm not there. Have you found something on him,
Morris? Because if you have, there's the problem of my father.'

'No one of that name has shown up on our radar,' he said
as if he was choosing his words carefully.

So my sigh wasn't one of relief. More frustration. 'One
thing you could do,' I said, playing with my pasta, which
didn't seem as tasty all of a sudden, 'is to make sure no one
can move between the two parts of the hall without anyone
knowing. Not just the official door, with the keypad. But the
other ways in and out, too.'

'Other ways?'

My voice sounded very thin and hollow. 'Ways I don't think
even Lord Elham knows. I found them myself. It could be
that someone else has. Hell, Morris, does this mean I'm a
suspect?'

'I hope not. How am I going to get to see these here secret
doors?'

'That makes them sound very exciting, as if you need a
magic potion to shrink you.' A copy of both *Alices* had been
one of my father's few gifts to me. Admittedly I'd turned one
present down – the one worth a million – but perhaps sometimes I wished he'd hand me a pretty item and tell me to keep
it just for myself.

Morris laughed. 'What did it say on the bottle in *Alice*?
Drink me!'

'Quite. But seriously, taking you through the public side might
make that administrator think my father's to blame. He's had
enough tussles with the trustees not to want another one.'

'But I bet he's won them all by simple attrition,' he said.

'What's that? How do you spell it?' It was a very good
word and I jotted it in my vocab book. Which reminded me,
I still needed to see if Darren Harris was in my father's book,
which didn't contain words, of course, but details of women
like my mother, and their children, if any. There were records
of other details too.

Frowning slightly he explained.

'Don't start banging on about the education system,' I said
hurriedly. 'It's just that I didn't go to school much. Being

fostered,' I explained. 'But that doesn't mean I don't like learning now.'

'No need to sound so defensive. It's a crying shame the fostering system lets down kids so badly. As for you – well, you radiate intelligence. That's why I'm genuinely asking your advice.'

'Maybe when I've finished eating I shall think of some to give. They do a wonderful treacle tart here,' I added.

'So you've no idea how we can sort out these doors?' he asked, looking wistfully at my dessert.

The tart had come with both a fork and a spoon. I pushed the spoon over: 'Help yourself. Go on, you can't be worrying about your waist line.' For his age he had a remarkably trim figure. He'd kept his hair, too, even if it was a slightly regrettable ginger.

'I can. How many policemen have you seen who wear their bellies over their waistbands? I don't want to end up like them. And I loathe the gym, so prevention is better than cure.' All the same, he picked up the spoon and dug in.

'I didn't say that I couldn't sort out the doors,' I said. 'I said I didn't want to go via the main house. So it'll have to be via my father's wing. And that means spinning a good story. He may not be bright, but he's cunning. And I don't want to put ideas into his head, either.'

'God, no!'

'And I don't want him getting the idea he's still under suspicion.' I pushed the rest of the tart in his direction. I'd have thought a sugar rush might have helped, but my brain felt horribly furry. 'Not without a lawyer handy.'

'Who'd end up in as much of a mess as we did. OK, Lina – softly, softly catchee monkey. But swiftly, swiftly catchee him too.'

He'd left one corner of the tart for me. I couldn't resist it. And suddenly the idea came. 'I could always tell him that people had been nicking stuff from the Hall and you wanted to make sure they didn't get into his half and start stealing from him too.'

'Good idea. Do you want me to return that silver-gilt dish to him, by the way? It's in the car.'

I pulled a face. 'On the whole, no. It's safer with me, and I can ration the cash when I manage to sell it.'

'Fair enough. I'll hand it over when we've finished. Do you want a coffee? No? I'll settle up, then. My treat. Or rather, my expenses' treat. After all, I needed your help and I'm taking your time. And maybe more, when we go to Bossingham.'

'Thanks,' I said. I checked my watch and followed him to the bar. 'Do you want to go now? With luck he'll be watching some TV programme he can't miss and he'll let us get on with it.'

For some reason, however, Lord Elham was as alert as I'd seen him, and worried with it. He actually grabbed my hands when he opened the doors to me, the nearest he'd ever come to physical contact. There was no looking to Lord E for a fatherly hug.

'But what are you doing with that policeman chappie?' he asked, eyes widening. 'He's not going to arrest me, is he?'

'It depends what you've done, Lord Elham,' Morris said jokingly.

'He doesn't do jokes, you fool,' I hissed.

And he could see that for himself. The poor old guy was clearly ready to bolt.

'No, my lord, I'm here to advise you on your security.' He was almost bowing. 'There have been some thefts from the main part of the hall, and Lina's afraid some of your treasures might be at risk. You know how she worries about you, sir.'

'You do, don't you? All that food and the washing and stuff? Yes, you're a good girl. I'm proud of you.' He squeezed my hands. Releasing the left one, he lifted the right nearer his face. 'I don't know about that ring, though – not the sort of thing a lady should wear during the daytime.' He screwed up his eyes and looked into my face. 'Not on that hand.' In anyone else that look would have been shrewd. Perhaps it was shrewd.

'I'll tell you if it ever moves to the other one,' I said. And meant it, funnily enough.

'Ask me, you mean, and before it moves!' He peered behind me to the van. 'Any chance of any fizz?'

'Sorry, not this time. Are you running short?'

He ushered us into his living room. 'Darren's taken to

bringing me some. But it's strange stuff. A glass knocks you clean out. Wake up the next day feeling as if your brain's turned to cotton wool.' He leant closer. 'Gives you trouble with your water works too. Good job you made me buy that washing machine thing, Lina. Not like me at all. And I have these weird dreams. And now you tell me I might be getting robbed.' He sat down heavily.

Morris squatted beside him. 'Lina and I will go and check your security, like I said. Make sure no one's getting in here to rob you.'

To judge by the furrows on his forehead, a thought was oozing round Lord Elham's head. I waited, but it didn't find its way out. So I said, 'Don't worry about us. We'll sort things out. And – cheer up – I might find something else to sell for you.'

'He's really worried, isn't he?' Morris observed, as we set off together.

I nodded. 'I've never seen him like this before. Tell you what, let's pop in here – it's not on our route, but it's got something important in it.' The room itself was even more important to me, as it had once been the only memory I had of my early childhood. It was seeing it for real that had convinced me that Lord Elham was my father. It had been something he'd taken into it that had convinced him that I was his daughter. Now it lurked in a bureau he kept locked, but which I could always open with a key from a bunch I kept in my bag.

'Bloody hell!' Morris exclaimed. 'A burglary kit! Lina, I don't want to know.'

'For goodness' sake! We buy furniture from time to time – wardrobes and bureaux like this. And we need to look inside them. Back in the eighteenth and nineteenth centuries, there weren't many different types of lock, not for everyday furniture. So we have a range of the standard keys. Anyway, this one fits this bureau.' I demonstrated. 'And this key opens that little pair of doors here inside.'

He opened them very gingerly, and reached inside. 'There's only some old school exercise book here. French Vocab.'

'Thank God it's still there!'

'What's up, Lina?'

'I was afraid Darrenarris might have got his paws on it. And it's more important to me than anything.' I opened the book and showed him the columns inside. 'Surname; Christian name; when, where and how; offspring, if any, M/F . . . That's my mother there – Helen Townend. Now, let's see if there's a Harris.'

He took the book. 'Is this what I think it is? A list of all his mistresses? What's that? Diseases? Payments? Bloody hell – Lina, you poor kid.'

Before I knew it I was in the middle of a giant hug. I don't know if it was to comfort me or to comfort himself. Hugging wasn't my top priority at the moment, not even with the accompaniment of head kissing and hair stroking, so I eased myself away. 'Can you see a Harris here?'

'The writing's awful, isn't it?'

'I think today they'd call him dyslexic. Ah, yes. That looks like a Harris.'

He nodded. 'Just one problem, Lina. In the M/F column – Ms Harris has an F, not an M, against her name.'

FOURTEEN

'Lord Elham isn't a man to confuse an M with an F,' I said. 'Is he? Not with his pro . . . propi—'

'Especially not with his proclivities.' He said the last word very slowly.

I fished out my vocab book. 'Could you spell that?'

He did so, a curious smile round his eyes. 'You seem very laid-back about your father's proclivities.' This time he said it at normal speed.

'You mean I should get upset? Well, look where it's left him.' I took the other vocab book from him, weighing one in each hand. They were pretty well the same on the outside, though not on the inside, of course. Then I returned mine to the little cupboard, locking it and the bureau carefully, and stowing the keys and Lord Elham's book in my bag.

'Did I see you do that?' he asked sternly.

'Is that your official voice? This book means a great deal to me, and nothing at all to my father. And it might mean

enough to Darrenarris for him to come looking for it, mightn't
it? To ensure my father can't check up on him.' For some
reason Arthur Habgood's face swam into my head. 'Of course,'
I continued, rather pleased with myself, 'Lord Elham could
always insist on a DNA test for him.'

'You'd need, as I'm sure you know, Darren's permission.'

'You're sure? I've read about getting hairs out of brushes,
that sort of thing. Come on, I'm sure if a crime's being
committed, you people don't worry about written permission
and all that. Not always, anyway. And nicking things from a
man you claim is your father and isn't would be a crime twice
over, wouldn't it? Now, should we change the code on the
security pad on the official door, or do you want to see the
unofficial ways in first? We pretty well have to pass the official door. You'll have to do it – I've no idea how these things
work. And we must remember to tell my father.'

'Or not,' Morris muttered.

It took him a matter of seconds to change the code to the
number I gave him – the year of my birth. When I explained,
I couldn't read his sideways look.

'And now for the first door.' I set off slowly.

'What's the matter?' he asked, looking at me closely again.
'You still don't really know whether to trust me, do you? I
promise not to arrest you as an accessory before or after the
fact. And I promise not to strangle you, steal all I can and
flee the country.'

I managed a smile. Sort of. 'You know pretty well everything about me. What you see is what you get. But you—'

'I've told you before. Not all policemen are bent. You can
phone my ex-partner and ask if you want.' He held up his
mobile. Then he put it down again. 'She's probably in the
middle of a rehearsal at the moment. She plays the cello in
the BBC Symphony Orchestra. We broke up because we never
saw each other, what with my shifts and hers. Here's my home
address.' He flipped me a business card. 'And I'm sure Farfrae
would be happy to talk to you again.'

I looked him in the eye. 'Griff liked you. That should be
enough, shouldn't it?'

'I hope you like me.'

'I'd rather rely on Griff.' I set off up the stairs into one of
the bedrooms now used as a dump.

We stood in the middle of the room, surrounded by piles of newspapers. He gaped but pulled himself together. 'So where's this here door?'

'Beside the wardrobe. God knows what's in there. I've never looked.' I jangled the little keys temptingly.

'Not this time. We've got work to do.'

'OK. It's all yours.' I pointed. 'It's pretending to be part of the wall.'

His face lit up as if someone had switched on a bulb. 'It's one of those hidden doors! All those times I've been to a National Trust property and seen one of these and not been allowed to cross the red cord and open it – let alone go through. Why were they designed like this, Lina? With the same dado, and wallpaper and everything?'

'So a great slab of magnolia paint doesn't spoil the decor? I should think that's the main reason. And maybe you want the servants to come and go without using the posh gilded doors and the state corridors. Especially if they're carrying chamber pots and things. One of these days I'll get round to researching them.'

Again he gave me a quick look, before he asked, 'Which magic key fits?'

'You don't need a key, I'm afraid. That's why it's a security risk. Just finger nails. You try. Hell,' I said, slapping my face, but only lightly, 'I forgot to ask if you've got a torch.' I fished mine out of my bag's outer pocket.

'There's one on my mobile. Do I gather a torch is a normal piece of feminine equipment?'

'Yes, if you're an antiques dealer,' I said. 'Now, turn left. We're heading for the main part of the house.' I counted the doors as we went, finally reaching one I'd marked. I pointed to a lipstick dot I'd put on the china handle. 'This is the one. After you.'

We stepped into the west-facing bedroom, lit up by the setting sun.

'It's not very grand, is it?' Morris said with a sigh.

'Better than the one we've just left, though.'

'What do the punters think, I wonder?'

'It's not one they see.' I opened the official door and stepped through. 'I don't remember their being allowed into this corridor, actually. I can't see any sensors or any cameras. Can you?'

He followed me, peering round. 'No. So I could literally walk down into the main part of the house?'

'Well, eventually the cameras would pick you up some-where, of course. And I presume after your conversation with the administrator they're all working again.' I raised a finger. 'It sounds as if they've got the climate controls back on again, too. Well done, Morris. Now, do you want to have a close look round here or would you like to see unauthorized access two?'

Since we couldn't lock the hidden door in Lord Elham's wing, Morris and I moved some piles of newspapers in front of it. It meant we now could reach the window, and the amount of dust we stirred up settled nicely on the carpet so it was hard to tell what we'd been up to.

'Onwards and upwards, then,' I said. I had an idea I was quoting someone but had no idea who. 'Up to the next floor. And another secretish door.'

'Where?' he asked, after a few minutes' peering round.

'In that cupboard.' I pointed. 'Again, no key. Just twist the knob to your right.'

I followed him up a very steep flight of stairs, almost a ladder, really. Another door at the top opened into the attics, a series of barn-like spaces. The dormer windows along the back let in enough light for us to see it was full of yet more junk. Morris was like a dog let loose in a wood, not knowing which target to head for first.

'There must be rich pickings for you here,' he said. 'That card table alone—'

'One of the drawers is missing. In any case, I'm not absolutely sure where Lord Elham's part ends and the trustees' begins.'

That earned me another look. 'You really are incredibly moral, despite your genes, aren't you?'

I dug for a phrase I'd heard Griff use. 'Is it nature or nurture? If it's nurture, I have Iris, my last foster mother, and Griff to thank. Anyway, you see that hatch there? Near the chimney stack? All you have to do is lift it up and drop down. You land on a bed. But that's one that the punters do get to see, so I presume there are cameras.'

Lifting the hatch, he laid it back carefully and dropped on

his knees to peer through the hole. He flashed his torch round but then got to his feet. 'There's no way of securing this?'

'Not that I can see. Unless we could put something on top of it. Trouble is, our footprints will show up in this dust, whatever we do.'

'Not if we leave enough of them. What about that chest of drawers? Could we shift that?'

'We have to get the drawers out first. It'll weigh a ton.' I pulled out one of the smaller ones at the top. Thanks to the cabinet maker's skill it slid as easily as if someone had waxed the runners only yesterday. There was no treasure inside, though – just bed linen speckled with iron mould. The other drawers were full of the same. All we had to do was move the carcase over the hatch and slide the drawers back in.

It was getting so dark that even Morris realized there was no point in staying up much longer – there was only so much our torches could light up. But I had to promise to bring him back another day, as if I was a mother dragging a child from Toys R Us.

'No bolts, no padlock,' he said, jabbing a finger on the door as we shut it behind us. 'It wouldn't do the wood any good, but I think we should fit one.' He made a note. 'Anything else I should see?'

'We could cast our eyes over each room as we go down, to see if anything's obviously missing.'

'Lead on.'

We established that several silver candelabra and a couple of pretty hideous silver-gilt epergnes had gone, plus a cardboard box or two I'd never got round to opening. Someone had torn open a box containing enormous buttons and shoe buckles but left them. I didn't.

'They could have been made by Matthew Boulton,' I said. 'And he's got a bicentenary or something coming up. Could keep my father in champagne for a bit.'

'But not as valuable as the stuff you say has gone astray?'

'Probably not. Seems as if Darrenarris is keen on silver, doesn't it?'

'Him or someone who's nipped over from the other side. Probably using the official door – 1234 isn't a hard code for your average burglar to crack. We'd better notify the administrator we've changed it, by the way.'

I shook my head, releasing a cloud of dust. 'Let them find out the hard way. Anyone from the house is supposed to come to my father's front door and ring, anyway. Now what? My goodness, we're filthy.'

'We ought to make sure no one can get into the house via the attic. They'd be hard put to push down all the papers and get in from the service corridor. They can't use the official door. What about any other doors?'

'There's one at the back, another to the kitchen. And plenty of rooms with grade one listed windows that have those discreet little bolts in the frames, but nothing else. Nice old glass – very brittle indeed. I've already found keys that will fit the doors to those rooms. We might just check they're still locked.'

We did. They were. Just in case it was Darrenarris who'd been on the prowl, I removed the keys and pocketed them.

'How will you know which is which?'

'They're all the same. The kitchen and back doors have different ones, but the locks could easily be picked.'

'I don't want to know how you know that.'

'No, you don't,' I said with a grin.

He fished out a notebook. 'So we need modern mortise locks, some bolts, a new lock for the front door and a security chain. Where's the nearest B&Q or Homebase?'

My turn to look hard at him. 'Why are you doing this, Morris? Why not tell Lord Elham to call a locksmith and skedaddle back to the Smoke?'

'Because I know I can trust me to do it tonight. He might be an old bastard, Lina, but he's a frail old bastard. And once people get a taste for easy pickings, they get cross if they're thwarted. So I want to make sure whoever is behind the thefts is kept properly out.'

It sounded reasonable. 'Bear with me a second – I want to see if he's got anything left in his freezer.'

He trailed after me to the kitchen, peering at the contents of the sink – again, pairs of glasses and plates.

'Just as I thought. When I bring his supplies I know pretty well to the last frozen pea how long they'll provide for him. There's only a couple of things left. He'd have been back on Pot Noodles if I hadn't noticed.'

'So what do I bring in? A lot of healthy option ready meals?' Again he jotted.

'And some green tea bags. He likes those with a touch of jasmine best.'

'Will he be expecting us to eat with him?'

'Not if there's anything worth watching on the TV.'

'OK. Shall we snatch a bite together after we've sorted everything out? It might be late, of course, by the time I've finished my handyman stuff.'

So did he want me to join him or not? Or was he after something else? I'd better say yes, then talk to Griff.

It must have been possible to give Griff enough information without thoroughly alarming him, but I couldn't manage it. I did my best when I phoned – I'd even worked out in my head what I needed to say before I dialled. It sounded good enough there.

'Hi, Griff – Morris says a couple of locks here at Bossingham Hall could do with upgrading, so I'm staying to hold the fort while he goes and buys them.'

But it obviously wasn't good enough.

'So you're alone with that old idiot while an able-bodied man goes swanning off to B&Q, eh?'

'Yes. And then we might go and have a spot of supper together,' I said casually.

'Indeed? And what about young Piers, whose ring you are no doubt still wearing?'

'It's a friendship ring,' I said, with a theatrical sigh he'd have been proud of if he'd heaved it himself. 'And more to the point Morris is a mate too. He must be forty if he's a day, Griff. Far too old for me.' I might as well get a little dig in. 'And far too young for you, while we're about it!'

Griff took the bait. 'Aye, me!' OK, my sigh was nothing to his.

'And how's Aidan?'

'He sends his regards. Not Nella's, of course, but you'd hardly want them anyway. We had a pleasant lunch, thank you.'

'And did you have a trip to Waitrose?'

'Of course. And I bought no end of lovely end-dated goodies. What heaven that shop is.' But I hadn't diverted him enough. 'And what time can I expect you safely home, dear heart?' he demanded, in his extra-plaintive, I'm-a-very-doddery-old-man voice.

'When you see me,' I retorted firmly. And then I had an idea. 'Unless you've got enough goodies to knock up a meal for three? Something that won't spoil if we're late?' And – because it had taken me a long, long time to learn to say it – I added, 'Love you!'

'And you are the light of my life, my child.'

I wasn't sure if I could claim the same for my father, but at least I could make us a cup of green tea. I couldn't say I was at all keen on it, but neither Griff nor my father was grown up enough to drink it unless I did. We sipped in silence, apart from my father's boos at the weakest link.

I turned my mind to the missing silver. None of it was especially good – the trustees had naturally kept any obvious collector's items, and no doubt volunteers like Mrs Walker had been applying elbow grease to it, with or without the eyes of CCTV upon them. Some hideous pieces had good hallmarks; some elegant pieces didn't. And a mixture of both types had gone. I wished I knew what was in those boxes. More silver, maybe. No china and no books had gone, as far as I could work out. Perhaps he didn't need them. Or perhaps my father had rem . . . remon . . . hell, perhaps he'd told him off for selling that Meissen figure below the market price.

The buttons and buckles made a wonderful display when I laid them out on the table that dominated his living room. When I'd first seen it it had been foul with encrusted Pot Noodle pots. Now at least it had a coat of wax to protect it, though I'd never shifted the white rings left by endless champagne glasses.

'Hey, those are quite valuable,' he said, picking one up. 'Didn't someone famous start out making these?' Perhaps the green tea was more effective than I realized.

'Matthew Boulton. The guy based in Birmingham.'

'Brummagem ware. City of a thousand trades. What's the matter? You've found more stuff's gone missing? More silver?'

I nodded and told him what I thought was gone.

He listened carefully, and suddenly switched off the TV with a decisive gesture of his zapper thumb. 'They do what they do with cars. You know, take two that have been in a crash and take the front half of one and the back half of another and weld them together. Same with silver.'

'How on earth do you know that?'

'There was a programme about that the other day. I watched it because I thought you might be interested. Ah! Time for the rugby!' His thumb leapt into action.

I was beginning to make sense of what he said, but clearly he wasn't going to offer any more information for a bit. If only I'd known more about silver. If only I'd taken the trouble to carry on studying the book that had brought Piers and me together. My feeble excuse was that the Nella episode had rather put me off silver.

One person who knew more about dodgy antiques than most was Titus Oates, who was unshockable, to say the least.

The best mobile signal was in the kitchen, so that was where I went to make my call. As usual, Titus answered first ring.

'I thought I was supposed to be phoning you?' he greeted me.

'I've got a problem with stolen silver.'

'If you're offered any make sure you check the hallmark.'

'Even I know that.'

'And check the silver around the hallmark – it's possible for a skilled man to transplant it, but it always leaves a bit of a scar. What have you been offered?'

'It's more what's gone missing.'

'Not from the old geezer's! Hey, you're not accusing me, my girl—'

'Of course I'm not. I'm not accusing anyone. But someone's walked off with a load of stuff, all sorts, really. I'm wondering if someone got through from the main house.'

'Same someone as nicked all that ivory? Word on the street is that that was nicked to order. Maybe the silver was, too.'

'It's such a mixture of good and bad, though.'

'You can always melt down the bad. Or you can use it to make good stuff even more saleable. Now, no one wants a brandy saucepan these days—'

'I didn't even know there was such a thing.'

'There you are then. So you take off the handle, which is at the front, and replace it with another handle, opposite the spout. And – Bob's your uncle – you've got a highly desirable jug. OK? Is that all? 'Cos I've got other things to worry about than Lord Loopy's silver.'

'You're glad enough of Lord Loopy's skills!' I snapped,

foolishly. 'There is another thing, actually. Someone's got all this ringed silverware – how does he shift it?'

'Invent a provenance of course. And make sure it's a good one. Tell you what,' he said at last. 'Seeing as how it's Lord E, I'll keep my ears open. Can't say fairer than that, can I, doll?' He cut the call before I could answer.

So he'd said much what my father had said. Did that make it better or worse? I wanted to tear apart whoever was doing it, just as they were slicing up lovely objects just to make more money. Yes, I was a bit vague about how they did it. But the fact that they were doing it at all made me feel as I did when people faked tables or sideboards by taking apart items that wouldn't sell well and putting them together with other tops or legs or whatever. And then, of course, selling them to unsuspecting punters. The red mist made me want to punch the wall until my knuckles bled.

And what would Griff say if I came home with my hands in bandages?

Nothing. He'd just gather me into his arms and weep over the damage. 'I'd hoped you were over that,' he'd say.

I couldn't do that to Griff. So I did what the therapist he'd taken me to had told me to do. I took a deep, dizzying breath, and sat down. She'd told me to identify my emotion. OK, this was anger. The cause: someone else's wrongdoing. The cure: well, even as I sat fuming on Lord Elham's back stairs, I realized that it wasn't my job to punish the wrongdoers. It was the law's. So I breathed a bit more. It would be nice to help the law find who was doing wrong, but not if it meant hurting my hands and especially if it meant hurting Griff.

There. I felt better now. And my brain was beginning to work. Was I barking up the wrong tree? Maybe it wasn't Darrenarris that was up to no good. Maybe it was my father and Titus Oates.

'Your father? Dealing in dodgy silver? Forgive me saying so, Lina, but he doesn't look as if he's got enough marbles for that,' Morris said, as he tightened the last screw in the last lock.

'You're right, of course,' I said quickly. Possibly too quickly. I could hardly tell him my father was actually a master forger of historical documents, and might even have the skills to create an authentic-looking set of papers to give any silverware a decent-looking provenance, the sort Nella insisted on. And obviously I couldn't suggest Titus was his accomplice. The less Morris knew about Titus the better. But just as I'd dismissed the idea that Titus might have stolen the Meissen, now it dawned on me that he was so good at dealing in one thing he wouldn't want to risk dealing amateurishly in something else – why, he'd been cross at the thought of pot being smoked at the hall, in case it attracted unwanted attention.

Morris looked at me sideways.

I checked my watch. 'Time we were heading for home, Morris – Griff's cooked a meal for us both and he'll be worried sick if we're late.'

He said nothing about the way I'd changed his plans, only observing, 'You're a grown woman, Lina!'

'Not in Griff's eyes. I'm still the china figurine he rescued from the scrap heap and glued back together.'

'What will he do when you marry Piers and leave him?'

'I told you, it's only a friendship ring.'

This time he looked me straight in the eyes. 'So you say. Does he know that?'

'They were his own words. Mind you, we haven't seen each other for a bit. Work and so on,' I added defensively. 'I'll just pop and say good night to my father and we'll be off. Don't want whatever Griff's cooked us to spoil.'

Lord Elham flapped his hand, his eyes still glued to the TV. But then he really shocked me. He got up to see us out. And even held my hand back a second, while Morris headed for his car. 'Good bloke, that Morris. You could do a lot worse.'

'But I'm with someone else, remember,' I said. 'In fact, I'm seeing him tomorrow – we're at the same fair.'

'Hmm. Well, we shall see. We shall see.'

FIFTEEN

One reason for taking Morris back home to eat was that Griff and I had an early start the next day, and Griff was a dab hand at getting people to leave when he wanted them to – though he always gave the impression that it was they who had made the first move and that he was heartbroken to see them go.

We were heading to a fair at a village church hall in Sussex, not our usual sort of venue. We were only going because one of Griff's old actor mates living nearby had invited us to dinner. On the other hand, Piers was going to be at the fair too, so it might be that he and I would nip off somewhere and leave the old dears to it. Always assuming we were still an item, of course.

We arrived at the village hall to find that no one had got round to turning the heat on and no one seemed to know where the switch might be. In the cold, Griff's knuckles turned bluey-white, the rest of his fingers purple. I knew he'd have liked a nip of brandy, but I caught his eye and shook my head firmly – his alcohol intake was strictly rationed.

Piers' hug and kiss suggested we might still be together, and who was I to argue? We hadn't time to talk because punters were already queuing, and the organizer proposed letting them in out of the sleet, rapidly turning to snow. Not that they'd notice much improvement inside. Somehow we all managed a speedy set-up, with no breakages.

All of a sudden, Piers nipped over to our stall and presented me with another ring. It was a sapphire version of my ruby, with a lovely Sri Lankan stone, much lighter than you get these days but fashionable in the Victorian period.

'I'm not asking you to choose between them,' he said pettishly, as I slipped off the ruby so I could display the sapphire.

I bit my lip: I'd better not tell him I preferred it.

'I'm asking you to sell it,' he explained. 'Usual terms, of course. It's too good for my stall. It'll just disappear amongst all the collectibles. But you've got nice, classy stuff.'

I nodded. Even Griff and I were out of place here. We and a lady who dealt exclusively in fine cups and saucers were the only people dealing in high quality goods. Some dealers even made Piers' stall look good.

'China, glass and treen,' I said cautiously. 'No jewellery.'

'Then it'll stand out all the better, especially with a spotlight trained on it. And your hand to model it.' He kissed it with enough passion to tempt me.

'I'll have to ask Griff,' I said.

'He lets you fly solo with your restored china,' he pointed out. 'I can't see how he could object if you want to branch out into jewellery, particularly stuff as nice as this.'

'I'll ask,' I said, 'because I value his opinion.' He should have known by now never to argue about anything concerning Griff.

The sapphire spent a whole day winking seductively under the display lights, but no one so much as asked after it. Everyone was going round hunch-shouldered and with their hands in their pockets, only removing them by the second-hand book stall which did a brisk trade in paperbacks, seven for a pound. A couple of Piers' Beanie Bears went, and at last someone wandered our way. But it was only to tell us that he'd got a better lustre jug at home, and ours wasn't worth the forty we were asking for it. (It was, take my word for it.)

Frankly, if Griff hadn't been booked in for supper, we'd have packed up and left an hour before closing. But Griff didn't want to impose himself on Felix so early, and I was rather hoping for an invitation from Piers to go on what passed for the razzle in this part of Sussex. After all, I was wearing his ring. And trying to sell another one for him.

Eventually he drifted over, and put very possessive arms round me. I felt foolish for ever having had any doubts. He was just outlining our proposed evening together, his lips tickling my ear, when his mobile went. Since Griff really doesn't approve of anyone snogging in public, especially me, and since it was probably the one thing my father and he would agree on, I pulled away from Piers so he could take the call. His face instantly serious, he moved away and spoke urgently. I wanted to go and stroke better the furrows deepening in his forehead. But a customer – a single, solitary customer – was hovering by my Worcester china. I was far too well trained to pounce, but as soon as he was ready to catch my eye, my eye was ready to be caught. I passed him the mug he was interested in – on a white ground, a jolly blue parrot was pecking blue fruit; the crescent mark underneath was nice and clear. Since the mug was in perfect condition, with no help at all from me, it would more than pay for our day if he bought it. As he handled it, I could see him falling in love. I could have fallen in love with him, as he fished fifty-pound notes from his wallet. A lot of them.

By the time I'd wrapped it there was no sign of Piers. And there was no sign of any other customers, either. So Griff and I did what every other stallholder was doing – we packed up. Griff had so many years of experience he could have done it in his sleep – or, more likely, in an alcoholic fog – without so much as a chip. But I made sure I carried the plastic boxes to the van. I might be small but I was very strong – thanks to some unknown genes. I rather expected to see Piers in the car park, but he wasn't there, either. Meanwhile, his stall was the only one intact. Griff had found another old friend to natter to, so I did the obvious thing – I started packing the Beanies. But should I do it by colour or by type of animal?

I'd done no more than pick up a box and put a turquoise teddy into it when Piers turned up, a strange expression on his face. My activities didn't seem to meet with his approval. But he managed a smile, and explained his system, so we got through the task very quickly, bears and other animals being much easier to stow than china and glass. I'd expected us to laugh a lot, but he was as serious as if he was packing original Steiffs. As we loaded the last box into his van, he said, 'I'm afraid I'm not going to be very good company this evening. Grandmama's been taken ill. The one living in Arundel. A stroke, they think. She's a dear old stick and I—' He swallowed hard.

'You should go and see her,' I said. 'Be with her. If Griff were ever ill, that's what I'd do, Piers. Hell, if you'd told me I'd have packed up all your stuff and taken it with ours!'

He kissed me and my knees literally weakened. 'If you're sure you don't mind . . .'

'Of course I mind. But we can be together any time. And if your grandma's poorly . . . Now, off you go and don't give it another thought. Thank goodness the snow's turning to slush . . .'

Although Felix was nearly as good a cook as Griff, and a brilliant mimic, reducing me to helpless and painful giggles, I was glad when Griff declared that he had had a hard day doing nothing and needed an early night. Since Sussex doesn't seem to run to anything approaching a decent road, and we didn't leave till well after ten, an early night was certainly not on offer. But at last we picked our weary way into the village, and I stowed the van in the garage with its state of the art security. Nonetheless we carried the boxes with the most valuable items into the house itself.

'Griff,' I declared, smacking my forehead, 'I've only kept that ring Piers wanted me to sell. I meant to give it back to him.'

'Put it in the safe, loved one. And we'll worry about it in the morning.'

'My darling child, if I'm not mistaken you have a birthday very soon,' Griff mused, pouring his breakfast coffee the following morning. He never allowed himself (or me) to oversleep, but on days like this appeared in a gorgeous old dressing gown that he'd once worn as a pantomime Grand Vizier. I sported an embroidered silk kimono. But it was understood that as soon as we had eaten we would go and change into what Griff considered proper clothes. 'It occurs to me that you are so attracted to that sapphire ring that it would make an ideal gift.'

I looked him in the eye. 'Not so much attracted as suspicious, Griff. You look.' I passed the lovely thing to him. And my eyeglass.

'The sapphire looks exquisite,' he sighed. 'But I take it you'd like me to look at all the stones under a light?'

'Please.'

He pottered off. I finished the toast while I waited for him to come back. It tasted like cardboard.

'And how many dodgy stones can you count, sweetling?' He sat down heavily and reached for his coffee.

'Five this time. If I put it in the shop I shall have to mark it sold as seen.'

'And the price? If you do that it'll never reach what he's asking.'

I put the two rings he'd given me side by side. The splendid centre stones winked enticingly at me. I stared them down. And put the sapphire into the shop.

Buckles and buttons are a pretty specialized area, especially eighteenth-and nineteenth-century ones. I'd never so much as touched any like these, let alone tried to sell any. I certainly didn't want to repeat the experience I'd had when I'd put Lord Elham's silver in someone else's hands, so I'd have to sniff around a bit. Griff's contact book wasn't any use – the one person he thought would help was now dealing buttons at the big fair in the sky. So after cleaning them all – they must have looked magnificent on the coats and shoes for which they were made, especially glittering under candlelight – I stowed them all in our increasingly crowded safe.

'Dear one, Aidan's phoned to ask me to lunch,' Griff declared, as I set the combination and stood up. 'Ah – I see you've not put your ruby in there.'

'It can live on my ring a little longer. I think.'

'It's on probation, as it were.'

'Exactly. Off you pop, then – I'll keep an eye on the shop. I've got some straightforward restoring to do which will keep me busy if we don't get too many customers.'

He snorted. 'Too many flying pigs, more like. I'll take the smaller van, Lina. And – I know – I'll drive carefully, not drink very much, and phone you to let you know I'm on my way home.'

If I knew him, he'd phone, all right – and then be absolutely forced to go and have a root round Waitrose, so he'd be at least an hour later than he told me to expect him.

'Mind you do.' I hugged him. 'Have you got your driving glasses? Good. Remember to put them on. My regards to Aidan. Now, off you go, and have a lovely time.'

When I work on china, I tend to lose all sense of time. So it was a real surprise, when a punter came into the shop, to see that it was well after four. She talked knowledgeably about the plate I was repairing; I explained our policy of never selling restored items without a warning. Then she bought a perfect Locke potpourri vase and cover, one of those pinkish ivory ones, with a pretty pierced cover, and I promised her comps for our next fair. All very easy and civilized. There were unlikely to be any more customers, and I might as well work in the better light of my workroom in the cottage. So I gathered everything up and locked up as thoroughly as I always do.

As I let myself back into the cottage, setting the alarm for access doors only, it dawned on me that Griff hadn't phoned. Maybe he'd had an extra glass at lunchtime, and was waiting for his alcohol level to drop before he drove. That wasn't unusual, but he always phoned in to confess.

I let the worry nag at me till nearly six. Then I reached for the phone. Voicemail. Which suggested he might be on the road. Why hadn't he phoned to tell me? OK, he was a grown man, but I always worried about him when he drove on his own. Always. Just as he worried about me, to be honest. I'd learned not to let it irritate me, and I think he quite liked it if I bollocked him for letting me down.

I made myself wait another ten minutes before phoning Aidan.

'But Lina, he left at three,' Aidan said. 'My God, what's happened to him? Listen, I'm going to get in my car now and trace his route.' He cut the call before I could argue.

These days I didn't even know which hospital you got taken to if you were ill or in an accident. Maidstone? William Harvey, in Ashford? Not the nearest, not if the administrators had anything to do with it. So I decided to pull in a favour.

'Morris? I need some help.'

'Tell me.' Down the phone his voice sounded solid and unflappable.

'There's no sign of Griff and I'm afraid he's had an accident on the road between Tenterden and here—'

'I'll get on the phone to my Kent colleagues now,' he said. 'And then I'll call you back. Promise.'

As I sat on the stairs, two things occurred to me. I was probably panicking needlessly. But Morris hadn't once suggested I was.

SIXTEEN

Within seconds I'd got the van keys in my hand and was ready to set off – for wherever. But it made more sense to stay in the cottage till I heard from either Aidan or Morris. It was all very well driving here and there in some vague hope of finding Griff, but throughout Kent mobile coverage was poor and Aidan or Morris – even Griff himself – would find it hard to contact me. So I sat and stared at the landline phone, willing it to do something. And then I wondered if I shouldn't be putting together an overnight bag in case – though I didn't even spell out to myself what it was in case of.

I'd no idea how long Tim and I had been sitting staring at both phones begging for one of them to ring. I wasn't sure how his fur had got wet, either, but it was. I never cried. Never. Well, hardly ever.

If only I smoked or bit my nails. If only anything, and Griff was safe.

The landline rang first.

Morris. 'He's in A and E at William Harvey. Not badly hurt. I've sent one of the local lads to sit with him until you collect him.'

'How badly?'

'A black eye and a bruised but not broken nose. The van's OK, but I want SOCOs to check it over.'

'SOCOs? Why on earth?'

'Because it seems it wasn't an accident, Lina. Griff will explain. I'll be in touch.'

I'd locked the front door and was ready to drive off when I remembered that Aidan would be as worried as I was. Nearly. So I called him. He'd got a hands-free system in his car, so he picked up the call at once. I explained.

'I'm almost at Ashford now, Lina. I'll pick him up,' he said.

'Like hell you will. I'm on my way.'

'Then I can only suggest you turn round and go home. For goodness' sake, travel in your van when he could have the comfort of a Merc? If you like, you can meet us back in Tenterden.'

'If I like! Tenterden! This is his fucking home, Aidan, and this is where he fucking belongs!'

'My dear child, you can bring a case for yourself too if it would make you happier.' And he cut the call.

I didn't appreciate his grand concession. Before I could redial and treat him to a few more words Griff would hate, the landline phone rang again, so I dived back into the house, screaming at every second's delay as I fiddled with the locks. I grabbed the phone.

'Hang on – I must stop the alarm.' There. 'Who is it?'

'It's me, Lina.'

It took me a second to register it was Lord Elham.

'Darren was here. And something made him very angry. I thought I should tell you. Only I couldn't find your number.'

I took a deep breath. If I shouted, I'd get nothing out of him. 'I thought we'd agreed you weren't going to let him in?' All Morris's efforts buying and fitting locks had been a waste of time.

He said nothing. No doubt Darren had waved a case of champagne under his nose.

'OK, what made him angry? And when?' I slapped my face. Stupid, stupid cow – he could only manage one question at a time. But I underestimated him.

'Sometime this afternoon. He couldn't find something. And said you must have it.'

'Any idea what?' He couldn't have wanted all those buttons and buckles, could he?

'I really don't know. But he was very angry. Please be careful when you see him.'

'When I see him? How will he find me?'

'He's seen your van, Lina, hasn't he?' For once my father spoke quite sharply, as if I was the dim one, not him.

'So he has. Now, go and lock up properly so if he's still angry and comes back to take it out on you, he can't.'

'I've got an old army swagger stick I keep under the bed. That's what you need – that sort of thing. You know what, I think you should ask Morris round. Or that young vicar chappie who's sweet on you.' He muttered something else and put down the phone.

I thought the something else might be to do with the next TV programme, so I didn't call him back.

Once again I sat on the stairs, Tim for company. If my father thought I needed protection here in Bredeham, it was, though I hated the thought, logical for Griff to stay with Aidan safely in Tenterden. But I wouldn't be taking up Aidan's terribly generous invitation. I wouldn't even if it had come with gold knobs on. Leave the cottage and shop unattended? No way. We might have a brilliant alarm system, with fire sprinklers and everything, but anyone trying to hurt us would have something else to reckon with – me.

Me and a friend, though, my father had said. And what more obvious friend than my lovely broad-shouldered boyfriend? I dialled his number, praying he'd pick up. And he did. And said all the right things about it being lovely to hear from me.

'Piers – I'm in a spot of trouble,' I said in a rush. 'And it'd be great if you could come over and help me out.' I explained.

'Well, of course I'd like to help,' he said, in an apologetic tone that said more clearly than words that he wouldn't be stirring. 'But I'm up in Leeds at the moment. At a fair. And with the best will in the world, I can't be with you before – what? Midnight? My advice would be if you're in danger, get out. You and Griff, of course. Hang on.'

I could hear him muttering to someone.

'A mate here reckons I might make it by eleven, if the roads are OK. Do you want me to come? Mind you, I'd need to be on the road back up here by five, wouldn't I?'

'Of course you can't come down. It'd be silly,' I said firmly, hoping to be overruled. I said all sorts of Griff-like things about driving when tired, the perils of the M25 and more – and still hoped to be overruled. But he agreed. Very sadly, very tenderly, he agreed.

'So where does that leave us?' I asked Tim, still sitting patiently on the stairs. 'Don't worry, if I go, you come too. But I'm buggered if I want to go anywhere.'

There were other people on my father's list of likely protectors, of course – Morris and the clergyman he'd mentioned. Robin Levitt was the Bossingham-based vicar who still visited my father and asked me occasionally to go with him to concerts in Canterbury Cathedral. He'd already saved my life once, and I was sure he could be relied on to do it again. On the other hand, just because someone fancied you it didn't mean you could summon them whenever you needed them to do a bit of dirty work. Which left Morris, of course.

Maybe my hands were shaking a bit. Somehow I speed-dialled Farfrae's number, not Morris's. I was just about to gabble an apology and get off the line, but he seemed quite happy to chat, and even passed the phone across to his wife so she could tell me how much she loved the print I'd found for her.

Eventually I got Farfrae back again. I might as well say it: 'Bruce – is Morris kosher? Really truly? Because I've had it up to here with bent policemen, and I just want to make sure.'

'I'd trust him with my life,' he said simply.

'Then I'd better trust him with mine.'

I'd hardly put the phone down and was thinking about popping Tim back into my bed when it rang again.

'Farfrae says you're in trouble,' Morris said. 'I'm on my way.'

I couldn't argue because he'd cut the call.

'I really do not want to leave you here,' Griff declared, leaning on our front gate, Aidan still in his Merc and drumming his fingers on the wheel. His engine was still running too, as if he'd never heard about cars and global warming. 'Morris or no Morris. And Aidan's already invited you to stay in Tenterden, he tells me.' He glanced over his shoulder, to see Aidan nodding in confirmation.

'Of course he has,' I said, trying to smile convincingly. Since the only light was from our security system, perhaps I'd get away with it. 'And I certainly think you should go with him. But I want to chew things over with Morris, and we can't expect him to swan over half Kent just because I've changed my mind.'

'In that case I'll stay too. I'm sure he'd like to hear all about my little local difficulty this afternoon.'

'He has. From the Kent police,' Aidan put in sourly. He cut the engine and got out, jiggling his keys very ot . . . ost . . . Hell, in a very obvious way. So I knew he wanted to be back on the road. And who could blame him? Poor Griff really ought to be lying down and having a mega-cosset. Only one eye was closed, but the other was colouring up, and his nose seemed inclined to bleed again.

'I've packed enough things for several nights,' I said, handing Aidan a bulging overnight case and a Sainsbury's long-lasting carrier bag, which he took with a look of distaste, as well he might. In any case, Griff always kept some clothes in Tenterden. 'Mrs Hatch says she'll help me look after the shop. And as soon as Piers gets back from his antiques fair in Leeds, he can help.'

'Antiques fair? Leeds? This week?' Griff repeated. Then he stopped dead. It was almost as if he was being pulled towards the Merc by Aidan's willpower. I added mine to give him a bit of a shove.

There. Between us we managed it.

But when I'd locked the front door behind me and reset all the systems, I found Tim's fur getting wet again.

*   *   *

'When you sit in a room like this,' Morris said, looking around him at Griff's centuries-old paintings and furniture, 'you don't think that anything nasty can happen in the world.'

'Except all the people that originally owned all this stuff are dead,' I pointed out. 'More rice? And the last of the stir-fry?'

'Please. I thought you said Griff was the cook in your household.'

'He's teaching me. And it's useful because I can make sure Lord Elham gets a few vitamins and minerals from time to time.'

Morris put his elbows on the table, and leant his chin on his clasped hands. 'Has it ever occurred to you, Lina, that a young woman like you, who anyone else would say needs a bit of care herself, is looking after not one but two old men? Yours is – let's just say a very strange set-up.'

I nodded. 'The villagers didn't like me moving in with Griff at all: I think they were ready to dob him in as a child molester. And one or two thought I should be sent to a young offenders' institution, though by then I hadn't done anything wrong for ages. But we stuck it out. Mrs Hatch was a big help.'

'Mrs Hatch?'

'She helps out in the shop from time to time. As a favour. She's far too genteel to say she works.'

He nodded, grinning.

'She never gossips, of course, but she let it be known that I helped her nicely and had such good manners, and of course Mr Tripp was an ex-actor with such *distinguished* friends.' It wasn't often I tried mimicking people but Morris roared with laughter.

'Another old person, though, Lina – do you have any people your own age to turn to? Anyone to have a nice girlie time with?'

It seemed a strange question, but I did my best to answer. 'I had to leave behind my old mates. Small-time crime – sometimes not so small: drugs; drink; prostitution. That was what my mates were doing or ended up doing. There aren't too many people my age in the village, and those that are here seem to think there's no life outside the pub. There's a very nice vicar, over Bossingham way. At one point I thought . . . But he's got a bit of a prior commitment, hasn't he? God,' I explained. 'And of course there's Piers. We do all sorts of lovely crazy things together.' Or we did, for about a month. And then he gave me this dodgy ring and seemed to make himself scarce. But I wasn't going to worry about that now. Not with the attack on Griff to worry about.

And, I suppose, the possibility of an attack on me. Which was why I'd made Morris stow his car in the garage, out of harm's way.

'Would you mind if I phoned to see how Griff is?' I asked.

'Of course not. But he might. He's probably in bed with a couple of aspirins by now and sound asleep.'

I nodded sadly. 'And Aidan's had me up to here for today. I still can't understand why Darrenarris should rough up Griff. He could see it wasn't me.'

'First we don't know it was Darrenarris: we've got to wait to see if there's any useful bits of DNA in the van. Second, if he'd gone to the trouble of forcing the van into the lay-by, only to find it wasn't you at the wheel, I think he'd feel like roughing up someone. But he could have done a lot more damage, if he'd felt like it. And probably would have done, to be fair, if that lorry driver hadn't stopped and he had to drive off sharpish.'

'I can't understand why the lorry driver didn't get his number. Isn't that the obvious thing to do?'

'He says he was more concerned making sure the old man wasn't too badly hurt and then calling an ambulance. And from what the local lads say, he may not be able to read all that well.'

'Imagine not being able to read!' I said. 'Good job I was at school long enough to suss that out. Though I rather think I learned before I went. I remember being ever so bored in infants' school. And told off for looking at the end of the book to see how the story ended. Hang on, we don't know how *this* story began – how on earth, if it was Darrenarris, did he know Griff or I would be on that road at that time? Or actually, not me but Griff?' My brain was beginning to feel tired, as if I was like that character who had to believe a whole lot of impossible things. Alice again?

'He might not have. It might have been an opportunistic attack. If it was, it's all the more likely his DNA will be on the van somewhere, because he won't have been wearing gloves and so on.'

I was in the middle of gathering plates when a thought crept to the front of my brain. 'Griff had two black eyes – right? But no cuts? He should have been wearing his driving glasses, Morris. Wouldn't he have had cuts if someone had punched him? Or did he take them off so the guy could punch him?' Still holding the plates, I sat down very hard.

'There was an assailant, Lina. There's no doubt about that. But are you suggesting it might have been more a case of road rage?'

Without his specs, with a glass or two of Aidan's wine, Griff might have been weaving around all over the place. But I'd already said a lot too much. 'I'm not suggesting anything. I just have a horrible feeling I've dragged you out all this way because I thought there might be a connection with Darrenarris and – Hell, Morris, I'm sorry.'

'But Lord Elham was worried enough about Darrenarris to phone you and warn you to take care. So even if Griff's assault isn't connected, you did right to call me. And I'm glad to be here.'

If I made a big deal of it all, I might do more harm than good. So I finished clearing the table and peered into the fridge for inspiration. 'Do you like cheesecake? Because there's some of yesterday's here.'

'Love it.'

He watched me divide it into two and put the slices on two plates. Then I remembered Griff had always told me to ensure there was enough left to offer the guest a little extra. *Sorry Griff. And sorry for wondering if someone got so cross with your driving on that horrid windy road from Tenterden that they pushed you off the road. But where were your glasses?* I'd seen him put them on before he left here – had Aidan taken as much care?

He took his plate. But why was he getting up, opening drawers? I'd only forgotten to give us spoons – or should it be forks? He seemed happy enough with the spoons he found, passed me one, and sat down, not saying anything else until we'd finished. Then he took my plate.

'You look done in, Lina. Why don't you go off to bed? I'll load the dishwasher.'

'Because I've not stripped and made up Griff's bed for you yet.' I managed a grin. 'I think you might find sleeping in Griff's room quite interesting.'

'I'm sure I would. But in the boot I've got a bed roll. All I need is a piece of floor.' He kissed me gently on the cheek.

While he got it, I washed up the china – like much of Griff's china, far too delicate for a dishwasher. As I did so, for the tiniest moment, I wondered if Morris might be better company in bed than Tim, but I said nothing – not to either of them. Tim was a very dear friend and I'd have hated to upset him. As for Morris, what was he?

And – more to the point – what was Piers?

SEVENTEEN

The next morning, more than anything else, I wanted to know how Griff was. But Aidan wouldn't have welcomed a call before eight thirty, and tended to regard even nine as uncivilized. Morris and I had had breakfast and he had returned his bed roll to his car well before eight. He showed no signs of leaving, however.

It seemed he needed to make some phone calls before he hit the road, so I left him busy in the living room, while I checked our email for any Internet orders. Nothing, which was unusual these days. Griff hadn't wanted to go electronic, but since everyone else had done, he'd had to give in. Thank goodness he had, because the shop, like a lot of our friends', wasn't exactly flourishing these days. As for today's stint behind the counter, I'd promised Griff I wouldn't leave Mrs Hatch on her own, so I gathered some work to do over there. Within ten minutes I was at an entirely loose end. But Morris was still on the phone, getting quite excited by the sound of it. In fact, so excited it was hard not to hear that he was talking about Bossingham Hall. I didn't exactly want to eavesdrop, but the place did involve me, so I kept my ears open as I came downstairs. I certainly didn't tiptoe, but I didn't make any particular noise, either.

In the event, all I really heard was a barked announcement that he'd be there as soon as maybe. He turned, first finger raised, as I joined him in the living room. I wasn't used to being told to keep quiet in my own home, and could have got stroppy. But this was a man who'd appeared from nowhere and spent a night on a hard floor just to protect me – from some unknown risk. So I bit my lip and drifted off to the kitchen, to make sure everything was tidy in case Griff got it into his silly head to demand to come home.

It was. It seemed Morris's perfections even included drying everything I'd left on the draining board and stowing it in the right cupboards. It was still too early to phone Griff, though. I gave the sink a bit of a polish.

'What time does Lord Elham get up?'

I nearly dropped the dishcloth. 'No idea. Why?'

'Because it seems there's been an attempted robbery at Bossingham Hall. And I thought you might want to come over for the ride. Not to mention checking if the old guy's all right.'

'In other words, if you think he's a suspect, you want me to try and get some sense out of him. Hell, Morris, I know I ought to be there to hold his hand. But I promised Griff I wouldn't leave Mrs Hatch alone, in case Darrenarris had a go at the shop, too.'

He pulled a face. 'It might not have been Darrenarris duffing up Griff, Lina. One of those calls was to my contact in the Kent Police. They've got some CCTV footage – there's this guy in a big rush who didn't think Griff was driving fast enough. They can see him tailgating him and trying to over-take even on blind bends.'

'Plenty of them on the Tenterden road,' I said. Please God, don't let the cameras show Griff without his glasses. 'Did they get a number?' I thought my voice sounded a bit stran-gled, but Morris didn't seem to notice.

'They did. And our Kent colleagues will be talking to him this morning.'

I had to say something, didn't I? He was waiting. 'Can I tell Griff, when I phone him?' I managed.

'Best just say we're following a lead,' he said. 'Now, are you coming or not?'

The road from Bredeham to Bossingham is mostly pretty good, though with a lot of speed restrictions which Morris didn't always pay attention to. There was enough mobile coverage for me to speak to Griff, but with Morris sitting beside me I couldn't ask about his specs or how much booze he'd sunk at yesterday's lunch, could I? I told him to stay put and be sensible for a couple of days, and cut the call before he could argue.

Then I made another call, this one to Mrs Hatch. 'The police say there are a couple of suspicious people about,' I said, more or less truthfully. 'Keep the shop door locked, Mrs Hatch. Don't let anyone in you don't like the look of. And if you do let anyone in, stay by the panic button and if in doubt, use it.'

'My dear child, I've been assisting in that shop for ten years. I can look after myself.'

At that point I lost the signal, and couldn't argue. In any case, Morris wanted to know my dodge route to avoid Canterbury's rush-hour traffic jam on the ring road, so I gave that my attention instead.

At my suggestion, Morris didn't drive up to the Hall and park in the main car park. He took the lane leading to the track going to my father's wing. When we'd spoken to my father, I said, we could always get access through the official door into the main house.

'Bloody hell! Hasn't anyone ever thought of filling in a few of these potholes?' he grumbled, eventually having enough sense to drop down to first gear and creep round as many as he could.

'I have, many a time, especially when I've been ferrying a load of my father's china to sell. But it seems there's some legal dispute about who should do it, the trust or Lord Elham. They're having what Griff calls a Dickensian bicker. He reckons it will last till well after Lord Elham's death.'

'Or ours, which may well be sooner,' he said through gritted teeth as he tried to go through one I always miss.

I didn't argue. I was trying to phone Lord Elham to tell him to let us in, and nearly swallowed the mobile. Don't ask. And then the phone rang and I nearly swallowed it again.

'Lina, is that you? There's some funny business going on here. You might want to bring that Morris chappie.'

'I'm on my way. In fact, I'll be with you in two minutes.' If I lived that long. 'You will be there to let us in, won't you?'

He was actually standing on his front step, but held a long polished baton in his hand, ready for use. That must be the swagger stick he'd mentioned. Apart from that he was wearing a dressing gown so filthy it wasn't possible to tell what colour it might have been. I made a mental note to pop in to M and S men's department next time I was near. Some new slippers wouldn't be a bad idea, either.

'My burglar thingy on the door went off in the night,' he said, running across the gravel to me. He turned to Morris, whose presence he didn't question. 'The door to the other side. Couldn't stop it. Tried the usual number – didn't make any difference.'

I caught Morris's eye – had we got round to telling him we'd changed the code? He pulled a face. Perhaps we hadn't.

Morris obviously thought it was better not to look guilty, so pulled himself up so tall and alert you'd have thought he was back in uniform. 'So someone from the Hall side has been trying to access your wing.'

'Exactly. Just what I said. And then your lot come round here at the crack of dawn, saying I'd been trying to get into the hall. Why should I want to do that?'

I could think of several million pounds' worth of reasons, but said nothing. I just hoped he wouldn't add anything that might make him sound a lot less innocent.

'Quite,' I said quickly. 'Now, it's blowing a gale and any moment now it's going to pee with rain, so you go in and get dressed. You might want to shower and shave too. Morris can have a look at your door. And I'll make us all some tea.'

'I could kill him within two minutes of starting a conversation, but you don't even sound exasperated when you talk to him,' Morris remarked, as we stood at the open door to the main part of the hall. He closed it again and tapped in the code. Then he opened it again. 'It likes the new number. But I bet it doesn't like the old one.'

It didn't.

'I'm going to see what happens if I go through and try,' he said. 'If I don't manage on either code, you will let me back in, won't you?'

I shut the door firmly on him and waited. Yes, an almighty racket. He silenced it; after a few moments, he reappeared.

'So that's one thing we got right. Tell me,' he said, closing it and keying in the code, 'why did he let Darrenarris in after we'd made sure the place was well-nigh impregnable?'

He stared while I looked for something to write the word down on. Since my vocab book was in my father's bureau, I could only find an old envelope. When it dawned on him what I was up to he said it again, very slowly.

'Means no one can get in – right?'

'Right. So why did Lord Elham let him in?'

'Think champagne. My guess is he'd already sunk a lot and Darrenarris came with some more. He'd drink it even if Darren's sort does make him feel odd.' I frowned. 'He's drunk fizz all his life, Morris – why should it suddenly make him forgetful?'

He snorted. 'Suddenly?'

'OK, point taken, but why should it also make him sleepy and incontinent?' I insisted.

'Because he's really going down hill.'

'He was sharp enough to notice what's happening. And to want to wash the things he'd peed on. OK, he's not got round to washing his dressing gown, but if I get him a new one he'll take care of it.'

'And what does he give you in return?'

I wouldn't let him see how much that hurt. 'I don't pay,' I said, trying to sound like a teacher with a dim pupil. 'He pays, with the money I make for him. Where are you going?'

'The kitchen. I want to see if there are any unwashed glasses that might have the dregs of Darrenarris's champagne in them.'

We were in luck. Lord Elham had tidied the kitchen itself, but got no further than putting the glasses in the sink, where he knew I'd deal with them. While I made us all tea in pretty nasty 60s mugs, Morris put several unwashed glasses in evidence bags. I insisted on wrapping them very carefully in some of the bubble wrap I kept on the premises, bearing in mind the return journey down the track. They weren't just any glasses, after all, but pretty Victorian flutes, some just tat, but three or four worth a hundred or so each.

While he stowed them in the foot well of his car, I explained to my father that Morris was going to go round to the main part of the house to talk about the attempted burglary.

'But you must go with him! As my representative! I'm not having those damned Johnny-come-latelies making that sort of accusation against me. You go and tell them, Lina.'

Morris, who'd come into the living room halfway through

my father's speech, blinked so hard I almost laughed. He accepted the green tea, with a bow, muttered a couple of *my lord*s, and nodded in agreement.

The administrator, Ms Pamela Fielding, hadn't met me before, of course, and Morris simply introduced me as Ms Townend, a consultant. Thinking it might not make things easier if I reminded her that I'd recently left her a note about a damaged plate, I nodded politely and took the seat I was offered – much more comfortable than those available for the other staff and in a very much more airy and well-decorated and equipped office. A thought cropped up which quite surprised me: once it was the lord who made sure he had the best; now it was a manager doing just the same. A very well-dressed manager, too, considering she was working for what was supposed to be a charity – a suit as well cut as Morris's, with spiky shoes more at home in London offices than on the fragile carpets of a place like this. Griff would have found her make-up a bit unsubtle, especially the vivid lipstick and nail polish, but if you could still get away with it when you were in your forties, why not? Her roots needed attention, but the cut itself was excellent. I touched my own hair – Griff liked me to spend as much on it as I could afford, and if I had a lean patch would sneak me a few fivers to help out.

'I've already been through all this with your colleagues,' Ms Fielding said, 'and I can't imagine what good it will do to repeat it.'

'Indulge me, Ms Fielding,' Morris said, in a steely way he'd only used with me a couple of times. 'This property holds items of national importance. It's unlikely anything stolen will end up at Ashford Market boot fair.'

'The constable who took all the details of the missing silver said it was ten to one everything would be in France within two hours of it leaving the Hall.' .

'I don't deal in racing odds. And I am aware that while getting stolen goods across the M25 may not be as easy as taking them on a ferry or Eurostar,' he said dryly, 'there are plenty of outlets in this country. You've already lost ivory and silver – what was taken this time?'

'Nothing. That's the strange thing. Several cases were forced, but the contents were just disarranged.'

I thought of the locked door. Had someone thought he could get them out via my father's wing? And, finding he couldn't, shoved them back where he'd found them?

I was only there because my father had bulldozed Morris into taking me, and though Morris hadn't told me in so many words to button it, I didn't think he'd welcome an interruption. But I must remember to mention it when we were alone. To remind myself, I slipped the ring from my right hand to my engagement finger. It was much too big and slipped off immediately, rolling from my lap to the floor.

Scrabbling to retrieve it I was aware of things I hadn't been able to see from where I was sitting. There was Ms Fielding's huge fashionable handbag for a start. Real leather. It would have cost a mint. It was firmly closed. I turned my eyes to the filing cabinet I'd had my back to. It seemed that Ms Fielding liked to have her family photos where she could see them – two kids and a dog; two kids and their dad; two kids and their mum; two kids, their dad and their mum. All happy, smiling faces.

And I knew one of them. The dad.

If only I could remember where I'd seen him before. I concentrated so hard on placing him I lost the thread of the others' conversation, and came to with a great jolt as they got to their feet. Since I'd no idea where they were heading, I attached myself to Morris as tightly as if I were planning to pick his pocket, which was crazy given that I knew the hall so well. Put me in any room and I could have found my way back to my father's door. And this happened to be where we were heading, it seemed.

I touched Morris's arm. 'Can we see the display cases she mentioned?' I asked quietly.

His eyebrows shot up, but he simply repeated my request to Ms Fielding, who shrugged and turned down the next corridor. I was a bit surprised because I knew this only led to the visitors' loos – I'd been down it enough times, carrying stuff from my father's wing to wash it in the nice hot water there, before, of course, the security had been stepped up. In any case, now I'd sorted out the kitchen and made sure the water heater worked I didn't need to.

She muttered a word Griff wouldn't have let me use before seven, turning on her high heels and rejoining the main drag.

I had to bite my tongue to stop myself asking her where the cabinets were and offering simply to lead the way.

By the time we got to the library corridor I was fizzing with fury: how dare someone working in the place full time – apart from sloping off during spring-cleaning – not know her way to such a vital place? But she was right about the display cases. Someone had forced the locks, which should surely have been enough to set off a million alarms, and then apparently simply shuffled round the silverware inside. There was a dusting of powder everywhere – no doubt the scene of crime people had been busy.

I stared at the nearest case. Something was setting my nose twitching. But I'd better say nothing, not until Morris and I were on our own. In any case, Ms Fielding was on the move.

When after a couple of false starts we got back to the connecting door we found they'd been busy there too.

'What's the code?' Morris asked idly.

'It'll be on file in my office,' she said, quite clearly not keen to go and find it.

He waited. At last she unclipped the little two-way radio all the women carried and spoke sharply. Someone called Eileen was sent to find it – it was apparently in the back of Pamela's desk diary. Pamela cut the call, and drummed nails, which even I found a bit bright and certainly too long, on her crossed arms. At last a muffled reply came back – giving the old code, as Morris must have known it would. So what had he been up to?

'Do you want to key it in?'

The numbers didn't work, of course. At her third attempt the alarm went off, just like a hole in the wall swallowing your card if you made three mistakes.

Whatever his plan, it was certainly noisy.

At long last he covered the keypad with one hand and tapped in the new number. Wonderful, wonderful silence.

'Standard override number,' he lied. 'A trick of the trade. Meanwhile, we need to ask Lord Elham if he's changed the number.'

'That old soak? Wouldn't know how to do anything except bend his elbow, I'm told. I bet it was him who came in and had a rummage round last night – that would explain why nothing was put back in its place.'

I know Griff would have corrected her and told her to say, *I bet it was he*, but I still said nothing.

'Very well, have you finished here, officer? Because I do have work to do, you know.'

'I'm quite sure you do.'

If I'd been Ms Fielding, I wouldn't have been quite sure about his tone. I'm not sure she was, actually. But Morris gave me a little push, and I set off back down the corridor, trying to think of something to say so that she wouldn't notice he wasn't with us.

Griff would have coped. He'd have asked a question that made her talk about herself.

I took a deep breath. 'What brought you into this line, Ms Fielding?' There, that should do it.

It didn't. Instead, she came to a halt and stared at me. 'Do I know you from somewhere? Your name's familiar, anyway. What are you a consultant in?'

'Fine art and antiques,' I said, smooth as if I were Griff. Nearly.

Thank goodness, before she could ask anything else, Morris caught us up and kindly put himself between her and me, still keeping going at a terrific rate so we had to stride out to keep up. Easy in my low heels; tricky in hers. At last we were back at her office. We made our farewells and bowed ourselves out. Via the servants' door.

EIGHTEEN

At the bottom of the steps, Morris stopped. 'Why did you take your ring off and drop it?'

I'd been expecting a few questions but not that one. 'I took it off to put it on the other hand. I sometimes do that if I don't want to forget something.'

'Which was?'

'I just thought that someone had broken into the display cases and hoped to get the stuff out via my father's wing. And when they couldn't, they'd just put it back again. But I'm wondering . . . I don't know quite what I'm wondering. But my antennae are twitching.' I was really proud of that word, not to mention

knowing it was *antennae,* not *antennas.* 'Really hard. I think
we ought to go back and look. Without Ms Fielding. And there's
something else. Those photos of Ms Fielding's family – I know
her husband from somewhere.' I turned to him in exce . . . ecs . . .
exasperation. 'Hell, Morris – this crap memory of mine worries
me silly. Griff reckons it's something to do with not having the
right food and not having had it trained at school. He plays little
games to help me. Puts twenty or thirty things on a tray and
then covers it up and makes me write down what was on there.
That sort of thing. But it hasn't worked with that face.'

'Maybe if I showed you some mug shots on computer you
could pick him out. Like my Kent colleagues will be showing
Griff this morning.'

'That'd only work if Mr Fielding was a criminal, wouldn't
it? And I'm sure I've seen him somewhere really respectable.
I suppose you couldn't ask her about him?'

'Not without a reason, Lina. Looking at the display cabinet's
another matter, however.' Fishing out his mobile, he didn't
use it but pressed the other thumb hard on the bell. 'I've just
had an enquiry from one of my colleagues,' he told the anxious-
looking woman who opened it. Now I understood about the
phone. 'No need to disturb Ms Fielding again. We'll go straight
to the library corridor.' He set off like a rocket, as if he knew
his way around. Once we were out of sight, however, he
slowed down so I could lead the way.

'There can't be all that much wrong with your memory,'
he said, as we turned into the library corridor, 'not to get us
through this rabbit warren without a compass.'

'But I had to leave a trail of breadcrumbs so we can get
out again,' I said, with a grin it took him a moment to return.
'Now, this is the cabinet that set me off. And I don't know
for the life of me why.'

Side by side we stared at it. All that beautifully polished
silver, including some early Matthew Boulton. I wished I liked
it more, but I didn't. Perhaps the NEC experience had put me
off silver for ever.

Morris started pointing at one piece after another, counting
not quite under his breath. 'I think Griff's games have paid
off,' he said. 'There are seventeen information cards, and only
sixteen pieces.'

'Perhaps the other case has one extra.'

It hadn't. So we played a game that Griff would have been much better at – matching each piece to its card. Eventually we found one card without an object: *A George III* silver-gilt musical snuff box, of rounded oblong form, with engine-turned base and sides, the cover decorated in high relief with fox-hunting scene, no apparent maker's mark, London 1819.

'Tell me about it,' Morris said.

'No idea. I told you I'm hopeless when it comes to silver.'

He grabbed me by my shoulders and shook me – but only gently. 'Lina, when will you get it into your head you're not hopeless about anything. It's just you haven't learned about it yet.' Frowning, he added, 'Who used to shake you? You froze just then. Hey, hang on!'

For some reason my hands were flailing in front of my face, as if to fend someone off. Or maybe it was something. A memory.

'Lina? Lina? Are you all right?'

My therapist had told me to concentrate on my breathing. So I did. Great gulps at first, then smaller breaths. 'I'm fine. Sort of,' I added with a bit of a smile. 'Sometimes I remember things I'd much rather not. Some people say you should explore them. Other people say there's no point in digging up things you'd rather leave buried. Yes, I'm OK.' I held out my hand to show it wasn't shaking. Not very much, anyway. He looked so concerned I made a huge effort. 'Griff might have an idea about this here snuff box. But even he's not an expert. I gather you don't want to go and ask Ms Fielding about it?'

'I'd rather have a few facts to impress her with. And I did introduce you as a consultant,' he added, eyes twinkling nicely.

We found a corner where the signal wasn't too bad, and I called Griff. He sounded so much his normal self when he picked up I could have danced for joy. And his brain was ticking over nicely. He gave me a quick rundown on snuff boxes, musical and otherwise, and even recalled a George III one in working order going up for auction three or four years ago. 'It fetched over £5000 then,' he said. 'So goodness knows what it would be worth now. A real collector's item, of course. For some reason people are really attracted to anything depicting sport – as of course you know. The person to ask, of course, would be Nella Cordingly, but I can't imagine you'd want to contact her.'

'I'd rather stick pins in my eyes. And don't you go calling her, either. Promise. Griff, promise!'

'I promise, my child. And I'll go further – I won't even ask Aidan to ask, either.'

As we finished the call, I turned to Morris. 'Hang on, you're an expert too. A bloody police inspector in precious things.'

'I'm more into graphic art, with special reference to Renaissance religious pictures. And I'm really hot in altarpieces. Farfrae knows everything about Impressionist brushwork and can tell a fake a football field away. We really do have to consult experts like you from time to time.' He grinned as I clocked the word *expert*. 'So, something worth upwards of five thousand quid has gone walkabout. Something small and portable. Highly desirable. I'd better have another word with Ms Fielding. I suppose you couldn't lead the way, could you?'

'Let's go through the library.' I could never resist it, and almost jigged with pleasure just at the thought of it. 'There!' I flung open the double doors with as much pride as if I owned the place.

'Tell me what you like about it,' he said, laughing.

'Apart from the perfect proportions, the – drat.' My phone rang. 'My God! It's Mrs Hatch! I'll have to take it.' In less than the time it took me to press the green button, I saw her robbed at gunpoint, beaten up and—

'Lina, my girl – I told you I knew how to look after the shop, didn't I? I've sold that sapphire ring! And for only £200 less than the asking price, too.'

Piers' ring! I said all the right things, and then asked, 'You did sell it as seen, didn't you? *Caveat emptor* and all that?'

'Of course I did. And the credit card's gone through and everything's just as it should be. And it looks as if I may have another customer.'

'Be careful! You will be careful, won't you?' But I was talking to thin air.

Far from impatiently tapping his watch, Morris was staring open-mouthed at the family portraits. 'If I was going to steal anything it would be that Gainsborough. Or the Reynolds. Or maybe even that gorgeous Vigée Le Brun.' Since none of them had a label identifying the artist I could tell he really did know his stuff, even that out of his period.

'Make sure it's that one. There's one down the corridor I'm sure is a fake. OK, good news. Mrs H has sold a ring for Piers so we've got a bit of commission coming our way. I'll shout you lunch, if you like.'

'You're my consultant – I can put you on expenses. Now, do we tackle Ms Fielding? She doesn't even know we're here.'

'Oh, yes, she does. Or someone does. Not just the poor minion that let us in. CCTV, remember. It seems to be working again, thanks to you.'

'Drat. I wouldn't make a very good burglar, would I? Very well, I suppose it has to be now. Are you going to stay silent as you did before or are you going to do the talking?'

'It's very tempting. But you could be acting on information received, couldn't you? And I've always wanted to hear someone say that to someone else.'

But Ms Fielding wasn't about to hear it. Ms Fielding had been called away – a meeting with one of the trustees, according to her diary. I couldn't help catching Morris's eye, and was pleased, because he caught mine at the same moment.

We turned on our heels and left. Once again at the foot of the servants' steps, I said, 'I know I've got a suspicious mind, but she does carry a handbag, and you'd easily fit that little snuff box in there. Well, half a dozen of them.'

'I'm glad you didn't make that allegation within anyone else's hearing.' He was so pompous I stared – only to realize he was holding back a laugh.

When he'd let it out and I'd shared it, I asked, 'Now what?'

'Let's see if we can get Lord Elham to tell us what made Darrenarris so cross. And if he uttered any specific threats against you.'

We went round the outside of the building rather than use the door, because I wanted to see if my father was doing as he was told and locking up properly. He was. He'd kept the safety chain on and peered round it before letting us in.

But even a new brew of green tea couldn't make him recall why Darren had lost his temper. 'Thing is, I seem to get so dopey when he's here. I drift off for forty winks and he's gone.'

'Maybe you should stick to the champagne Lina brings you,' Morris said. 'And green tea, of course.'

'Trouble is,' my father replied, leaning towards him as if

he was going to tell him a big secret, 'I've never tasted a compost heap, but I'm sure it would taste like that stuff. She brought some the other day that was flavoured with jasmine – that was a bit better; she's a good girl. I'm proud of her,' he said, patting my arm.

Despite myself I felt a little glow. 'How much champagne have you got left – the stuff I buy?'

He shook his head. 'Not much. And I can't work out why. I'm not drinking any more. And Darren's been bringing a lot.'

Morris caught my eye. 'How would you feel, my lord, if I took Darren's away with me and replaced it with your usual tipple?'

'The police would do that?' His eye gleamed.

'Non-vintage,' I put in quickly. 'The sort I buy for you. And maybe we should find somewhere else to store it – somewhere only you know about. OK?'

While the two men dealt with the cheap booze, I took myself off to the bureau in which Lord Elham had kept his notebook, now in our special safe at home. I didn't need to open the bureau, or its inner compartment. My vocab book was in shreds all over the floor. I was still staring at it when Morris joined me.

'I thought I'd find you here.'

I pointed. 'All that effort torn up and discarded.' I was ready to weep.

'But you've finished with it now, Lina. Nearly. Most of it's up here.' With a smile as kind as Griff's he touched my forehead. He held my gaze so long I thought for a moment – no, he couldn't have been going to kiss me. Suddenly he turned away, fishing a polythene bag and purple gloves from his pocket. He knelt to gather up the shreds. 'No, don't touch any of it. I'm hoping he was so angry he forgot to put on gloves and has left lovely clear fingerprints all over the pages.'

We nipped into Canterbury Sainsbury's, and found the usual brand of champagne on offer, so we stocked up, leaving the checkout girl wide-eyed at our drinking capacity. I also bought a range of green teas and a supply of healthy ready meals, in case I didn't have time to cook my own for him. But my enthusiasm didn't run to wanting to share them with him, and when we'd delivered them and reminded Lord Elham to lock up behind us, we returned to Bredeham. Via a very nice gastropub, actually, the Granville, on Stone Street, where he stood me lunch.

'Now what?' I asked when we at last pulled up outside the cottage.

'I ought to go back to London to consult my colleagues about this and all the other cases we've got in our in trays. I'm still not happy about leaving you on your own, though.'

'I shall be fine.' I rather hoped I wouldn't be on my own. Piers should be back down south soon, and we had something to celebrate. Something told me, however, that wasn't what Morris wanted to hear. 'You've seen how well fortified our place is. Fort . . . Fort . . .'

'Fort Knox. Even so . . .'

'Fort Knox. I shall be fine.'

'Any problems, anything at all, you'll phone me – right? Promise?'

'Promise.'

Because he was so nice I hugged him and kissed him, aiming for his cheek but getting his lips instead. He turned away quickly and got in his car, but seemed to have trouble with his seat belt. Eventually, though, he set off with a smile and a wave.

As soon as I'd killed the alarms and sorted the day's post, I phoned Piers to give him the good news about his ring.

'You've sold it! That's excellent. Well done. Thanks very much.' Piers' words were enthusiastic enough, but I'd only have given him four out of ten for the warmth of his voice. It inched towards two when I told him we'd got £200 less than he'd asked for.

'That's the way the markets are at the moment, Piers – haven't you noticed?' I said, stung. I couldn't bring myself to point out it was probably more than it was worth, given the dodgy diamonds.

'I suppose so. Thanks, anyway.'

I thought an unasked question hung between us – when would he get his money? But I told myself he'd know that we'd have to make sure the purchaser didn't change his mind and that the card transaction was OK and all the other things that can go wrong didn't. And he could trust me to hand over a nice fat cheque as soon as I could. Maybe as soon as I saw him.

'How's Leeds?' I asked.

'Where? Leeds? Oh, pretty quiet. I shall be glad to pack up and come home. Are you doing anything this weekend?'

We made a few nice-sounding plans, and I began to feel better. He didn't have time to ask how things were down in Kent, though, because he said he'd got a customer. At least he promised to be in touch the moment he could.

All the same, I felt flat. I couldn't think why, unless something was troubling me about the way he'd said *Leeds*. As if he'd forgotten where he was. Or was supposed to be.

If only there was someone to take my mind off the niggling doubt. No Griff, of course. No Morris. Not even Mrs Hatch – she'd locked up the shop (I checked) and gone home.

For the first time for a long time, I actually felt lonely. Morris was right. I didn't have any mates my own age, no one I could have chewed Piers over with. So I'd better lock myself and the van in our Fort Knox and get on with a bit of sensible restoring.

NINETEEN

When Titus Oates phones, you feel you ought to curtsy, or something, because it's such an honour. He never gives his name, and always talks in a sort of gruff whisper as if he's afraid of being overheard – not that Titus ever talks when there's anyone within earshot.

'Provenance,' he said.

'Provenance?' I repeated stupidly, putting down my paintbrush and trying to think about something other than a shepherdess's chipped nose.

'For silverware. The word is some bloke's busy getting his mitts on as many old auction catalogues as he can. So that when he tries to sell his ewer or his salver, he can show where it came from. Old dodge, doll. All that silver nicked from Bossingham, you can bet he's waving his catalogue under some dealer's nose proving his dear old grey-haired granny bought it a hundred years ago – well, give or take – and she's just popped her clogs and left it to him. That's what he'll be doing.'

'Thanks, Titus. That's really helpful. I owe you.'

'Right. You do. So get the filth out of Lord Elham's face, there's a good girl. There's a few jobs I need him to do. You might tell him.'

'I didn't hear that. In any case, the police won't go away until folk have stopped nicking stuff from him and the Hall itself. Some more silver went last night. Small. Portable.'

'Bloody hell. Got to put a stop to that.' And he cut the call. That was Titus for you.

Tell my father there was more dodgy work for him? Not likely. But I'd better let Morris know about the catalogues, hadn't I? Was half nine too late to call him? I hoped not. It would be nice to hear someone's voice. The cottage was horribly empty without Griff. Was it empty for him, when I was away? And what if I ever married and left him? Marry! How many girls of my generation thought that was the way to have a relationship? But they hadn't had Griff to guide them.

Morris answered straight away. 'What's up?'

'Nothing. I mean, there's nothing wrong. And I'm sorry to bother you at this time of night. But someone's told me something you ought to know.' I explained.

'And I suppose you wouldn't want to name your source?'

I snorted. 'Not if I ever want any more information from him.'

He laughed. Then there was a little pause.

'Are you OK? Really?' he asked.

'The place is a bit quiet without Griff,' I admitted.

'Perhaps you should have accepted Aidan's invitation after all.'

'I'd only be in the way. I'm quite busy, actually. All this nipping round the countryside's made me get behind with my work.'

'If you need me to come down, you've only got to say the word. You know that.'

'Thanks. But I'm fine.'

'Really truly?'

'Really truly.'

We started to talk about all sorts of other things. At last, we had the previous exchange about being fine all over again. And by then I really did feel a whole lot better. To cheer us up, Tim and I had planned to treat ourselves to a really creamy hot chocolate, not to mention a slice of one of Griff's wonderful cakes, but we didn't need cheering up now, of course. But we had them anyway, and tucked ourselves in for an early night.

When Piers had made all those romantic plans for the weekend we'd both forgotten Griff and I were due at an antiques fair in Westonbirt, down in Wiltshire. Or it might just be in Gloucestershire. Anyway, not far off the M4.

'I'm afraid the sight of my face would put off all but the keenest punter,' Griff said, when I popped over to see him. I couldn't argue. 'So why don't you ask Piers to help you? He won't be selling collectibles there, for goodness' sake.'

Three days together, and spending the nights in our caravan – I was over the moon at the thought. But it seemed Piers had forgotten something on his own account – a big collectibles fair in Devon. My heart sank. Not just because I'd really been looking forward to seeing him but because at a fair like Westonbirt I felt a bit out of my depth, socially that is: lots of other dealers talked horribly like Nella and Aidan, and everything about them was intimidatingly and effortlessly chic. On the other hand, Griff and I always put out our best items, so although many other dealers were top of the range, we weren't outclassed professionally. Setting up was a pain on your own, too. So it would have been nice to have Piers beside me.

'But my fair doesn't start till Saturday,' Piers said. 'Why don't I meet you at Westonbirt and help you put out your things, and then I could go on to Barnstaple from there? Maybe we could have a nice meal somewhere. I don't think Gloucestershire goes in for discos and that. And then on my way back I could come and help you pack up?'

'Oh, yes, please!' Damn. I sounded overeager, a bit like a puppy being offered a treat. I ought to learn how to do cool, a bit stand-offish. *Whatever,* would have been better, with a huge shrug.

We agreed to meet at Westonbirt School itself. From a distance, the house looked genuinely Elizabethan. But according to Griff it was actually built for a very rich Victorian, whose family had made its fortune supplying London with drinking water. He'd made enough to start the National Arboretum just across the road, too. Now his house was a posh girls' school. I suppose even all the young ladies' fees wouldn't run to keeping a place as grand as this in the condition it deserved, and to make an extra buck it stooped to hosting antiques fairs. It was nothing like the schools I never quite went to – full of beautiful wood, silk-covered walls and ornate ceilings with genuine-looking gilding. None of the graffiti you'd get in your average comp. It was almost a sin to hide the walls by erecting stalls and lighting. But I set to and got on with it – because Piers had called in to say he was stuck in a jam on the M25 and would be late.

As he cut the call I looked at my watch. He was going to be very late indeed if he hadn't even got on to the M4. What time had he started out, for goodness' sake? But I didn't have time to think of all the cutting things I should have said to him, so I simply got on with what I had to do.

Some dealers were strictly specialist – oriental silk; seventeenth-century portraits; boudoir paintings. Our stall had what Griff called an eclectic mix. And I knew that was the right word because I'd written it down and learned it. I'd picked up a couple of tricks about display from Nella – about the only thing I'd ever thank her for! – and maybe they were responsible for a run of sales that left obvious gaps. In fact I was so busy I didn't notice the time. And to be honest I didn't even miss Piers, except that an extra pair of hands would have been useful. I was quite startled when he suddenly appeared, rather red-faced and with an angry glitter to his eyes.

'They only charged me for coming in! I told them I was a dealer, coming to help you, but they didn't believe me, the buggers. I had to fork out five quid!'

Should I offer to pay him back? I was on the point of fishing out some coins. But bother him. If he'd even grabbed me and kissed me before telling me how cross he was maybe I wouldn't have minded.

'Would you mind holding the fort for a minute or so? I'm desperate for a loo,' I hissed, not waiting for a reply. Well, I couldn't. But while I was away from the fair, I thought I might nip down to the tiny canteen area and pick up a sandwich and some water – I'd had no lunch, after all. As an afterthought I bought double, just in case he'd been so keen to get down here he'd not stopped.

There was something different about the stall. Hands full, I stopped and stared. He'd reshuffled the things on display, so the gaps didn't show. Excellent. But there was another difference.

Not like at Bossingham Hall, where there were more cards than items. It was the other way round. Sitting in pride of place was not the perfect Barr and Barr sucrier, with gilt handles and little painted scenes of jolly, well-fed peasants – goodness knows where the artist had found his models – but an elaborate leather jewel case, lined with watered silk. It contained a dazzling pair of earrings – free-hanging emeralds and diamonds on tiny springs.

I gaped and pointed.

'I was hoping you'd shift them for me. Victorian, of course. Got this aunt who's fallen on hard times. Doesn't want anyone to know.' He tapped the side of his nose. '*Noblesse oblige*, and all that.'

'All the same,' I muttered, putting down the plates and water bottles. I fished my eyepiece out of my bag and held out my hand. Eventually he twigged and passed me the case. Not a dodgy diamond in sight. In fact the gems were so fine I'd have expected to see the earrings at Christie's. 'These are well above our usual range – you can see for yourself,' I said, gesturing. 'What sort of price were you expecting?'

The figure he named was high, but not excessive (thanks, Morris) for such lovely pieces. I nearly asked out loud, 'Are you sure these aren't off the back of some lorry, Piers?' but managed to be a bit more tactful: 'What's their provenance?'

'They're from the collection of Lady Olivia Spedding.' He looked coldly down at me, rather like the Duke of Wellington, now I came to think of it, holding out his hand for the earrings.

I returned them, shrugging. 'No skin off my nose,' I informed him, my voice all accent and attitude.

I wasn't so much surprised as taken aback when he just said, 'Usual commission,' and disappeared. What the hell?

But I couldn't say it aloud or do anything except smile: a punter was pointing to the sucrier. He wanted to look at it. And remember, if a punter handles, he'll usually buy.

To be fair, there was no sign of his tantrum when Piers re-appeared. In fact, he really grovelled, blaming the awful journey and a lot of other things.

'Maybe this will cheer you up a bit,' I said, fishing out our chequebook and sitting down to write the amount we owed him for the ring. Griff had already made it out and signed it, so all I had to do was add my name. 'There.'

It went straight into his wallet. 'Thanks. Now about this
evening—'

Why didn't I want to hear the next bit?

'I've booked a table at the Hare and Hounds, just up the
road. My treat.' He patted his wallet. 'Glad rags – I hope
you've brought some? But then I'm afraid I shall have to slope
off as soon as we've eaten: an old friend of my mother's heard
I was going to be in Barnstaple, and insisted I stay with her.
A pain. But I really can't offend her. She's expecting me to
stay over into next week, too.'

It was on the tip of my tongue to tell him what to do with
his table and his glad rags. But I didn't want to spend a whole
evening on my own, even with Tim Bear for company, and I
would make sure I picked the most expensive food on the menu.
And my father had taught me about choosing champagne, hadn't
he? Yes, two could play at that game. And I rather thought,
now I had those earrings as hostages, I might well win.

I still had enough good china and glass in the van to fill up
the empty spaces on the stall, but there wasn't much left by
the end of the fair. I got together with an old-lace dealer, a
lady in her fifties, for supper on Saturday – it seemed she
didn't like eating alone in public either – and we helped each
other with packing up. The earrings hadn't sold, though there
had been some interest. Piers hadn't been keen for me to offer
a reduction even if anyone asked me for my 'best' price. So
I was stuck with beautiful but overpriced earrings, which were
the first thing I showed to a multicoloured Griff when I eventually got him home on Monday morning. Aidan had been
touchingly reluctant to let him go, Mrs Hatch had been inclined
to gossip when he visited her in the shop, and even the postie
wanted a few minutes of his life.

'Leave the post and emails till later,' I said, relieved to find
the cottage in one piece after the weekend, 'and sit down
while I make you a cup of tea. Here's your eyeglass: have a
look at these.'

'What am I looking for? Not more dodgy stones?'

'None that I can see. But I'd really value your opinion.'

'Continental,' he said, when I put his tea beside him.
'Beautifully clean. Everything just as it should be for the
period. Feel the weight. Lovely quality stones – all of them.

No reason why we shouldn't sell these. And for the price he
wants, too.'

Just then the phone rang. I thought I heard Griff add something about sprats catching mackerel, but perhaps I was
mistaken.

The whole day was tarnished by the fact that sooner or later
I'd have to ask Griff about the assault. He knew something
was wrong, and made himself busy checking what I'd sold
and exclaiming with pleasure at the profits. When I came back
from a stint in the shop – Mrs Hatch had a dental appointment – wonderful smells were wreathing themselves round
the outside of the cottage, courtesy of the powerful but fairly
quiet extractor fan that he'd recently treated us to. He was
obviously preparing one of his best meals. I felt worse and
worse. As I retired to work upstairs on that poor shepherdess,
I heard noises from the street. The police were returning our
van. I'd been bracing myself to have to go and collect it, but
it seemed someone had taken pity on Griff and dropped it off
on his way home, a mate hanging on to give him a lift the
rest of the way. It was all very friendly, with Griff offering
tea and generally chatting up the man in overalls – I think
Griff has a thing about overalls. He was just waving them off
when Overalls shot out of his mate's van, waving something.

'They're not going to be much use, I'm afraid. But you
might as well have them anyhow.'

Griff's glasses, the lenses shattered. I was nearly sick with
relief. I tucked the van in the garage, and returned to find
Griff with the phone book.

'I thought I ought to make an appointment with that nice
Mrs Pybus,' he said. 'It must be a year since she tested my
vision and generally had a poke round in my eyes. If I've got
to have new specs then they might as well have the latest
prescription.'

I wouldn't put it past him to have understood why I hugged
him so hard, but he said nothing.

The next offer of tea was to a uniformed police officer, a
young woman a bit older than me.

'This is PC Sally Monk,' Griff announced, 'who showed
me a lot of mug shots while I was at Aidan's. Pray come in
and sit down.' He ushered her into the living room,

'I've come to update you, Mr Tripp – Griff,' she corrected herself, as she sat down.

'Well, you must sit down and have a cup of tea while you do so. I don't suppose there are any biscuits left, Lina, my darling?'

She waved a hand. 'Not for me, thanks. Lent. I know it's not fashionable to give things up these days . . .'

'Don't apologize, Sally. I've just spent the best part of a week with someone who's given up alcohol for Lent. So I found I had to join him in his abstinence. I can't wait for Lina to tell me it's officially evening and I can have a glass. She bosses me terribly, the dear girl.' He squeezed my hand. I squeezed his back. Fancy the old bugger learning to read my thoughts.

Sally's news was that on the basis of the mug shot he'd picked out, they were on to a local speed merchant who was currently driving despite a ban. The DNA they'd got from the van should prove it.

'I thought they could do it like that.' Griff clicked his fingers. 'They do on *The Bill*.'

'Their budgets are fiction. Ours are for real. In fact,' she added, lowering her voice, 'if we hadn't especially wanted to get young Dean Pardoe, we probably wouldn't have bothered, since no material damage was done. Except to your glasses.'

'Hang on! Assaulting a man Griff's age!'

'Priorities, Ms Tripp. But as soon as the DNA results come through we shall be on to him, don't you worry. If you don't mind appearing in the witness box, Mr Tripp. A lot of people won't go to court. It can be quite a stressful experience.'

Griff chuckled. 'If you are suggesting that defence counsel will allege that I am an appalling driver who would drive our own dear queen to violence, I am prepared for that. But I trust any witnesses will tell you that while I was slow, I was purposeful – at least until he did his best to commit sexual assault on my exhaust pipe.'

She returned his smile. 'CCTV does show your driving and his to be much as you've described it, Mr Tripp.' She got to her feet. 'I'll be in touch as soon as I know anything – I promise,' she added, looking really nonplussed as Griff kissed her hand in one of his lovely courtly gestures.

It was only five thirty when she left, but I thought Griff deserved it.

'I've got a bottle of the champagne Lord Elham recommends,' I said. 'And it's been waiting in the fridge to welcome you home.'

TWENTY

Whoever this guy Pardoe was, it sounded as if he wasn't Darrenarris. At least I thought it did, until I remembered that the police hadn't finally ID'd him, and that in any case Darrenarris might not be my half-brother anyway, but just a con artist robbing a vulnerable old man. And whatever his name might be, he'd been angry enough for my father, who didn't do things in a hurry, to pick up the phone and warn me. So I locked up as carefully as usual, something that didn't escape Griff, although he'd got at least half a bottle of champagne inside him.

'Morris isn't staying here tonight?' he asked mildly.

'Not with you to strong-arm any would-be assailants,' I said. 'Actually, things seem to have gone quiet on the Darrenarris front. The theft of that little musical snuff box apart, of course.'

'Nor Piers?'

He looked well enough for me to tell him a few details of my weekend. I filleted out some of them, but not enough to stop him deducing that Piers had behaved like a louse.

'So you sent him to the rightabout?'

'Not exactly. The thing is, Griff, we both suspect he's up to something, don't we? Even if we've no proof? If I just stop seeing him – not that I see much of him anyway, but if I make a song and dance about it – then he'll find some other mug and keep on with whatever the scam is. So I thought I'd go along with it – and him – a bit longer. Actually,' I added really casually, 'I might have an idea.'

He sighed. 'I'm not going to like it, am I?'

'OK. It involves Lord Elham. Those earrings are supposed to belong to someone called Lady Olivia Spedding. Lord

Elham might just know something about her. I'll ask next time I see him. But you're involved too – no, not with Lord Elham. With that gem . . . gemmologist friend of yours.'

He smiled – I'd got the term right. 'Wally Brown?'

'Right. I want him to look at this ring and tell us about the dodgy diamonds. They may not be just bad stones – they might actually be fakes, good fakes, if you see what I mean.' I pulled the ruby from my finger and put in his hand. 'We'll send it tomorrow. Before I change my mind.'

'I'll ask him to prioritize it. What about the earrings?'

I shook my head. 'We're both sure they're kosher, aren't we? But I bet the next thing of Lady Olivia's won't be.'

'What does Morris have to say about this?'

'Why Morris?'

'He might not view your involvement so lightly.'

I frowned. 'Aren't we covering ourselves if we sell "as seen"?'

'I wish I could be sure. We have a reputation to maintain, my sweet one – we have to be careful where we dabble. And you have a valuable friendship with a man whose job demands he take action against fraud.'

'There's no harm in selling the earrings anyway, is there?' I said, needing time to think.

And we did sell them – very quickly indeed. And for the sum Piers had asked for. A couple of days later at a fair near Oxford I was doing on my own, since I didn't think Griff was quite well enough to venture further than the shop, I handed over the cash in the traditional brown envelope. It was hardly out of my hand when another slightly battered jewel-case appeared, purple leather outside, purple silk in, showing off a filthy diamond pendant and matching earrings to perfection. Little emeralds on minute springs danced like leaves. Once it was cleaned the set would be exquisite. Perhaps.

'You know I always ask about provenance,' I said, as if I might have been joking but wasn't.

'Same as before.'

It was all so low key we might have been just business partners, not close enough for me to have been wearing his ring. Not that I was, today – my ring finger was swathed in bandages from tip to knuckle, as if I'd had an accident with my restoring scalpel. If he'd shown any concern, even asked about it, I might have told him everything. Grassing someone up was something not to be done lightly. But in a trade that totally depended on trust, what else could I do?

When I got back, Griff had had news from Wally. It wasn't good. The suspicious stones in my ring were actually man-made. Fake, in other words. I handed over the pendant and earring set without a word. Equally silently Griff popped in his eyepiece and inspected them, stone by stone.

At long last, Griff removed the eyepiece and rubbed his face. 'You buy a couple of these so-called man-made diamonds for a song, remove two decent-sized stones from pieces where no one will immediately notice the exchange, replace them with the fakes, make the whole item filthy dirty so people think they're buying from someone with an aged relative who doesn't know they'd sell better clean and pocket the difference. If you got brave enough to replace a one carat diamond, say, with a fake one, you could profit by four or five thousand pounds.'

I nodded. 'To get away with it, you really need someone totally reliable like us. If by any chance people found they'd bought a wrong 'un they'd hotfoot it back to us and complain. And we could only say we'd had them from someone else and terribly sorry and here's your money back.'

'You complain to Piers, who laughs in your face. Or says his aunt must have replaced them to raise cash for her gambling habit or booze or whatever.'

'And in any case he reminds us it's *caveat emptor*.' There weren't many Latin phrases I knew but that was one of them. 'But to my mind it's more a case of *caveat*ing Trading Standards or even the police. I really ought to involve Morris, oughtn't I?'

'Oh, dear one, you can't use *caveat* like that,' he sighed. 'But you're right about the legal implications. To my mind, the only question is how much Piers knows about it.'

'If his genes are anything like Lord Elham's, a lot.'

He kissed me. 'Now, that chicken should be cooked to perfection.'

Over supper we debated long and loud what we should do next. Now I really wanted to pack up the so-called diamonds and send them straight back to Piers. With the offending 'friendship' ring. But, as I'd said, if we did, he'd certainly try to palm them off on someone else less canny than us.

'Equally, of course, Piers might be a dupe of someone to whom he'd innocently taken old items to be cleaned,' Griff observed resignedly. 'And it's the cleaner who's at fault.'

'Not the cleaner – look at the state of those.' I pointed. 'I've got to talk to Lord Elham, haven't I?'

'Or Morris. And Morris.'

I nodded. 'It had better be face to face. So I can make sure they don't get the wrong idea.' Morris especially.

I couldn't do it first thing next morning, however, because I had to set out early for a house sale the far side of Tunbridge Wells. These days Griff often let me go to small auctions like this on my own, trusting my experience, not to mention my antennae, to pick up bargains. I didn't need either today. Nothing was going for its proper value: even a little collection of Ruskin, usually the sort of thing dealers fight over, went cheaply enough for me to buy the lot.

'Good for you, doll.' Titus' voice sounded like gravel in a bucket as he came up behind me in the queue to settle up. 'Doing the right thing – buying while the market's down. It'll go up, you mark my words.' Then he dropped his voice even further. 'You got one of them clever phones that'll take pictures? You see that guy over there, leather coat? No, the brown one. Get a snap of him if you can. Because he's the one as says he's Lord Elham's son.'

'Darrenarris!' I was ready to abandon the queue and my Ruskin and tackle him.

Oates kept me where I was by gripping both shoulders and keeping me facing front. 'Hush your noise. That's his name, is it? No, he's never said as much, not in so many words – boxing clever, see? Just letting it go round that he's the illegit son of a mad lord, him with the daughter who's a dealer. Only to my mind he don't look much like the old bastard. You do – got something of his eyes about you. Honest. Only at least yours aren't bloodshot!' he cackled.

I let him rattle on, doing as he suggested and taking as many photos as I could without drawing attention to myself. By now I'd reached the front of the queue, though, and had to pay attention to money and forms.

Darrenarris'd gone, of course, by the time I'd finished. So had Titus. I didn't need him to tell me I owed him.

I swathed each piece in loads of bubble wrap before stowing it carefully into one of the plastic boxes I keep in the van, which I then locked securely – the Ruskin might have been cheap but that didn't mean someone wouldn't take it off my hands. Then I looked round. No sign of either of them. But at least, thanks to Titus, I had something for Morris to go on when I spoke to him.

I'd only been on the road ten minutes, a dodge route avoiding the worst of the traffic, when my phone rang. Not a lay-by in sight. I'd just have to hope whoever it was left a message. Only to find out, when it was safe to pull over into a side road and look, that they hadn't. And they didn't want the call returned either. I'd just hope they'd try again. And then I got scared. Here I was on a stretch of road with not very good mobile coverage, and if I'd seen Darrenarris at the sale, he must have seen me. Or at least the van. He might well have lurked out of sight and worked out which route I'd be taking back to Bredeham. There weren't all that many obvious ones. I didn't think he'd been tailing me, at least not close to, or I'd have noticed him in my rear view mirror. What if he'd shot ahead and was waiting for me somewhere?

If anyone knew anything, it'd be Titus. It took seconds to find his number and call it. But if he was on the road, he wouldn't pick up, would he? Law-abiding was his middle name, if it came to doing anything that might attract police attention. I was in luck.

'Hello, doll. Been trying to call you. You all right?'

'Fine.'

'So far. You got to that little B road to Maidstone yet? Well turn round and head back to the A228, that's all I'll say. Everyone's heard about Griff's accident. Some folks might like you to have one too. And you've got all that nice Ruskin in the van.' He ended the call.

Funnily enough, I didn't do exactly what he said. Yes, I turned round. But I picked up the B road going down towards Lamberhurst. Miles out of my way, of course. But it was a little closer to Bossingham Hall, if the crow was drunk while it flew, that is.

If Lord Elham identified Brown Leather Jacket as Darrenarris

I had to phone Morris. And sometime I'd better work out why I really didn't want to.

There's a most wonderful shop in Stelling Minnis, the next village to Bossingham, where you can get everything, from wellies to fresh lemon grass. Griff would have loved it. I grabbed a basket, filling it with fresh fruit, which I would make into a fruit salad for my father. He might not eat it all, not if I wasn't there to stand over him, but at least he'd pick up a few vitamins. Vegetables for a stir-fry. Meat and more vegetables for a casserole. I'd call Griff and tell him I'd be late, but not fill in all the details.

I'd just paid and had put the carrier bags on the van's passenger seat when I saw a familiar blond figure. It was Robin Levitt, the priest attached to the parish's two churches, neither of which was actually in the village. He had explained why, a matter of drifting populations and church politics, but since I went to neither it didn't really bother me. Robin was drop-dead gorgeous, it had to be said, Adam's apple apart. He looked frail, like a droopy Victorian poet in one of Griff's books, but in fact was extremely tough. I'd seen him in action when he'd saved me from some thugs.

'You might be smiling at me now,' he said, giving me a hug, 'but you looked pretty grim a few moments ago. Want to talk about it?'

You couldn't fend Robin off. 'I'd love to. But I wouldn't know where to start.'

He peered over my shoulder. 'You're going to feed your father?'

'He's not an animal in Lympne zoo.'

'They'd have a job trying to return him to the wild. Why don't I come too? It's been a while since I visited him. And it'd save me having to cook.'

'You make it sound as if I'm doing you the favour, not the other way round.' He always did, come to think of it. 'Tell you what, I'll just phone Griff and tell him I shall be late and not to keep supper for me.'

Usually Griff would have sounded a bit hard done by, but as soon as I mentioned Robin he perked up. The trouble was, by the time I got home he'd have spent a whole evening match-making, and would probably have worked out that the

Archbishop of Canterbury was the only one suitable to conduct the wedding service.

I just found Robin nice, easy company, but I had to admit, as we fastened our seat belts, that I was glad I wasn't wearing Piers' flashy ring.

Robin's presence brought out the best in my father, who insisted on joining us in the kitchen while we prepared the food. He made green tea in some very pretty eighteenth-century coffee cans, smirking as I registered them, and dug in a cupboard to find a bowl for our fruit salad.

'Lina says there's no market for cut glass,' he said, patting it. 'And I'm rather pleased. This is such a pretty thing.'

When it dawned on him he was missing the evening news, he toddled off. But soon he was back, demanding a cloth to wipe his table with. Robin's eyes and mouth made a trio of huge Os. I'd have laughed, except I dare say my own face had the same expression. Ten minutes later he was back for cutlery and champagne flutes.

I'd not yet shown him the photos on my phone, but if the evening was going to turn festive, I'd better do it now. He peered intently at the succession of images, but was so long responding I thought the worst.

'Cracking little machine, isn't it, Robin?' he asked, waving it under his nose. 'Have you got one like it?'

'Mine's a bit more basic,' Robin said, showing him.

'That doesn't seem right.'

'I don't need it for my work, like Lina does.'

'All the same . . . Lina, there must be something you could sell that would pay for a couple – one for Rob, and one for me too. You never know,' he added.

'Of course I'll find something,' I said, before Robin could argue. 'But first of all, tell me if you recognize that guy.'

'It's Darrenarris, of course. One of my sons, he says. One of these days I'll get round to looking in that book of mine, Lina. All I can say is he doesn't take after his mother.'

'What was she like?' Robin asked.

'Lord knows. Can't expect me to remember every gal I rogered.'

To my surprise, Robin found my hand and squeezed it.

'But she'd be a nice girl or I wouldn't have touched her.

And surely a nice girl would have had a nice child. Look at
Lina, now. Now, a spot of bubbly, everyone?'

He wandered off.

'How can I explain that it's Lent, Lina? And that I'm not
drinking?'

'He wouldn't get it,' I said. 'Hang on. Isn't God supposed
to be all-knowing and all-forgiving? I reckon he'd balance
one glass of fizz against all those onions you peeled. You
don't have to get pissed, you know. Any more than I do –
after all, I'm driving. Now, before my battery dies, I must
send these photos through to a policeman who's very interested in Darrenarris. Very interested indeed.'

When I'd finished, there wasn't even enough battery for a
text. If anything, I was rather relieved. I already had one dodgy
job to do – cornering my father about Lady Olivia Spedding.

On the other hand, did I want to talk about Piers in front
of Robin? My father would blurt out all sorts of embarrassing
questions about my relationship with Piers, and the whole
point of the conversation was to find out if the man was
committing a crime. I wasn't sure if a curate or vicar or whatever would want to hear about such a thing without feeling
honour-bound to do something about it – like tell the police.

On the whole, I decided to say nothing. Another day
wouldn't matter.

'So when are you seeing Robin again?' Griff rubbed his hands
together with even more glee than when I showed him the
Ruskin I'd bought yesterday.

'I didn't *see* him last night, Griff. We just fed Lord Elham
together, that's all, who asked me to flog a couple of bits of
Crown Derby so both he and Robin can have phones like
mine.' Let him chew on that.

'But why did you go to see Lord Elham, with a van full
of Ruskin, for goodness' sake? You're always complaining
about the state of that lane.'

I giggled. 'I didn't tell you I tipped Robin out at the bottom
and made him carry the best stuff.' But I knew I hadn't diverted
him. 'OK. I took some pictures at the sale of someone Titus
Oates thought was Darrenarris.'

'The one robbing the old man left, right and centre? Why
didn't you call the police at once?'

'Titus would have loved that, wouldn't he? In any case, I needed Lord Elham to identify him. And, before you ask, I've already sent the photos through to Morris. Do you want to look, before I delete them? Here. What's the matter? Here, sit down.'

I settled him on a kitchen chair and gave him a glass of water. 'You know him, don't you?'

'What if . . . You know, he's very like the man who ran me off the road. Very like. Lina,' he said, taking my hand, 'what if I've sent the police after an innocent man?'

I hugged him. 'According to Sally Monk, Dean Pardoe isn't at all innocent, and they wanted to talk to him anyway. He might not be the man who hurt you, but the DNA they get from the van will show that.'

'You'd better tell her I might have made a mistake. And you'd better tell Morris too.'

TWENTY-ONE

Since I could feel Griff's ears flapping – he seemed equally keen on Morris and Robin as possible replacements for Piers – I didn't phone Morris but texted him the news that Griff might have been mistaken when he'd picked out Dean Pardoe from Sally Monk's mug shots. I was quite happy to phone Sally herself, who promised to come over as soon as she could, though I could tell from her voice that she didn't think the matter was very urgent. I didn't tell either of them that Titus had warned me to change my route home, just that I was acting on a hunch.

I was just beginning to wash the haul of Ruskin when Griff came bustling in. 'Dear heart,' he said, 'I've just remembered I'm supposed to be having my eyes tested over in Canterbury this afternoon. I shall have to put off the appointment, I suppose, if the constabulary are about to descend on us.'

'You can't drive until you've got new glasses,' I said. 'I'll let Sally and Morris know you won't be in. Do you want me to take you? I know I'm supposed to be in the shop this afternoon, but Mrs Hatch would be glad of the extra hours, I dare say.'

'I could always go by train.'

Normally I'd have said yes. But it's quite a step from Canterbury West station to the optician's, which isn't far from the Cathedral. I wouldn't have thought twice about doing it myself, but I was still a little anxious about Griff.

'I'll pop round to the shop and see what she says,' he said.

I shook my head. 'I'll go. You stay and feast your eyes on these beauties,' I said.

'I'm not an invalid, my angel. You must let me out of your sight occasionally, you know,' he said, not quite joking.

'OK. I'll start cataloguing them. I can't make up my mind which to put in the shop and which to keep for good fairs.'

'Remember we've got Antiques for Everyone at the NEC in April,' he said, as he went out of the door.

Which meant some deep pockets, if we were lucky.

Cataloguing was a long and fiddly process, involving recording on our database where we'd bought an item, how much we'd paid and what we ought to ask for when we sold it. These days it also involved taking photos and adding them. And then we'd decide which to sell on line, via our website, which in the shop and which to save for when we wanted to make a big statement, like at the NEC. I was well into the task when I came across one – dark green and a very strange shape, but complete with the factory stamp – I needed Griff's advice on. It was only then it dawned on me that the house was very quiet. I called out. No reply.

Ten to one he was just having a nice gossip with Mrs Hatch. Or with a regular client.

Or—

And it was the last *or* that made me hurtle downstairs two and three at a time. Despite myself I locked up as I ran out of the back door, and set the alarm. Then I was across the yard and with my ear to the little airbrick at the back of the shop. Any voices? Any other sounds? Why should I think I heard a muffled scream?

Retracing my footsteps, I went back through the house – all the alarm and lock business all over again – and, grabbing a jacket, out into the street, walking towards the shop just like an ordinary customer. Rain? Good, I could pull the hood up without looking odd. So I mooched, hands in pockets, dawdling across the road to the pharmacy, as if really interested in hot water bottles, but trying to use the window as a mirror. Nothing. So I crossed back, and pretended to check out the china and glass on display. Griff and Mrs Hatch were where they should be, behind the counter. They were still on their feet. Thank God. Clutching each other? Not so good. The customer looked familiar, despite the ski mask. And the sword he was holding looked familiar too. I was more used to seeing it in its sheath, in our most secure display cabinet. Not with its blade bare, jabbing near their throats.

Why the hell hadn't one of them had the sense to press the panic button and set off the alarm? It wasn't just the house and shop it rang in – there was a direct line to Maidstone police station.

I had to rescue them. I stripped off my jacket, ready to sling it at the man, and then overpower him. The movement caught Griff's eye, but he looked away immediately, though I could have sworn he shook his head, ever so slightly.

What did he mean?

And then I remembered the words he'd made me repeat every time I'd served in the shop in the first year of my apprenticeship. If there's trouble, *Don't be brave, be clever.*

I couldn't move. I wasn't clever. I was bloody dim.

But suddenly I was cunning. Moving casually away from the shop, I prised a brick from a neighbour's wall – sorry – and heaved it as hard as I could through our front door. The alarm was on the same circuit as the shop, ringing straight through to Maidstone. You wouldn't be able to hear yourself think in the house; you'd be blasted in the shop, too. And hidden cameras would start working overtime in both buildings. Plenty of shots of a man in a bloody ski mask, of course.

Still with the jacket in my hands, I sprinted back. What I'd do was hurl it over the intruder's head as he fled. That should hold him up.

It would have done, if I'd thrown it better. Maybe it was one of the things I'd have learned at school – netball or something – if I'd hung round long enough. OK, it tripped him, and he'd have gravel rash on his palms, but he gathered himself up and simply hared off. I reckon I'm fast, but even in my blind anger I was no match for him. I didn't even see his car, just heard it roaring away from the village. Or was it a bike? I was too panicked to tell.

In any case, I was into the shop by then. And then even more scared – no sign of either Griff or Mrs Hatch.

'Griff?' I screamed, over the racket of the alarm.

'Behind the counter, angel. Heart attack, I think. Dial 999, for God's sake.'

Even as I jabbed the numbers into the phone I heard the twin horns of a police car. I dashed outside to flag it down. 'The attacker's gone. But my partner's having a heart attack.'

One officer shoved me to one side so he could get into the shop more quickly. The other spoke into his radio – I heard the words, 'Ambulance urgently required.'

Don't be brave, be clever.

There'd be aspirins in the house. Weren't they supposed to be life savers? I was in our bathroom before I even knew I'd killed the alarm. The silence was almost shocking.

My Griff. He mustn't die. Mustn't. God, I'll do anything if You let him live.

'What the hell's that?' one of the cops asked, as I shoved the packet under his nose.

'Aspirin. To put under his tongue. Let me get to him, please!' I was ready to fight.

'Get out of the way, miss. For God's sake, get out of the fucking way. We've nearly lost her once.' But he took the aspirins.

Staggering as if I was having an attack myself, I stuffed my hands into my mouth to stop myself calling out. And then I thought of being clever again, and ran out into the street in case the ambulance needed to be flagged down too.

One of the cops came and put a gentle arm round me. He must be about to tell me that Griff had died. Something between a sob and a scream tore out of my throat.

'Dear one! Dear one! I shall have to slap your face if you don't calm down. Don't make me do that. Please.'

Griff.

The world turned. I didn't often faint, but my ears were rushing now. Only Griff would try to catch me and I'd drag him down. And that would hurt him.

I turned and threw myself into his arms. Or he threw himself into mine. I don't know.

At this point we heard the ambulance.

Mrs Hatch mustn't die. Or Griff would blame himself. Hell,

I'd blame myself too. All this Darrenarris business was my fault. And it was hurting other people. Not just me.

Mrs Hatch was still alive – just – when the ambulance drove away. At my insistence Griff had gone too: he might not have had a heart attack but he had had a terrible shock, and should be checked over. I promised to follow the ambulance over to William Harvey to pick him up. I didn't add that – whether he liked it or not – I'd take him back to Aidan in Tenterden.

'OK, Lina,' said a calm voice, 'let's go and have a cup of tea and you can tell me what's been going on.'

I stared. Where had Sally Monk sprung from?

'You've had a shock too, you know. I gather you thought it was your grandfather who was ill. But you did very well.'

Patronizing cow. She had me by the elbow and was steering me back to the cottage as if I was ninety.

'I'm fine.' Even to my ears it sounded as if I was lying.

She stopped dead when she saw the mess the brick had made, but said nothing, stepping over the splinters of glass and wood.

'Well, I could use a cuppa. I was just tootling over to talk about the road rage attack and I find I'm in the middle of a raid, with rapid response cars and ambulances hurtling round all over the place.'

OK, patronizing but kind, too. We found we both preferred drinking chocolate and this time, Lent or not, we both needed cake.

For some reason she wanted me to go through the whole story, bit by bit, stopping me from time to time to make things clear.

'This man waving a sword: you're sure about that? He might not just have been examining it with a view to selling it?'

I was beginning to get angry, but I wasn't sure who with. 'I don't know that he'd need a ski mask just to look at it.'

'And what happened to the man with the sword?'

I explained how I'd tried to stop him escaping by throwing my coat at his head. 'Didn't work though. And I didn't even see his car or motorbike or whatever.'

'Motorbike?'

'I don't know. I'm sorry, I'm hopeless, aren't I?'

'We all panic when there's a crisis. What I can't understand is why the man with the sword should suddenly bolt
from the shop – you didn't really confront him, did you?'
I shook my head. 'He was scared by the burglar alarm.'
'Had Griff or Mrs Hatch managed to set it off then?'
'No. I had. I put that brick through our front door. The
systems are connected. And very loud.'
'In that case,' said another voice, 'I don't think you're hopeless at all.'

It was only after several moments in the comfort of Robin's
arms that I realized I might, in Griff's old-fashioned words,
be leading him on. Eventually, I pushed away, but he kept an
arm on my shoulders. 'Who did this to you?'
'Did what?'
'Hit you about the face, of course. And no one's got any
ice on it, for goodness' sake.'
Sally scuttled into the kitchen.
Shaking my head, I touched a cheekbone. Hell. How did I
hide this lot from Griff? 'I didn't even know I'd done it. It
must have been when I thought Griff was dying. But he isn't.'
'Have you always self-harmed?'
I hated using the term. 'I do it without even knowing some-
times. But we've got to sort it out before I see Griff. And I've
got to get on to our glazier – he's an expert on old buildings.
And there's Griff's appointment with Mrs Pybus to cancel.
Where do I start?' Damn me if I didn't smack myself again.
And wished I hadn't.
'With the ice pack,' he said, taking a tea towel full of frozen
peas and dabbing it on my face. 'Where's your phone book?
The officer here can call and explain.'
I pointed to the address book next to the phone. 'She's
called Sally. The glazier's number's in there as well. If you
say it's for Griff he'll pr . . . por . . . put it top of his list.'
'Come on, Lina,' said another voice. 'You can do better
than that. Prioritize.'
'Hello, Morris. I'd say come in but you seem to be in
already.' It wasn't much of a welcome, but I could have wished
that he hadn't strolled in and found another bloke stroking
my face. It gave altogether the wrong message.
'Who heaved the brick?' He kicked the splinters of glass.

'Me. Long story.'

'So it won't wreck a crime scene if I get it up? Dustpan and brush?'

sweep

'Under the sink.' I took the peas and pressed them against my face myself, setting off upstairs. There was arnica in my bedroom, and cream from the pharmacy. I'd better hope they worked. Griff would understand, but he'd be disappointed in me. He thought I'd stopped. I thought I'd stopped. And now at least three people knew I hadn't.

Embarrassed and ashamed, I managed to trail back downstairs.

Morris was still busy with the dustpan, so perhaps I hadn't been as long as I thought, which felt like forever.

Robin, who'd just finished a phone call, said, 'I know it's a silly question, Lina, but I don't suppose you thought to take any pictures of chummy on that nifty phone of yours.'

I hadn't, had I? I was ready to smack my head again, but I stopped. And managed a smile, which wasn't actually too painful. 'Didn't need to. When I heaved that brick through the door it would have triggered the cameras in the shop. Automatically.'

'Good lord.' He produced that angelic grin of his. 'I really don't think you're hopeless. Not at all.'

Morris stood up, making me realize just how tall he was. 'Hopeless? For a long time I've thought her a most remarkable young woman.'

TWENTY-TWO

'**B**ut,' Morris continued without even pausing for breath, 'she's not very good at delegating. I bet you're jumping up and down wondering how soon you can collect Griff from the William Harvey, aren't you, Lina?'

'I would be, only I'd rather he didn't see me like this.' I touched my face. 'And I was going to take him to his friend Aidan Morley's house, in Tenterden. Safer than here.'

'Good idea. I'll make sure he's taken there when my Kent colleagues have interviewed him about this morning's incident. That will take quite a long time, I should imagine.' Before I could interrupt, he continued, 'And I bet you're working out who can look after the shop while you're dashing round like a scalded cat – well, my Scene of Crime colleagues will be keen on spring-cleaning that. And don't worry – they're house-trained. If they break things it messes up the crime scene. Hmm, drinking chocolate, eh? I don't suppose you could organize some for me, Constable?'

I sat down very heavily. Sally disappeared. Robin started to chuckle.

But Morris hadn't finished. 'So is there somewhere round here we can all get a bit of lunch? Sit down, woman – you don't have to organize food for the five thousand as well.'

'Pub?' Robin suggested, as I subsided. 'I should think they'd have enough loaves and fishes there.'

Morris grinned, as if they'd shared a joke. But I wouldn't ask them to explain, not the two of them. 'Go and save us a table, will you, Robin? We'll be along as soon as I've sunk my hot chocolate.'

Which was as unsubtle a way of getting rid of Robin as I could imagine. I was inclined to be cross on his behalf, but he waved a hand and was off.

Morris took the mug Sally was offering and shut the door in her face, not rudely but firmly. 'And now, Lina, you can tell me what the burglar was after.'

'Not an antique sword? No? Well, as you can imagine, we've got a hell of a lot worth stealing. Do you think he was a proper burglar? Or was it Darrenarris – did you get the photos I sent? – who's a bit peeved by our attempts to protect Lord Elham and thought he might have a go at a softer target? He must have been seriously pissed off to find poor Griff at the shop, not me. Maybe the second time he'd got the wrong person. And Mrs Hatch, of course. Have you heard if she'll be OK?' The words seemed to gush out. I couldn't stop them.

'There's something else you're not telling me. That's two things altogether, Lina – get it?' He waggled a pair of fingers at me.

I took a deep breath. Perhaps the oxygen would get to my brain. 'One, he must have seen me at a sale the other day. And when I took a different route home to avoid being in an accident it was after a friend's hint. But don't you dare let on to Griff! Two, he's after my father's notebook. Isn't he?'

'I'm sure he is. You took a risk taking it, of course. Come on – hand it over.'

'Of course. But just to show how security conscious we are, you show me the safe. How long would your average burglar take to suss out a place, especially with the alarm smashing his eardrums? Three minutes? I'll give you five, while I put a bit of slap on my face. Can't go out looking like this.'

He touched a bit that wasn't bruised. 'You're much more Griff's granddaughter than Lord Elham's daughter. Hey, you're not cheating, are you? You're not going to sit on it while you apply your – er – slap?'

'No. But I will tell you we've got the official office safe – where you'll find the silver dish Nella accused me of taking – and another, unofficial one.'

'I give up,' he said, popping his head round my bedroom door.

'Excellent. We had this one installed after a spot of bother with *Natura Rerum*.'

'That precious book?'

'Right. A guy Griff knows who's an expert on priests' holes fixed it. You take this mirror from the wall, and then put a nail file under the beam that the mirror hangs from – go on, try it.'

He held out his hand for a nail file and did what I'd said. Nothing.

'Just there. Opposite the knot. See.' The chunk of beam came away like a book out of a shelf. I passed him my pocket torch. 'I'd better do the combination, though.'

He looked at me sadly. 'You don't trust anyone, do you, Lina?'

'Only Griff. And that took a long time. Anyway, there you are – the special safe. With Lord Elham's notebook and a couple of absolute total treasures Griff's saving for a really rainy day. I suppose you'd better take this into custody.' As I handed him the book I looked him in the eye. 'It's the only evidence I am who I am.'

He shook his head. 'You're wrong, Lina. The evidence is all around you – from those lovely Georgian miniatures to that bear. Tim, isn't it? He recovered from Nella's cavalier treatment, I see.' He tweaked his ear. 'OK, let's see about lunch. I thought you were seeing this guy Piers,' he said, over his shoulder as he led the way downstairs, 'not a vicar.'

'Who says I'm seeing anyone at the moment?' I said. 'Did you ever get round to having Darrenarris's DNA lifted from the glasses and checked, by the way?'

'It costs so much I can't just do it on whim, Lina. There has to be a complaint about him from the public, alleging a crime.'

'Would I do? Or does it have to be my father?'

'Who complains or provides the DNA? Better if he does both, actually. As a matter of interest, are you still refusing to cooperate with your putative grandfather?'

That was a good word. I liked the sound of it. Another one for my new vocab book when I got it.

'If you mean Arthur Habgood, yes. I looked this stuff up on the Net. The test wouldn't give an absolutely definite answer, would it? And I've got enough questions buzzing round my head without wanting more. Actually, I suppose the simplest way would be for him to talk to Lord Elham. I could introduce them.'

'Bloody hell, there'd pistols at dawn! Maybe some food'll help you to think more clearly. Then I'll nip over to Ashford to see how the interview with Griff's going – I might have a few questions the regular team wouldn't think of. And – if you like – I'll run him over to Tunbridge myself.'

'Aren't you asking Sally to join us for a bite?' I asked, as he shut the door behind us.

'Someone's got to hang about for the glazier,' he said in an offhand manner.

'But—'

'Lina, Sally is armed with an ASP baton and a spray and a phone link to colleagues. If it's you or her that stays at home, who do you expect me to choose?'

'It's a good job they do takeaways,' I said.

Robin's presence kept the conversation pretty general, but I couldn't resist asking a couple of questions.

'Has the missing musical snuff box turned up yet? Someone nicked it from Bossingham Hall,' I explained to Robin.

'Nope. Nor any of the other goodies. But – and I assume you can be trusted to keep your mouth shut, Robin – we've got someone working under cover at the Hall. And no, I shan't tell you who it is, Lina, because that's not the way I do things. OK?'

'OK. But I tell you what'd be really useful – if he or she could get me a copy of one of the photos in the administrator's office. The whole happy family, with the father and kids. I've got to place that man's face.'

'It's relevant? You're sure?'

'I wouldn't ask otherwise. The other thing I need is some anonymous wheels instead of our van.'

'Dead right you do. Good job I've left Sally to organize it. She'll stay overnight to keep an eye on you too.'

Robin coughed. 'Surely I could – or Lina could sleep at the vicarage.'

I looked quickly at Morris, who picked up my appeal for help. 'I'm afraid it'll have to be here, Lina. I suspect the SOCO team will have things to ask you.' And he kicked me lightly on the shin.

Lord Elham actually turned the volume down on the TV when I arrived although it was well into his favourite quiz programme when I finally made it to Bossingham. Picking up the hire car had meant it was much too late to take him to Canterbury. Robin had looked so fed up I promised to organize a shopping trip for the three of us as soon as I could.

My father stared at my face. 'That man of yours been beating you up? Piers Whatever his name is? Time you sent him to the rightabout if he is.'

'Accident,' I said. 'But actually, I'd quite like to talk to you about Piers. Or at least his family. He's got this aunt, Lady Olivia Spedding. I don't suppose you know her?'

'Olivia Spedding! Good God! I didn't know she was still alive.'

'It seems she's fallen on hard times: having to sell bits and pieces of jewellery. And she's got Piers to ask me to do it.'

'Why not ask Piers himself?'

'Because basically Piers deals in tat. And you know I don't.'

'Quality will out,' he said, but I wasn't sure why.

All the same, I picked up on the word. 'The trouble is, some of the stones in the jewellery aren't the quality they ought to be. Dead dodgy, in fact. And I was wondering, would she have had a few stones replaced here and there?'

'More likely to have the whole lot exchanged for paste,' he mused. 'You sure she's still alive?'

'Piers ought to know: he's her nephew.'

'Is he indeed? Are you sure? That must mean I'm related to him.' He peered at me. 'More to the point, it means you must be related to him. Though not closely enough for consanguinity to worry you.'

I'd heard that word before, hadn't I? In fact, Piers himself had used it. 'Maybe I wouldn't worry if I knew what it meant,' I said.

Sighing, he shook his head as he often did when my education came up. '*Con* means *with*. *Sanguinity* means blood – more or less. A relative. Family member, as those awful social workers call it. So *consanguinity* means you're too closely related to marry and have children,' he concluded. 'Not that he'd be marrying you without asking my permission, Lina. Got to do the thing properly.' He reached for my bare right hand. 'I'm glad you took the hint about that ring – quite vulgar if you ask me. Just the sort of thing Olivia would wear.'

'Do you mean the bugger gave me his aunt's ring without telling me? Bloody hell.'

Griff would have quietly tapped his watch to remind me about our swearing rule.

My father smiled. 'Exactly. Nice to see you showing a bit of spirit, Lina.' He reached for the champagne he had cooling and popped the cork. 'Need to celebrate something like that.'

From the row of mugs on the table and absence of dirty glasses, I gathered it was his first drink of the day – also something to celebrate.

'That ring,' I continued eventually, 'has a couple of fake stones too. As did a lovely sapphire ring he wanted me to sell. And a Victorian earring and pendant set.'

'So you need to know if it's Olivia that's shoving the fakes in or young Piers.'

I was so pleased I topped up his glass. 'And I've no way of knowing,' I pointed out.

'The whole business has a lot of implications for you, doesn't it? Can't have you marrying a con man,' he declared, as sincerely as if he wasn't a master forger himself. 'On the other hand, you can't blame him if the old bat's palmed phoney sparklers on him. Hang on – if he's in your trade he should

know, surely? Ah, you said he only deals in tat. Have to do
something about that, Lina, if you're going to marry him.'

I shook my head. 'I'm not going to marry him. Diamonds
or no diamonds, I don't like him enough. All the same, I'd still
like to know if he's the one conning me or if it's this aunt.'

'I'll make a few enquiries – name of the family, and all that.
You leave it to me, young Lina. That's what fathers are for.'

TWENTY-THREE

M y father would have been shocked to see me wearing
the ruby as an engagement ring that evening, and
rabbiting on, all dewy-eyed, about my fiancé. So
would Griff. But they might both have applauded my motive,
which was to fend off Sally Monk's sudden attentions.
Somehow she'd mistaken my lunchtime doggie bag and the
supper I cooked for us as a come-on. I didn't want her to take
my refusal personally – as I said, she was a nice, kind woman
– but amongst all the questions dangling points-down over
my life, my sexuality wasn't one of them. She might well
observe that I was a lesbian virgin, and didn't know what I
was missing till I'd tried – actually, she made it sound much
more like an accusation than just a comment – but I'd have
found her upfront suggestions crude and off-putting whoever
had made them. Whoever. Either gender.

Feeding her was one thing; sitting down for a cosy evening
in front of the TV was quite another. So I dumped a duvet
and pillow on the sofa and bolted upstairs.

I even locked the door behind me. In my own home, I felt
I needed to lock the door! I was so furious I was ready to
start hitting myself again. Furious? Was that it? I made myself
sit down and breathe deeply. What was I actually feeling?
Was I outraged? Scared? Or what?

At this point I realized that Tim Bear was laughing. Morris
would certainly split his sides when I told him. And then I felt
very ashamed. Hell, no one was camper or gayer than Griff, and
I didn't raise so much as an eyebrow at his flirtations – even
when we were both making eyes at the same bloke. So why

should I even think of sniggering about Sally behind her back? Actually, there was some part of me that wanted to laugh at myself. I hadn't wanted to sleep under the same roof as a really decent guy who'd never have made a pass at me while he was my host – or even my guest. I'd been happy to be guarded by a woman. And this was how it had turned out.

Actually, it wasn't a laughing matter. It was sexual harassment, wasn't it? I should report her, shouldn't I? But it would have been my word against hers, and most police officers, in my experience, stuck to each other like shit to a blanket.

So what should I do? Maybe I'd better speak to her myself. Or not.

I exchanged a rueful grin with Tim and then joined him in bed.

Next morning, I tried to behave as if everything was normal but Sally didn't make it particularly easy.

'So where do you go for breakfast?' she demanded. Was she looking grumpy or just tired?

What did she mean? 'Here, of course.'

'But where here? I had a quick look round the village but I didn't see a Starbucks or Costa or anything.' She kept rubbing her neck and stretching as if to reproach me for making her spend the night on the sofa.

I wondered if I should reproach her for leaving me unguarded while she'd been exploring the fast-food possibilities of the village. 'No. You wouldn't. That's why we eat here.' I pointed at the table.

'So where do you get it?'

'Out of the fridge or out of the cupboard.' Apart, of course, from the lovely dense granary loaf I fished out of the bread bin. 'There's porridge, muesli, toast . . .' I felt like that character in *The Wind in the Willows* describing the picnic he would have. Getting little response, I added, 'The bread doesn't toast well, but there's home-made jam and home-made marmalade.'

'I'll stick to coffee, thanks.'

'I have to make sure Griff eats well, you see,' I explained, reaching out both the butter and Griff's Benecol spread. It sounded like an apology for offering a feast, not a load of fast food. I suppose I'd have felt like she did about doughnuts and muffins if Griff hadn't taken me in hand. I was cross,

though, because she didn't even want to try the good things
on the table.

'Look, Sally,' I said at last, 'you might be looking after me
but you're my guest, too, you know. And I have to say you
were really out of order last night. On both counts. Sexual
harassment, that's what it's called.'

Her head went back. 'But—'

'And you know you were out of line. So just bloody well
don't do it again. To anyone. OK? And if you don't promise
me, I'll report you.'

Feeble, really.

But it was enough to irritate the socks off Sally.

Thank goodness the phone rang.

Griff. He wanted to know how I was – as if I'd been the
one held at swordpoint and had someone collapse on me with
a heart attack. I'm not sure he entirely believed me when I
assured him I'd come off unscathed, but thanks to Robin's
prompt demand for ice for my face, with luck the bruises
would have faded by the time I allowed him to come home.
Feeling very brave, I asked to speak to Aidan, who made an
effort I could almost hear – Morris would know a nice neat
word for that – to reassure me that Griff was safe.

'I will personally ensure that he remains in Tenterden. Even
if I have to hide his shoes to keep him here,' he added. There
was a pause, and I'd have sworn that he wanted to say something else, but he didn't, except to promise again to guard Griff.

So we all parted on good terms, and I could work out what
to do next.

Sally was taking a call on her mobile when I went back
into the kitchen. 'She's just come in, sir. Inspector Morris,'
she mouthed as she passed me her phone.

'You mentioned that you thought your raider might have
escaped on a motorbike,' he said.

'And good morning to you, too,' I said. 'Only might, Morris.
And there'll be no CCTV. There's this local councillor who
doesn't believe in street lights or cameras, I'm afraid.'

'So I gather. And your shop footage just shows the ski
mask, of course. Nothing for our facial recognition program
to work on. Just a big man waving a lethal-looking sword in
the direction of two terrified pensioners. Only don't tell Griff
I called him that.'

'Why the hell did they unlock the case and hand it over? And not press the panic button? It's an absolute rule not to let anyone into the shop unless we can see their face, let alone letting them get their hands on anything valuable or dangerous.'

'Unfortunately she'd already unlocked the case and handed over the weapon when Griff arrived. And she's still too ill to question. If it hadn't been for your initial suspicions and prompt action, plus flagging down the mobile and my colleagues' first aid training, of course, she'd be a goner. She still may be, Lina – I have to warn you. So what are you doing today?' He made an effort to sound brighter, but it was clear Mrs Hatch was very ill. If only I'd tried to like her a bit more.

'Working, of course. Dispatching Internet orders; serving in the shop; restoring china; planning what we take to the next antiques fair. And I shall be sticking to all our safety rules.'

'Do you want Sally to stay?'

I should have expected that. But even if I wanted to tell him the truth, the fact she was standing only a couple of metres away would have stopped me. 'I shall be all right.' Let him make of that what he would. If ever there was a man who could read between the lines, it was Morris.

He sounded very doubtful as he asked, 'You sure you're all right?'

'Anything scares me and I'll be on to that emergency alarm before you can say knife.' He didn't need to know that my father's parting gifts to me had been his swagger stick and an instruction to keep a can of hairspray or deodorant by me and aim for the eyes – how he knew about that I didn't ask.

'And will you be out and about?'

'I might have to go across the street to the post office, to send off some orders and get a new vocab book. Maybe Londis. No need for that hire car, I hope. But thanks for organizing it. Maybe Sally could drop it back to the depot. That'd be really helpful.' And get her out of my hair.

'What about that trip to Canterbury you were talking about?'

'If I go, I shall get Robin to come and pick me up and bring me back.' Some devil inspired me to add, 'If it's very late I could always stay at the vicarage, or have him doss here.' In fact, I had no intention of leaving the place unguarded.

'Oh. Very well. Put me on to Sally again, will you?'

Griff had told me it was rude to listen in to others' phone

calls – Sally obviously didn't know the rule – so I nipped off
and cleaned my teeth and generally started my working day.
There were a couple of Internet orders – small items that need
very careful packing; three or four enquiries to respond to and
a couple of thank yous from grateful customers that I'd get our
webmaster to copy on to the site. Someone wanted to be allowed
to post adverts on our site – I referred that to John as well.

At last I thought it safe to go downstairs. Safe? Sally had
actually left without telling me. Five years ago I should have
thought it quite normal to behave like that. But not since Griff
had dinned into me the importance of good manners. Fuming,
I stripped the duvet and pillow, shoving the bed linen into the
machine and starting it off.

Morris had been right about the SOCO team: presumably they
had searched and photographed and done all they were supposed
to do, but they had left the shop immaculate, as I found when
I went round, locking myself in, of course. There was even a
little Post-it note saying that a mug full of paper clips and rubber
bands had fallen during the efforts to resuscitate Mrs Hatch; it
was wrapped and in the bin if I wanted it.

On weekdays it was always quiet enough for me to work,
either reading up on areas I was weak on or low-level restoration. Today, however, the reporter from the local paper arrived
– yes, I made her pass her ID under the door before I let her
in – and wanted photos and an interview. Morris hadn't told
me whether this was a good idea. So I gave her a sniff of a
story, no more, pretending my arrival at the shop had just
been a co . . . *oh, come on, woman* . . . a coincidence, and
referring her to the Kent Police Press Office. (I only hoped
they had one.) I'd no sooner got rid of her than another two,
a reporter and a photographer – a freebie paper this time –
arrived with the same questions. I gave them exactly the same
story and refused to be photographed, especially the bruises
they assumed had been inflicted in the course of my heroic
activities.

A couple of neighbours waved and popped in to offer me
sympathy and cakes, and to get the full low-down on Mrs Hatch
and Griff. One of them offered me supper, not liking to think
of me rattling round the cottage on my own; the other offered
to bring round a portion of the casserole she was cooking for

herself. Whichever I accepted, I knew I'd offend the other. So I said I had a feeling a friend might be dropping by.

Morris, of course. Peeved by the thought I might need Robin's protection. He hadn't phoned. All the same I'd wait and see.

And got egg on my face and a meal from the freezer on my own.

It dawned on me as I washed up the solitary plate, that if I could send photos, I could receive them, too. In response to my text, Morris sent through a copy of the photo I'd seen in Pamela Fielding's office. At least I had the whole evening on my own to sit and stare at it. Or not. Sometimes the harder you try to remember something, the more you forget it.

A little later a text message from him came through. Words for my new vocab book, it said – followed by a list. Must have taken him ages. So with some music on the radio, the sort Griff wanted me to learn to love, and a dictionary on my knee, I got to work. I even found some more words in the dictionary I'd heard people use and never jotted down.

'Actually, I've had a really good evening,' I told Tim as I joined him. And I had. But I still hadn't placed the face in the photo.

I managed to stop myself slapping my face. I wasn't that cross with myself. But I was cross enough to go downstairs again and bring up the phone. I'd stare at it half the night if necessary.

It wasn't.

Of course I knew that face.

Was it too late to phone back? Not to text anyway.

Mr Fielding @ LAPADA show @ NEC. CCTV?

Mr Fielding was none other than the man Nella had gone off to lunch with. But that would take far too long to text.

TWENTY-FOUR

'**M**orris? Sod it, it's only six o'clock!' I was quite proud of myself for forcing my eyes wide enough open to see the dial.

'I thought you'd be on the road by now. Haven't you got a fair down in Hastings?'

'Bloody hell, so I have. At that posh new hotel. Well, I can't go to that and keep an eye on the shop.'

'With all due respect to your stock, Lina, I don't think Chummy really collects antique swords. I think he was after a person. You.'

'That's supposed to cheer me up, is it?'

'It means if you activate all those clever alarms the shop should look after itself.'

'There's an awful lot of road between here and Hastings,' I pointed out.

'A nice busy A road, mostly. Lots of camera coverage. You'll be all right.'

'And at the fair?'

'Plenty of people around. Look, Lina, don't argue. Just get your arse down there, there's a good girl.'

I thought of all the boxes and bags and the cash point thing and . . . 'Can't be done,' I said. I spoke to thin air.

As I drove into the Mondiale car park, having smashed the speed limit if not the china in the back, the first van I saw was Argentia Antiques'. Well, that might make for an interesting conversation in the ladies' loo. I had to park at the furthest point from the hotel, of course. It would take for ever to shift everything. Before I could even swear, however, I was greeted by a young man who produced an ID and announced himself as DS Valentine Farthing.

'I'm your muscle,' he said. 'Known to my friends as Tiny.' As a clincher, he added, 'DI Morris sent me.'

I didn't argue. If anyone could carry our display cabinet single handed it was DS Farthing. He'd probably have managed it with me sitting on it, actually.

'You carry in; I'll set up. Just remember to lock the van between journeys.' I tossed him the keys, grabbed one of the boxes and set off as fast as anyone could when she was carrying £5000 worth of china.

I'd just unpacked the last box and tweaked a final spotlight on the display when who should stroll up but Piers, with another little jewel case. An opal ring, this time, with a blaze of diamonds around it.

'Two and a half K, I should think.' He popped it into the display case alongside the earring and pendant set. '*As seen.*

What the hell do you mean by that?' he demanded, jabbing a furious finger at the card beneath it. 'And I asked for more than that!'

'I haven't had time to clean it and check the settings,' I said, kicking myself for being a coward. 'What else do you expect me to say? And would you rather I sold it, or had it sitting on the stall for months? See that dealer over there – she's had the same spectacle case on sale for £400 for a year to my knowledge. That tortoiseshell one. I've got a client that would have her hand off if she reduced it to £350. That's a lot of money to have missed out on. And times aren't good, remember.'

He hesitated. I'd not realized until this moment how like a horse he could look when he pinched his lips together.

I unlocked the cabinet. 'Here, have it back if you think you can do any better.'

Holding the case, he stared at it and then at me. 'Lina, you're not wearing my ring!' he cried, looking really upset.

One thing I did not want – any more than Nella had done, all those weeks ago – was a scene. I was spared one by my mobile. 'I've got to take this,' I said, turning away. No need to tell him the caller was Morris.

'OK, I'm here at the fair. What next?'

'Are you busy fighting off customers?'

'Only Piers, so far.'

'And are you wearing his ring?'

'I'm not even wearing any make-up yet. Didn't have any breakfast, either.'

'My heart bleeds. Teach Tiny all you can because you may have to leave the stall this afternoon.' End of call. Just like that.

'I hope you're a quick learner,' I said to Tiny, who had simply reappeared by the stall, just as Piers' so-called diamonds had reappeared in the display cabinet. How such a large man had managed to be invisible until I'd needed him I don't know. He was like the Cheshire Cat, not the group but in that book my father had given me – *Alice's Adventures in Wonderland*.

But he didn't smile. 'I'm in Mensa, if that helps,' he said.

'Bloody hell.' Sorry, Griff. 'In that case, you can probably work out all the price codes for yourself, while I go and apply some slap.' Being a total coward I went back to the van to do it. I really didn't want to face Nella in the loo in waif or stray mode.

'You look a different woman,' Tiny declared when I returned ten minutes to the second after leaving him.

'Thanks. And have you broken the code yet?'

'It's not too hard, is it?'

I shook my head. Even I'd managed to suss it after half an hour. 'Tell you what,' I said, 'it's pretty quiet and I didn't have time for breakfast. Do you fancy a sandwich too?' I reached for my purse.

'On me,' he said, making off before I could even tell him what I wanted. Perhaps it was because Piers was circling.

'About the ring—' he began.

'Went clean out of my mind. Griff's staying with Aidan and I'd forgotten I was supposed to be here. God knows how many speed cameras I waved at.' He didn't need to know about the goings-on back in Bredeham.

'So what was that guy doing here?'

'He saw me struggling with my stuff and offered to help. He's something to do with security. I spy a punter,' I said, looking over his shoulder.

Tiny arrived back in time for me to demonstrate how to use the electronic card reader for the punter who'd just made the day worthwhile with a single purchase, a framed Rockingham plaque.

'That was the boyfriend, was it? Piers Hamlyn?'

'Soon to be ex-boyfriend. Thanks for the sarnie.' Smoked salmon on brown, with a glass of fresh orange juice. 'Ah, another customer.'

I was busy enough not to have time to worry about either Piers or Morris, but I still felt a weird tension around me. If I'd been a dog I'd have been sniffing the air and kept a growl waiting in my throat. Was it because of Nella? Her stall was at the far end of the suite of rooms we were using, and there was no need for our paths to cross. Arthur Habgood? Yes, he was there, but after our last tiff he was studiously avoiding my eye, which was fine by me. Piers was doing such a poor trade in vivid animals I almost felt sorry for him. But not quite. I should have tackled him about the dodgy diamonds. I should even have dobbed him in to Morris. But I still hoped for another solution.

My phone rang. Tiny was quite capable of holding the fort so I took the call. My father!

'Your young man's a fraud. Far too young to be Olivia Spedding's nephew – even her great nephew. Popped her clogs years ago: no stamina, those Speddings. In any case, she spent all her dosh on the gee-gees: never wore a diamond in her life. So wherever he's getting his sparklers from, it's not Olivia. So that Piers of yours is a lying bastard.'

I didn't argue with the term, though it still grated.

'And I know just the way to deal with him. You leave it to me. Though you may have to take me to London,' he added as he cut the call.

You leave it to me. That was my father speaking?

I was just about to send Tiny off for a lunch break when I saw something that made me grip his arm instead.

'That good-looking guy there. In the suit.'

'Over by the stall dealing exclusively in willow pattern? I wouldn't call him good-looking.'

'Let's not worry about the details. He's Pamela Fielding's husband—'

'She's the administrator at Bossingham Hall, right?'

'Hell's bells, you haven't half done your homework. Anyway, he's also close to Lady Petronella Cordingly—'

'Who runs Argentia Antiques and did her best to get you in the shit. And is fencing a whole lot of silver nicked from your father's place – well, the main house. Oh, didn't Morris tell you? That's why he wanted you here, Lina. To see a nice dramatic arrest or two.'

My legs wobbled. 'I thought she had immaculate provenance for everything. Ah! There was a rumour someone was buying up loads of old auction catalogues: it must have been her. Things have obviously moved on a bit since I spoke to Morris. Tell.'

He checked that he couldn't be overheard. 'SOCO – that's the scene of crimes boffins—'

'Yeah, the white suit brigade.' There was a customer drifting our way, and I didn't want to miss him.

Tiny followed the line of my eyes, and waited with a really queasy smile until the punter had checked the price of whatever had brought him over. 'SOCO have picked up traces of DNA in your shop that matched the DNA in the van in which your grandfather was attacked. And they match the DNA in the glasses DI Morris found in your father's kitchen.'

'So you've got Darrenarris?'

'The *soi-disant* Darrenarris. That means—' He quailed as I gave him the sort of look I wanted to give Morris. How dared he betray my vocab problems to a stranger!

'So Darrenarris was just the motorist driving while banned—'

'Nope. Your grandfather got the ID wrong. It was Darrenarris who pushed the van off the road thinking it was time to have words with you. He's a con man used to fleecing old people out of their goodies. Just to make sure he drugs them—'

I might have smacked my head. Instead, I clicked my fingers and pointed. 'Yes! The champagne that made Lord Elham wet himself. And left his brain even furrier than usual. That date rape drug? Isn't it called Rohypnol?' I patted myself on my back.

Morris would have rewarded me with that nice grin of his. Tiny didn't. 'He used a variant.'

'But how did he get my father to trust him?'

'I'd have thought you'd be the best one to find that out. If you can. Darrenarris's version is that he'd read about that Lord Elham's trust and the spin some of the papers put on it and thought he'd have a go. And your father didn't ask any questions. It's a good job he's got you to keep an eye on him, Lina. Anyway, it seems Darrenarris has been branching out. Which is why we're all here today. To mop up his friends and associates.'

I looked wildly round. What if someone had fingered Titus Oates? Old devil he might be, but he was a mate. I saw not him but Morris, looking so intently at something on a jewellery stall I'd have sworn he wanted to buy it.

'Tiny, why didn't anyone tell me all this was going on?' I asked with no attempt to sound patient.

'Police work. We just get on and do things. Especially when people's lives are at risk.'

'Mrs Hatch? I never even asked—'

'Not good at all. Touch and go in fact. Darrenarris could be looking at a manslaughter charge. And we shall nail him for it, I promise you. We've got phone records, mobile and landline, CCTV footage – we've been using all the technology available. So all you have to do is sit back and watch the fun. And absolutely no joining in, DI Morris said.'

I stuck my tongue out at his back, only to have him turn round as I did it. He didn't give a flicker of recognition. 'The only thing is,' Tiny continued, 'that we thought your stalls might be closer together. If you want to watch, you may have to go and find a colleague to talk to. But not, repeat not, too near Argentia Antiques. Get it?'

I didn't like being treated like a child. The best revenge would be to give him a dose of his own medicine.

I said, very managerial and cold, 'Tiny, I think that lady's trying to catch your attention. Was it that vase you wanted lifting down?'

He got the message. And made a very good job of apologizing to the customer. So good she didn't even ask our best price, but bought the Moorcroft full price.

Of course I had to wrap it – I couldn't trust him to do that. But at last, her money safely in our account, I left him in charge and drifted towards Argentia Antiques.

There wasn't even a commotion to guide me.

Nella sounded as if being arrested was an everyday event. It was so low key it might have been. Not like the arrests I'd known – not personally – when I was a kid. They involved a lot of running, the sort of language Griff wouldn't have liked even after midnight, and then some violence on both sides. Quite a lot, sometimes.

Nella merely eyed the search warrant Morris showed her as if it was an inaccurate bill, and listened with complete boredom to the arrest incantation, which he spoke so clearly that Griff and his actor friends would have applauded. Her shell of calm cracked when she saw the handsome toy boy in handcuffs, but she soon regained control over her features.

As she gathered her bag and coat, she said, 'You will be careful packing away these items. Most are extremely valuable.'

Only *most*. Did that mean that Titus' suggestion that someone was cobbling together two unfashionable things to make one desirable one was true? And that she was involved?

I couldn't ask, of course. But I was sure that Morris would. Meanwhile two officers took up position by her stall. They wouldn't need to know price codes or how to work the credit card terminal, would they?

'I'd have expected a triumphalist dance,' Tiny said, as I

returned to our stall. 'And a few handsprings. But you've got a face as long as a fiddle.'

'I know her brother. And a more upright and law-abiding man you couldn't meet. And I'm worried about the lovely silverware. She's right. Whoever packs it must be very careful.'

'Are you volunteering?' Morris demanded, appearing from nowhere. 'It'd be great if you would.' And he was gone, before I could tell him what to do with his great idea.

Actually, why not? I left Tiny in charge, ready to charm cash out of a really sweet old lady looking up at him and fluttering her lashes as if he was a Greek god, and headed off to supervise the team dismantling Argentia's display.

Which was how I came to find an eighteenth-century musical snuff box with a hunting scene, stolen from Bossingham Hall. I wrapped it and slotted it in with the rest. They'd be looking for a new administrator, wouldn't they? I just hoped it would be someone who loved the place and the things within it.

TWENTY-FIVE

'How's Aidan taken this business?' I asked Griff, as we prepared supper together his first night home.

'Quite hard. It was very tactful of you to keep out of the way when he brought me back, my sweet.'

'It wasn't just for his benefit, Griff,' I admitted. 'Mine too. That woman!' I looked at the clock but it wasn't quite seven, so I couldn't use the rude words I wanted to. 'Thieving's one thing, but trying to shift the blame to poor old Lord Elham is another.'

'Not to mention trying to implicate you, dear one.' Griff put down the vegetable knife and allowed himself a sip of champagne. 'Tell me, did I hear aright when you told me that your father proposed to rid you of your troublesome boyfriend? I misquote, of course.'

I frowned. The words rang a distant bell. 'Troublesome *priest*? Thomas à Becket?'

He put an arm round me and kissed me. 'Exactly. It should actually be *turbulent priest*, but let that pass. What does he intend to do?'

'He won't say. Except I have to take him to London.'

'London!'

'I've already taken him shopping for the right clothes – that gents' outfitters in Canterbury. It was like stepping back a hundred years or so. And then we nipped off to Jones's for some shoes. He had a haircut too. And bought a Dictaphone. Don't ask me why – I've no idea, and he's really enjoying keeping everything to himself. He tells me he'll let me know when we have to go. I shall just – and I never thought I'd ever say this – have to trust him.'

'So soon you will be footloose and fancy free? Ah, do I sense a little hesitation? Have you lost your heart to young Robin at last? No? Oh, Lina – it's Morris, isn't it?'

I couldn't tell whether he was pleased or alarmed. I sat down. 'He's nice. He's lovely. But he's nearly twenty years older than me. And he told Tiny that I didn't know long words.'

'A breach of faith.'

'He didn't need to. As I shall tell him tomorrow when we go out to dinner. And then we'll see.'

In fact, Morris and I didn't go out to dinner the next day. Or the next. He phoned to apologize twice, saying things had come up and hoping I wouldn't mind. As it happened, I did mind, very much, but then came something to mind about a great deal more. Mrs Hatch died. Poor Griff was very badly shaken; as soon as the funeral was over, attended not only by the whole village, but by the two policemen who'd managed to resuscitate her, I took him down to stay with an old theatrical friend now based in Devon. I'd been invited too, but my father phoned to tell me to stand by for the Day of Reckoning, as he modestly put it. And since there was a limit to the amount of theatrical nostalgia I could enjoy, I went back up to Kent. Maybe if I took my father a load of casseroles for his freezer he'd explain what he was up to.

The cottage was so quiet I understood a little bit of how Mrs Walker might feel, so before I went round to my father's wing I popped into the main part of the hall to take her off for a coffee and bun. There was no sign of her, so I asked another volunteer where she might be.

She looked carefully round before leaning towards me and whispering, 'I'm afraid she was sacked.'

'Sacked!' I repeated. Much more loudly. And marched into the admin hub demanding an explanation.

'Well, she broke a plate,' said the deputy administrator apologetically.

'She didn't break it! It broke because that Fielding woman messed with the climate control. Hey, now she's been arrested, can't Mrs W come back?'

'I don't think she could.'

'But I'd trust her with the china in my shop!' I shouted. And then stopped shouting. 'You don't have her address, do you? Oh, don't tell me it's more than your job's worth.'

It seemed it was.

My father looked dead shifty when he came to his front door. 'Could you come back in an hour or so, Lina? I'm engaged at the moment.' Since Titus Oates' van was tucked behind an outhouse, I knew better than to ask how on earth he could be busy.

'Pop these in the freezer and call me when you're free,' I said, putting the bags of home-made meals for one into his hands. 'Remember, I really do not want to know what you two are up to. Ever.'

The best thing about villages, especially those as small as Bossingham, was that everyone knew where everyone lived. So when I saw someone busy sweeping her front path, I pulled over and asked for directions.

'Mrs Walker? Three houses down. That way. I warn you, she's not herself.'

Nor was she. Her hair was a mess and her jumper and skirt could have been cleaner. I had a sudden fear that if I was kind she'd cry. So I had to be careful with my offer.

'I'm in such a mess,' I said, quite truthfully, though I hammed up my distress, so it seemed to match hers. 'I've got Griff convalescing down in Devon, a shop to run and antiques fairs popping up all over the place now spring's here. I just don't know where to begin.'

The biscuit she passed me was shop bought and on the stale side. She really did need a kick start. In fact, she looked so miserable I wondered if I was going to make an almighty mistake.

I sold her the idea slowly. First I said I was lonely and hated eating on my own.

'We could always lunch together?' she said hesitantly.

'There's a nice pub,' I said, 'over in Bredeham.'

She was off in a flash to change and comb her hair. At last, while we were tucking into our rather tough lasagne (I didn't even know lasagnes could be tough), I pointed out that she'd never seen our shop.

It was love at first sight. I think she'd have paid me to let her work in it. She even took the security system in her stride. She would start as soon as she'd had her hair done, she declared. We agreed a week's trial without prejudice on either side – her idea, and certainly her words.

Somehow I had to tell Griff I'd made such an important decision on impulse, and without consulting him. But I needn't have worried. He greeted the news as if he'd written the script himself. He even thought a woman who worried how her hair looked would be a credit to the shop. Somehow everything started to look a lot better, as I told Morris next time I texted him.

And so they did until the next phone call. It was Lord Elham's summons. I was to take him to London the next day.

For some reason I cleaned the van before I called for him. And it was a good thing I had. Not only was he wearing his new clothes; he'd even shaved.

'You look very good,' I said.

'It's not often I go to Town these days but I think it behoves me to look every inch the country gentleman.' And then he flinched. 'We are not travelling in your trade vehicle!' he insisted.

'I'm not going to turn up advertising it's me, am I? We'll do what Griff and I always do if we want to go to London. We'll park at the station and catch the train, and after that take a cab. There's nothing more incognito than a cab, surely.'

'And you're happy to lurk – in that cab, for preference – while I Do the Deed?'

'What deed?'

'You'll just have to wait and see,' he declared, with something like a chuckle.

I was glad Griff was still away – he'd have been very alarmed, not just at what I might be getting involved in but also at the thought that my father's sudden kindness might be a way of persuading me to move to Bossingham.

We could have travelled from Canterbury or Ashford International; I opted for Ashford because it has such a good – if dead expensive – car park. The downside was having to buy tickets from a machine. I prefer a person.

My father pointed at the screen. 'Travel first class? Dear me, I can't afford that!'

'Nor can I. I always travel second class.' I started prodding the screen, but I could tell he was sacrificing himself. However, he perked up considerably when he saw even the second-class areas were comfortable and our seats even had a little table on which to place the champagne he'd insisted on bringing but which I was determined to ration. To my amazement, he showed me how to tackle Sudoku, rattling through the *Times*'s fiendish puzzle as if he were a child with an abacus. The journey passed surprisingly quickly.

'Now, you won't drink more than one bottle of champagne at this club?' I prompted him.

'Shampoo at £600 a pop? You jest! And yes, I know how the Dictaphone works.' He patted a pocket. 'Taxi!' It seemed he didn't believe in queuing at stations. I kept my head down and hopped in behind him.

We found ourselves outside a posh-looking door in a very smart neighbourhood. My father pressed my hand, reminded the cabbie he had to wait, and disappeared inside.

'I never seen the like,' the cabbie gasped. 'Old geezer going into a knocking shop and leaving his lovely daughter outside while he has his shag. Don't hold with it.'

'It's a brothel, is it?'

'Bloody right it is. Claims to be a gentlemen's club, but it's a whorehouse all right.'

'I've never seen one like that,' I said. Those I'd seen were seedy little places claiming to be massage parlours. If it were the sort of thing I could discuss with Robin, I'm sure he'd say it was the hand of God that prevented me from working in one, when I was at my very lowest. And maybe I wouldn't have argued with him. 'He's actually not a punter at all,' I added, because the cabbie was still looking outraged. 'He's – let's say he's working undercover,' I said, dropping my voice and touching the side of my nose.

* * *

Some time later my father emerged with a very smug expression on his face, directing the cabbie to take us to the Savoy, where it dawned on me that we were to have a rather late lunch. But he was on his best behaviour, praising the beef as judiciously as if I didn't know that Spicy Beef Pot Noodles were his real preference, and gossiping about the famous faces he'd seen at the brothel. I'd spotted, from the depths of the cab, a further couple he'd missed. One face we'd both seen was Piers Hamlyn's.

At last Lord Elham extended a spatulate finger and pressed the Dictaphone's Play button, not your usual behaviour in a restaurant but since the tables were so widely separated perhaps no one would hear and complain. Now we could hear the clink of glasses twice over – once for real and once on tape. We could hear Piers' voice quite clearly. He was boasting about his fence, how it was like taking candy from a baby.

And then we heard Lord Elham's: 'Young man, it happens to be my baby from whom you are taking the confectionery. My little girl Lina. She will not be marrying you, of course. And, unless you want an exposé that would shock even your family to the roots, I suggest you listen very carefully to what I say . . .'

'The Falklands!' I repeated at last.

'I do wish, my love, you wouldn't squeak,' Lord Elham reproached me, just as if he were Griff. 'Yes, the Falklands. I believe he will find his niche out there: sheep or mineral rights, whichever interests him more. Not for ever. Just long enough for you to mop up all the fake gems he's scattered about the country.' He laid a wad of notes on the linen tablecloth. 'From Piers and his partners in crime. It should suffice. You will keep any change.' He looked at my ringless finger. 'You should find enough there to purchase genuine stones for the jewellery in your keeping, which is now yours.' He sat back, belched, and looked at his watch. 'Now, I don't want to miss *Neighbours*. I think it's time we made our way home. Do they have Sudoku in the *Evening Standard*?'

TWENTY-SIX

'And how much of your adventure with your father do you propose to tell Morris over the dinner table?' Griff asked. He was home again, at last, much to my relief.

'Nothing at all,' I said flatly. 'It's much safer if he goes on thinking Lord Elham's a demented old soak, several knives short of a canteen. What if he made a surprise visit and found Titus there, like I did the other day? Disaster all round!'

'And you're not going to mention young Piers either?'

'No. Except to say we've broken up. My father got a list of people Piers sold dodgy jewellery to, plus all that cash. I can buy the stuff back or pay to have new stones inserted.'

'So practical justice, if not legal justice, can be done.'

'Exactly. Now, which is far more important, what should I wear this evening? It's Eastwell Manor, remember – so smart.'

'More likely smart casual,' Griff said, with a sigh. 'I believe I even saw someone wearing trainers last time we went. And spring's such a confusing time of the year, sartorially speaking. One never knows whether to dress to keep warm or if summer finery's in order.'

So *sartorial* meant something to do with clothes. Perhaps it was a word I could drop out when I was bollocking Morris for telling Tiny that I was a dimwit with words.

In the end I chose a silk skirt Griff had found for me in that wonderful Thai shop in Tenterden, and a simple top that showed off the flower pendant I'd bought for myself, not Farfrae's wife. Griff checked my hair and adjusted my slap and popped me into the taxi he'd booked for me. I felt like Cinderella without the fear that everything would go pear-shaped at midnight.

Actually, it seemed to be going pear-shaped a great deal earlier. Morris was late, so I was left sitting in the bar like a lemon, my outfit attracting the attention of a couple of men old enough to be my father who assumed I was on the game. Before I could assure them in no uncertain terms – in other words, the sort of language that might actually have convinced them and the barman that they were right – in ran Morris, apologizing and explaining so breathlessly I couldn't make out a word. We sipped our drinks and nibbled our canapés, horribly tongue-tied.

At last I blurted out what I'd wanted to say ever since the Hastings fair. 'I was so miffed everything got tied up behind my back, Morris. I wanted to be in on the fun.'

He shook his head. 'Modern policing isn't like it is on TV, Lina. The team and I do the leg work. Then the boffins and Crown Prosecution Service get their heads together, and tell me I can do the next bit. The arrest. And if anything goes wrong with that, everything's scuppered. Then there's another long process of interviewing and correlating statements – Tiny will be talking to you and Griff again later this week, just to make sure everything hangs together.'

'Not Sally?'

He looked at me sideways. 'I gather there was a problem. Do you want to tell me what it was?'

'No. But I'd rather that Tiny was doing the talking. Sorry. I interrupted.'

He nodded slowly, like Griff did when he'd lost the thread of what he was saying. 'All this generates so much paperwork you get smothered in it. And then – please God – there's a trial and a guilty verdict.'

'So you can't tell me what's been going on.'

'Not everything. Not till after the trial. Because you're a material witness. As is Griff, of course. I'm not sure about involving Lord Elham – what do you think? Would he help or hinder?'

A few days ago I'd have said he'd have ruined the case for them; after our London adventure I wasn't so sure. Thank goodness for the arrival of a waitress to take our order, which gave me the chance to work out something that wasn't quite a lie. 'He has good days and bad, Morris. Well, you've seen.'

'If I've seen him on a good one than heaven help us if we get him on the stand on a bad one. You know that Darrenarris will be charged with manslaughter too? After Mrs Hatch's death?'

I spread my fingers and ticked off the items. 'Manslaughter; drugging a dippy old man he claimed was his father; running

Griff off the road and beating him up; lots of thefts from my father and from the Bossingham Hall trustees. I'm glad he's not my half-brother. Will the case get a lot of publicity? You never know how many more real or fake sib . . . siblings will pop out of the woodwork.'

'And how would you feel about that?'

'Depends if they're in my father's notebook – I will get that back, won't I?'

'James will, Lina – it's not technically yours, you know. And it's a good job you kept careful records of everything you've taken away and sold, or prosecuting counsel would make mincemeat of you.'

Why did I feel that despite the pretty outfit and all my efforts, Morris didn't approve of me as much as before? Or perhaps he didn't approve of the venue? A frown lingered between his eyebrows even when we were taken through to the dining room. Should I ask why? On the whole I thought it was safer to talk about our nice classy surroundings and the upmarket food before us and then tuck in and shut up.

When the first course plates were cleared, he made no effort to introduce another topic. I hated the way that despite the resident pianist's efforts the silence was deepening to the point it seemed quite threatening. So I started again.

'Has Ms Fielding ever explained why she turned off the heating as well as the security system? I can see why she didn't want alarms and CCTV, but I can't understand why she should risk damaging pieces she might want to nick.'

'I think she was contemplating another scam. To send precious items ostensibly damaged during a *failure* of the climate control system away for repair and to have them replaced with inferior versions – forgeries, even. With everything locked away in glass cases and cleaned once in a blue moon, she'd have got away with it for several years. Apparently there are people who specialize in replacing good with bad.'

My God, they weren't on to Piers, were they? It was all very well knowing he'd broken the law and deserved to be punished, but any enquiries would certainly reveal his sudden departure from the UK and might reveal why. And any trail involving my father would lead back to me.

Again I was saved from having to incriminate myself by

the arrival of food – what they called an *amuse-bouche* – a tiny cup of soup.

'It's a strange sort of life for a musician,' I said, thinking it was time to turn the conversation to something much safer. 'Playing in a room like this where no one wants to listen. As bad as playing at the NEC during the LAPADA fair.' I ventured a smile. After all, it was where we'd first met, and he'd been very kind to me.

To my amazement, he frowned even more. He even opened his mouth to say something, but shut it. When he spoke, I was sure it wasn't to say what he'd first intended. 'How's Griff getting on with Aidan Morley? It must be hard to have your sister sent down by your lover's partner.'

'I don't think Aidan and Nella were all that close, from what Nella said the first time we met. And Aidan was outraged by the way she treated me – even bought me a new bear to replace Tim. A mega-pricey one too.'

'That smart Steiff job that sits in your bedroom? I thought you collected them.' His face had fallen so much I nearly laughed.

'I can always start,' I said. 'But I'd find it difficult to sell them. It's really hard sometimes,' I added, 'buying something for the firm and then finding you can't let it go. Like this pendant. I was really looking for something for Farfrae to give his wife. But when it came to it, I had to keep it.' There, it was out.

'But I thought you'd divvied a print for him!'

I thought of what Griff had said. 'I might have divvied that too. Who knows how this thing works.'

'You make it sound like falling in love.'

I nearly dropped my spoon. Apart from Griff, I'd never heard a man use the L word.

The arrival of my guinea fowl and his beef gave me a little space for reflection. At last, as we both put down our knives and forks to take a sip of wine, I grasped the nettle. 'Is every thing OK, Morris? All evening you've looked as if you've lost a silver dollar and found a rusty button.'

His sip turned into a swig. But he took another forkful of beef. It seemed he needed time to think too.

At last he said, 'Your father, Lina.'

My God, they were on to him and Titus!

'Would your life have been any different if you'd known him from the start?' he continued, as if he hadn't noticed my awkward swallow.

'You mean I wouldn't have been dirt poor, shunted from one foster home to another, hardly in school, dabbling in crime and nearly into drugs? Yes, it might have been a bit different.'

'Point taken. But I didn't mean like that. I meant emotionally. You and he seem to be shaking down into some sort of relationship now – a very weird one, with you more his carer than his child, but a relationship.'

'Are you asking if I'd have liked a dad? One to love as much as I love Griff now? Do I have to tell you the answer?'

He looked down and shook his head, pushing away his plate as if he'd finished his meal.

'Morris,' I asked quietly, 'this is nothing to do with my father, is it? It's something else. But,' I added, 'you might just as well finish that beef, if it's anything as good as my guinea fowl.'

He gave a short laugh and retrieved the plate. We ate in silence, but a more companionable one now.

The word amused me, but suddenly I was cross. 'I have to tell you,' I said, finishing first, 'that I was really miffed you told Tiny about my problems with words. I thought you were my friend, Morris, and friends don't do that. It felt like a – a betrayal.'

'I'm sorry. It wasn't meant to be. I was telling him how hard you were working to overcome all your handicaps. All the things you said earlier. All the things that make you such a wonderful young woman.' His voice was so tight someone might have been strangling him. He stopped altogether.

The waiter whipped away our plates and hovered with the dessert menus.

'Just coffee,' Morris snarled. I didn't have the heart to tell him I'd really fancied the chocolate fondant. 'I was talking about fathers earlier. It seems . . . hell, Lina, my ex-partner's eight months pregnant and I'm the father. She only let me know about a week ago. You can guess how I've felt.'

'Not from the expression on your face I can't. I'd have thought you'd be chuffed to bits.'

'Not when I was hoping to start seeing another woman.' He took my right hand. The dent left by Piers' ring had completely disappeared. 'But now I don't think I can. I need to be there for my daughter, don't I? Especially the hours my ex . . . my *partner* works. And I work. If I tried to be a part-time dad, I'd be no use to my daughter or to the other woman I wanted to be with. Hell, Lina, I'm so sorry. But from now on, it's got to be a professional relationship only.' He raised my hand and kissed it before returning it firmly to the table.

It dawned on me that I ought to say something. I swallowed hard a couple of times, quite upset. Yes, I really liked him, didn't I? I blinked back the tears. Whatever I said would sound heartless or corny. Especially if it was about me. I took a deep breath. 'You mustn't just look after your daughter, Morris, you must love her too. And you must love her mother, or it won't work.'

I didn't really sort out what I felt until I was in the taxi on the way home, accompanied by another large Steiff bear, very handsome and stiff, with the sort of fur you definitely don't cry into.

Had I said all that was right? That I was very fond of Morris – could well have got even fonder – but I really honoured him for what he was doing? I hoped so. It certainly wouldn't have done to tell him that deep down I was relieved. How could you be in a relationship with a man and not be completely honest with him? Which I couldn't have been, not just for our sakes but for other people's. And I wouldn't have wanted to turn my back on old sparring partners like Titus just to give my conscience a polish.

You've no idea how glad I was to see our cottage lights still on. Griff had promised not to wait up for me, but as I was home rather earlier than expected, I couldn't shout. It's not often I drink spirits, but the thimbleful of malt whiskey Griff pressed into my hand hit the spot nicely.

'You did very well, my love,' Griff said. 'It sounds as if you've left his poor bleeding ego intact and have been sweet and dignified as well. And you were right to accept that dratted Steiff teddy bear, though it's a horribly sentimental farewell gift. I must say, he was too old for you, you know. Morris, not the bear.'

'Do you think I should send him that pretty coral rattle and teether we found the other day? When the baby's born?'

'We'll have to consider if that's wise. Perhaps we could send it from the pair of us. Now, young Robin phoned earlier – something about a concert in Canterbury Cathedral. I do hope you're free, because I told the poor love I'd go if you weren't . . .'